T0114836

The Church of Three Bells

Jesse P. Ward

authorHOUSE®

AuthorHouse™
1663 Liberty Drive
Bloomington, IN 47403
www.authorhouse.com
Phone: 833-262-8899

Published by AuthorHouse 09/28/2020

ISBN: 978-1-6655-0221-4 (sc)
ISBN: 978-1-6655-0222-1 (hc)
ISBN: 978-1-6655-0223-8 (e)

Library of Congress Control Number: 2020919131

Print information available on the last page.

This book is printed on acid-free paper.

Contents

The Cave

He opened his eyes and looked down at his leg. He could feel the pain, and he could see that he had lost a vast amount of blood. *How was I wounded, and where am I?* He could see by the faint light that he was in a cave. He was about ten yards from the cave opening, and there was enough light to see. Lying next to him he saw a young girl. She had a bandage on her left shoulder. She too was wounded and was covered with blood. *Who was she? How in the hell did I get into this cave?*

Looking back toward the cave entrance, he could see that it was daylight outside the cave. The light coming through the opening was blocked by a pile of rocks, and they were casting a shadow which looked like an enchanted castle on the cave wall.

He looked at the young girl. Her face was covered by her dark hair, and he could tell that she was asleep or perhaps passed out. She appeared to be fourteen or fifteen years old. *Who is she? Why are we in this cave?*

"If we are going to die here, I guess we should know who we are. My name is Jason. I don't know what your name is, but it does not look good for us." In the faint light he could see a used bandage lying near the girl. "Looks like someone has been here. Maybe there is hope for one of us."

He again looked down at his leg. His eyes were adjusting to the dim light. He had moved, and the movement had caused the leg to start bleeding. Looking at the crimson-soaked pants leg, he knew he was in trouble. *I am going to die here,* he thought. He felt sick at his stomach. Things began to fade. Voices pulled him back from the slumber that was being caused by his weakness. *The Germans have found us*, he said to himself as he realized he was a soldier, and the Germans were his enemy. He reached for his gun, but standing proved to be too difficult. He felt dizzy. One of the soldiers called out, "Jet, is that you?" He heard nothing because he had passed out.

A week later he awoke for a second time. A doctor was shining a light into his eyes.

"Good, you are awake. We were getting worried about you. You had lost a ton of blood, and it was touch and go for a while. Can you see me, and can you hear me? I need to ask you some questions."

His vision was blurred, and he was seeing someone he could not make out. It was like looking through the bottom of a glass. Blinking his eyes several times, he saw a man come into focus. "Who are you?"

"I am Doctor Eperson. The question is, do you know who you are?"

"My name is Jason. My rank is private, my tag number…"

"Stop, son. You are not in a prison camp. You are on a hospital ship. You have been in and out of consciousness for the last week. What do you remember?"

"I was in a cave. My leg was bleeding." Looking down, he could see his leg suspended above the bed. He began to get scared. "I don't remember anything. I don't know how I got into that cave. I do remember a young girl. I don't know who she was. She was bleeding. I think she may have been shot. I am sorry. I just can't remember."

Doctor Eperson could sense his fear and said, "Try to relax. You must have had a great shock. You have not suffered from any head trauma. Your memory will come back. Meanwhile, I have good news and some not so good news. The good news is that we did not have to take your leg. The bad news, it is a bad wound and will require more surgery. Surgery we don't want to do here. The leg is stable, the bullet has been removed and if you don't walk on it you will be fine until you get to England. There we can get you fixed up and maybe get you back to the war, or maybe they will send you home. We will just have to see."

"Who was the young girl? Is she going to be alright?"

"I don't know anything about a young girl. We were not told about her. You were brought here from the front. The doctors that treated you at the field hospital left written notes. All they did was stabilize your leg and give you blood." Doctor Eperson stood up and walked to the door. "Jane, come in here."

In just a moment a young lady came into the room. Looking at Jason she said, "Good to see that you are awake. I will get your vitals, fill out your chart, and then clean you up."

Standing in the door, Doctor Eperson looked down at his watch. "You are on a ship, and tonight it will pull out of here. I hope you don't get sea sick. I am going to tell Doctor Murphy you are awake, and he will come and see you and see if we can get your memory back."

Jason lay back on his pillow and watched as nurse Jane took his pulse, listened to his heart, took his temperature and wrote them down on his chart. She quickly left the room but soon returned with hot water, a wash cloth and soap. Not saying anything she went about giving him a sponge bath. He felt a little embarrassed, but the warm water felt so good he said nothing. He closed his eyes and let the nurse do her work. When she finished she said, "You are lucky. Most of the men on this ship are in the ward. They are lined up, with their beds very close together. Very little privacy."

He was getting sleepy again. "Why am I so special?"

Jane smiled. "I guess because you have been submitted for the Congressional Medal of Honor. This space was available. So here you are."

Jason did not hear what Jane said. He had drifted off to sleep and started to dream.

He was standing looking at a church. It was a picturesque small cathedral. In the front was a tall bell tower, and at the top of the tower were three large bells. The church was made of square stones. In the front was a large cross. Two large doors with oval tops were in the front, and there were two stained glass windows on either side of the doors. Carved in the stone above the doors was the name of the church, La Chiesa Delle Bellissime Campane. *In his dream, as he makes his way to the church it disappeared. All he could see was rubble and smoke.*

The dream brought him out of his sleep, and he was damp with perspiration and had a slight headache. He tried to raise up in the bed but found he could not. He closed his eyes and sleep soon found him again.

When he awoke the next morning, he could feel the ship was moving. It wasn't long until a man came into his room carrying a tray of food. He scooted up in the bed as the orderly placed the food on the bed above his lap and adjusted the bed so he could sit up.

Looking down he could see that he had oatmeal, a slice of toast, and a glass of some type of juice. "You don't happen to have a couple of eggs and some bacon on that tray, or perhaps a bowl of gravy and a biscut or two, do you?"

"I am afraid not," he laughed. "Only a country boy from the south would make such a request. Your menu has been set by the doctors. No solid food for a while. You have not had anything solid for several days. Let's see if your system can handle this. I will let the doctors know you wanted something more solid. That is a good sign."

The next day he had a visit from Doctor Murphy. He came into the room and took a seat next to the bed. For a moment he did not say anything as he looked at Jason's chart. "I see you have no head trauma, but have no memory of what happened to you. That was yesterday. What do you remember today?"

"Coming ashore at Anzio. Rome had been liberated, and my company spent a couple of days there. We moved out of Rome and then everything seems to go fuzzy. I was in a cave and I heard soldiers coming in. I remember being scared because I was not sure if they were American or German. I don't remember anything else until I woke up on this ship."

"You have no memory of going into the cave or the battle that took place before you were found in the cave. Do you remember the girl who was found in the cave with you?"

"I remember waking up in the cave. I did see a young girl not too far from me. I could see that she had been wounded, and someone had bandaged her shoulder. I heard someone coming into the cave, and then I remember nothing until I woke up here."

"The battle must have been horrible. I think your mind has blocked it out. Do you want to read the account of the battle and what your men witnessed? There were even some Germans that were questioned, and their accounts are part of the official record. There was also a priest that gave a good describtion of what happened before the battle."

At first Jason thought he should read about the battle, but then he said no. "I don't think reading about what happened is going to help." Thinking for just a moment, Jason said, "How was I ever found inside that cave?"

"You owe that to Lieutenant Robert Forbes. When the battle was over, he insisted that you be found. I don't think he expected you to be found alive, but after interviewing several soldiers and a few German prisonors, soldiers started looking for you with little hope that you would be found breathing. It was a soldier named Tony Martin that found the trail of blood leading up the hill and to the cave. The rest you know. You do know you have been put in for a medal. What you did will be read in a ceremony if you recieve the award. It might help if you have read it first."

"I don't want any medals. I want nothing more than to be remembered as a soldier who did his job. That's what most of us do. We are all just scared. We try to take care of each other. I think I may have been scared even more than most."

"We will talk about your medals later. Do you have any memory of your childhood, and things like that?"

"I do."

"Tell me about yourself, where you are from, your mother and father and how you came to be in the army."

Jason adjusted his pillow, lay back and started to tell his story.

Growing Up in Madison County

Jason was born in December of 1929 in Madison County. He had always thought that it was strange that the town of Richmond was in Madison County. Just about everything was named either Richmond, or Madison. There was Richmond Bakery, Richmond High School, Madison Laundry, Madison High, Richmond Hotel, Madison Movie Theater and the list goes on and on. He often joked that the city's residents had no imagination. His father, John W. Terry, was a carpenter. He did finish work. He was good at what he did but made just enough money to pay his bills. Jason's mother had died when he was four years old, and his father had lied about his age to get him into school, telling the school officials that he was six. His father cared very little about education but needed the school as a baby sitter, so he could work. School came easy for him and even though he was an indifferent student, his grades were good.

His father had plans for Jason. He was going to be a carpenter, and they were going to have their own business. As he got older his father started him working in his backyard shop. He found he liked working with wood, and the woodworking skills came easy. Unlike his father, he liked to sketch out his wood projects before he started working on them. As he got better, his sketches would just about always match his final project. When his father didn't have a job for him, he enjoyed playing with the boys in the neighborhood. The street he lived on was a dead end, and beyond the street was a large farm. He and the local boys played all over this farm. In an overgrown hollow about a mile from his house, they built a club house. They called the hollow Dead Dog Hollow. There was a large lake on the farm. He and his buddies would often go fishing. They also were run off the property quite often. Jason's father never gave him money. He always took his lunch to school and it mostly consisted of a cheese or ham sandwich, a piece of fruit, and a cookie. There were always fellow students who didn't like milk and would give him theirs. Even though his father never gave him money, he could always come up with some. He would gather iron to sell, pick up bottles, pick berries, and in the fall of the year gather up walnuts. On Saturdays he would go to the movies if he was not helping his father with a project. He loved movies. They became his great escape from life. With only a little change in his pocket, he could get into the movies, and buy popcorn and a coke. The movie theaters had continuous showings, and it didn't matter when it started. He would just go in. Sometimes he would watch the movies twice.

He and his friends walked to school. He would walk to the end of Cherry Street, make a left on Westover, and walk one block to Main Street. Taking a right on the main street took him by what he and his buddies would call the haunted house. It was a large four-story house that sat way off the main road. It was made of both brick and frame siding. There were lots of trees, and in the back of the house, there was a barn and several small out buildings. He and his friends were scared to go on the property. Once, on Halloween, Jason and several of his friends were on Main Street trick-or-treating when they saw the haunted house. They dared each other to go to the house. His friend Sammy took the dare and walked down the narrow road which led to the front door. When Sammy knocked on the door, it was opened by an old man. Sammy didn't say anything. He just turned and ran.

This all changed when he was twelve years old. His father took a job to put cabinets in the haunted house. He went with his father and was somewhat scared to be on the property.

His father had brought him to help measure the space where the cabinets were to be installed. It was then he met the man that would change his life forever, although he did not know it at the time. His name was Jake Winston. He lived in what Jason had always called the haunted house. They made the turn off Main Street, went down a small hill, crossed a brook, and drove up to the house. Jason then realized that the house was not old and ugly. It was an American castle. They pulled their truck up to the front door, and Jason got out and marveled at the structure. It stood four stories high. It was built into the side of a hill, and the basement was visible from the front but disappeared into the hillside. The second and third floors had four gables, and to the left side of the house was a turret that transverses all four floors. The roof was made of red shingles. The first floor was surrounded by a porch that wrapped around three sides of the house. It was truly the most magnificent house he had ever seen. Jason and his father climbed the six steps that led to the front door and knocked. A very mature lady opened the door and told them to come in and that they were expected. Mr. Winston was sitting in the front parlor. He did not get up.

"John, go into the kitchen. You can see the old cabinets and you can get your measurements. I will be in in a minute. Seems like getting up is getting harder and harder."

As he and his father were measuring the space, Mr. Winston came into the kitchen walking with the aid of a walker. "John, looks like you got some good help."

Jason looked at the old man and smiled. He was surprised that the old man knew his father by name.

John Terry stopped measuring for a moment and turned to the old man. "He does a good job. He and I are someday going to be partners in business."

"How old are you, young man?"

Jason was not sure if he should tell his right age or the one his father had invented for him, so he could start school early. "I am twelve. I will go to Madison High next year."

Mr. Winston gave Jason a smile. "I am sure you will. Everything in this area is called Madison or Richmond. Are you learning the woodworking trade?"

Jason's father interrupted. "He is. He is gifted."

"John, I want you to do me a favor. I have some wood in one of my outbuildings that I would like for you to use in this project. I know that you make a little money on the wood you use in the projects, but this wood is special. It came out of the home where my father lived before, he moved into this house. It is knotty chestnut. There is enough to do the cabinets and make a table. Come with me and I will show it to you. It is the first shed on the right."

The two men and the boy walked out to the back of the house. Mr. Winston had to walk very slowly because of the walker. Just behind the house was a small building. It was made to match the house and it had two stories, had two garage doors and a door on both sides of the two-car garage which opened into storage sheds. They opened the door on the left and went inside. Just inside the door was a large pile of wood. Jason could see that there were lots of chestnut planks, but there were other types of wood in the pile as well.

John picked up a piece of the wood. "This is marvelous, and it is old. This will do just fine. I will go home and figure how much wood I will need and come back and pick up what I need. How big of a table do you want, and do you have a design in mind?"

"There is quite a bit of wood here and even more in the barn if you need it. I think you might have enough to make a table with seating for twelve. I will leave the design up to you. I don't want anything with a modern look. I want it to match the room."

John was curious. "Do you ever have need for a table that would seat twelve people?"

Most people would think John was being somewhat nosey, but Mr. Winston just smiled and said, "No, I don't. I just think the room is so big, a smaller table would look funny."

The two men continued their conversation as Jason explored the outbuilding. It had a shed on the left, which had a workshop with tools and piles of old wood. It also had a shed on the right which had steps that led up to a loft, but he decided that he would not go up there.

The next day was Sunday. Jason and his father never attended church. This was something that Jason did not understand because next to his father's bed was a Bible, and he knew that his father often read it at night. The minister of the church would sometimes come by and encourage his father to come to church, and once Jason heard the preacher say, "John you need to come back to the church." He knew his father once attended but did not understand why he stopped going.

Jason went with his father to get the wood. They went straight to the door on the left side of the garage doors where the wood was stored. Looking at the pile of wood, John said, "I am going to go slowly through the wood pile and pick out the best pieces. You can wait here or explore the building. It will not take long. When I am finished, I will call you and you can help me load the wood."

Jason did not have long to explore, but he did have enough time to return to the stairs he had seen earlier. The steps led to a loft apartment which had a bathroom and a small kitchen. He found that this was strange.

"Dad, there is an apartment up here. It has a bathroom and kitchen and everything. It is small, but a person could live up here."

"It is common for some people to rent out rooms for extra money. I guess Mr. Winston did rent this out at one time. I don't know if Mr. Winston ever needed money. I have heard that both his mother and father had money, but if he was like everyone else, he lost most of it during the stock market crash. He is a strange man. He rarely leaves his house. He has a lady that does his cleaning and cooks for him. Hart's grocery brings him his food."

With the wood now in John's workshop, he started the project. Jason mostly watched his father but did help with the sanding of the wood. The cabinets and the table were works of art, and Mr. Winston was as proud as John was. As they were leaving Jake Winston's large house, Jason asked his father, "How does Mr. Winston know you? He calls you by your name."

"I have done work for him from time to time. He has asked me several times to do minor work on the house. I don't like to do that kind of work, but he pays good money and I really like him."

The next fall Jason started high school. School started in the first part of September, and he would not turn thirteen until December. It really helped that Jason had had a growth spurt over the summer and was as tall as most of the boys in the freshman class. It was not a good time for him. He wanted to play sports, but his dad wanted him to help in the workshop in the afternoons. It all became academic on December 7. The Japanese bombed Pearl Harbor, and by the beginning of the new year the sports teams didn't have enough boys to make up a team. Most had joined the army.

High school was easy, and he applied himself more than he did in elementary school. His grades were above average, and he made the honor roll. He did not know if his father was proud or not. He just talked about how they would start their business when he graduated. He asked Jason a couple of times if he wanted to quit school, so he could go to work. Jason had already decided that going into business with his father was not what he wanted. The problem was how to tell his father. He took shop, but his father had already taught him more than he would learn in the shop class. He liked art and history. He had a good memory and all he had to do was sit and listen in class and he could pass the test. Math came easy and his teachers tried to encourage him to go to college.

His senior year finally came, and Jason had made up his mind to attend college. The problem was how to tell his father, and how to pay for the tuition. He didn't have to worry too much about getting drafted. He could just pull out his birth certificate and show how old he really was.

In the spring of 1944, three weeks before graduation, his father had a heart attack and died. He wasn't sure how to arrange the funeral for his father. He went to the church and talked with the minister. Reverend Masters lived behind the church, and Jason was not sure what to say when he knocked on the door.

Reverend Masters opened the door. "Jason. I thought you might come by. I am so sorry about your father. Please come in."

After they had taken a seat, Jason said, "I have no idea about what to do. Can you tell me how to handle this?"

"I can, and I would be glad to help. Both your mother and father were members of this church. I will go with you and help arrange everything."

"I knew my mother was a member here, but I didn't know that Dad was. Why did he stop coming?"

"Your father loved your mother very much. When your mother got sick, we prayed together, and your mother died. He became somewhat bitter and felt that his prayers went unanswered. He never came back to the church. I came to visit him several times but could not convince him to come back. Let's take a ride down to the funeral home and get things started. The church has a fund to help with the expenses."

Jason was able to live by himself until he graduated. The teachers of Richmond knew of his situation and really gave him words of encouragement. Sometimes they would bring him food and some even gave him money to eat on.

His favorite teacher was a Miss Smith. She was in her sixties, never married and made every student feel special. A week from graduation, she asked him to stay after class. "Looks like you are going to make it. Only six days to go. Have you thought about what you are going to do?"

"Yes, I have. I want to go to college, but I don't have enough money."

"You are one of the most talented artists we have ever had at this school. You really could do something with that skill. I can write you a letter, and I think the college will give you a grant. I went to school with the president of the local college, and I would be glad to talk to him about a presidential scholarship."

Jason smiled and thought, *she is such a good person, but there is more than just college tuition that I need.* "It means a lot that you are trying to help me, but there is more involved here. We don't own the house we lived in. The owner has let me live there until graduation, but in about six days I need to move out. I have nowhere to go, so I am going to join the army."

Miss Smith came over and gave him a hug. "I know good things are going to come to you someday. If you do join the army, please write me a letter from time to time."

He didn't want to join the army, but he needed a place to live and food to eat. It was not hard to convince the army recruiters that he was old enough to join. He was tall for his age, and they needed men.

After graduation, he sold all his father's tools and everything else he owned and joined the army. Everything came to one hundred and thirty-five dollars, and his father had another seventy-five dollars in his bank account. When he went to the bank, he asked to see the bank manager. It was not long until he was talking to a Mr. Elmer Hall.

"My father has died, and you sent me the seventy-five dollars that was in his account. I have joined the army. I want to open an account and put that seventy-five dollars in that account. I am not sure what the army is going to pay me, but I think it is around forty or fifty dollars a month. I can get by on less. I am going to add another one hundred dollars to the account and send you half of what the army pays me each month. I will keep you posted on where I am, so you can send me receipts."

"I am sorry about your father. He was one of the best carpenters this town ever had. I will open you an account. You are wise to do what you are doing. Most young boys just waste their money. I guess they are scared and want to live as much as they can. I don't want to bring this up, but if something happens to you, what do you want me to do with your money?"

"I am not sure. Let me think about it, and I will contact you with the first deposit and with that information." For some reason he had never thought that he might get killed while in the army. *Have I made the right decision? Yes, I have, because this is the only choice I have.* Looking at Mr. Hall he said, "the Baptist church helped with my father's funeral. If something happens to me, give the money to the church."

The Army, a Way Out

Near the end of July, Jason found himself at Fort Benning, Georgia. Fort Benning was to be his home for the next eight weeks. His sergeant was mean as hell, but he did not take it personally. Most of the men in his outfit were from large cities. Under his breath he called them city slickers. He found he could outrun them on the obstacle courses, he could outsmart most in hand to hand combat, and he was the best shot in the outfit. He could thank his father for his skill with a rifle, because he had given him a rifle for his seventh birthday. It was during his stay at Fort Benning that he won his first award. He was awarded the Marksmanship Badge, and before he left Fort Benning, he was awarded the Expert Marksmanship Badge.

After about three weeks of training, on a Thursday morning they were awakened early. They all jumped up and scrambled to find their clothing, but before they could, a captain was standing at the end of the barracks as they lined up in front of their bunks. "Relax men. Today is special. I have exciting news and some news that you may not find too exciting. The bad first. We are going on a ten-mile walk/run this morning."

A low murmur could be heard in the barracks.

"Now the good news. Anybody who completes the run in less than two hours will get a pass this weekend."

Jason heard somebody say in a low voice, "There won't be any passes this weekend."

"Now more bad news. Anyone who takes more than two and a half hours will have to do the course again this Saturday morning while everyone else is getting ready to go into town."

Sergeant Benny Carr barked out an order. "Tee-shirts, shorts and shoes only. Out front in ten."

In about ten minutes, they were standing if formation waiting for more orders. Thirty minutes later, they were standing on a dirt road receiving their instructions.

"Men this is a loop course. You are going to start and end right here. You start on the road that you are standing on and go straight for about four miles. At four miles you will take a left and follow that road for about half a mile and then another right and you will finish on the road that is on your right. It is marked, but most of you won't need the markings because you will be in a group. If we happen to have a jet in our group who leads the pack, just follow the chalk on the road."

Jason nudged Tony, who was standing next to him, and said, "What is a jet?"

Tony scoffed, "You darn hillbilly. Don't you know anything? Have you not been reading the papers? The Germans have a new plane. It is extremely fast. They call it a jet."

A voice came from the front. "No talking until I blow the whistle. If anybody gets sick and passes out, we are going to throw your body over in the ditch on the side of the road. What I am saying is don't get sick. There will be a water station at five miles. Get your water and keep moving. Time is important to you, and I don't want to be out here with you on Saturday morning."

Sergeant Carr blew his whistle and they were off. At first Jason stayed in the pack but found it was slow. About ten men were going at a fast pace, so he fell in with them. After they completed the first mile, a soldier standing at the marker told them they had completed the first mile in nine minutes, and Jason still felt the pace was slow. Looking around, he noticed the lead pack was down to five. Again, he felt the pace of the men slowing, so he moved up to take the lead. At the end of two miles he was way out in front, and he felt good. At the end of five miles no one else was even in sight, but he decided he would not slow his pace. He grabbed a cup of water and continued. When he finished the course, he heard the time. He had completed the entire ten miles in sixty-two minutes. He got a cup of water and watched as the rest of the men came to the finish line. Less than half of the men finished the course in the required time and would not have to repeat the run on Saturday. The lucky finishers would get a one-day pass.

Jason had not buddied with the men of the outfit, but after the ten-mile run he knew that they respected him. Several men in his barracks had not completed the run in the required time, and they had to do it again.

On Saturday, several of the men were getting ready to go into town. "Hey Jet, do you want to go to town with us? Some of the guys were saying you would rather stay here and read a book. Surely not. This town has lots of women, but not many men. There is a bus heading that way in about forty-five minutes."

Jason turned and looked. It was Tony from New York. "I do want to go into town, maybe catch a movie and see some of the town. What did you just call me?"

"You mean Jet. That's your nickname on the training courses. Jason Edward Terry. JET for short. Besides you were like a jet on the run Thursday."

He had not been to the town since he had arrived at the camp. There had been one other time the soldiers had been given a leave, but he chose not to go.

On the ride to town, Jason said very little to the men around him. As the bus slowed down to drop off the men, Jason turned to Tony. "What is that pungent odor? That is awful."

"There is a paper mill not far from here. You will get used to it. I am going down to the Merry- Go-Round. We have been told that they have great drinks, and lots of women. Do you want to come with us?"

"I don't think so. I am going to find a place that serves a great hamburger, and maybe take in a movie."

Tony was smiling. "I did say women, but did I say they have naked women? I don't think you will be disappointed."

"I am tempted, but why don't you come with me? I have a feeling that when you come out of the Merry Go Round you will be broke. I don't plan to spend more than a couple of bucks."

Tony gave Jason a light punch on the arm. "I may come out broke, but I will be smiling all the way back to the barracks."

As the bus stopped, the driver got out of his seat and turned and faced the men. "There are several things to do in this area. I have maps, and the place where we are dropping you off is marked with a large x. Please remember who you are and act like gentlemen."

The men all laughed and cheered.

"Okay, okay, let me continue. There are places where you could lose your money and others where you could lose your life. The Merry- Go-Round is the safest place with adult entertainment. I would not go any further down E. Street. It really gets rough. Remember all you have is a Cinderella pass. We must be back by twelve o'clock. I will be back here at 11:30."

Jason waited until everyone was off the bus. Stopping alongside the driver, he asked, "Where is there a good movie theater, and a good place to buy a hamburger?"

"That is not a question I get asked very often." Pointing to the road the driver said, "Go two blocks that way, and then take a left on Mason Avenue. There is a movie theater about five blocks on the right. There is a shopping area there. It is like a little city, and I am sure you will find a hamburger to your liking. I like a place called Eric's."

It was not long until he was standing in front of the theater looking at the posters and prints which showed scenes from the movies that were showing. They were showing, *The Major and the Minor.* The times were posted, and he found he would have to wait about forty minutes until it started. Looking across the street he spied a restaurant. It was Eric's. It was too early for lunch, but he went inside anyway. Eric's was a two-story diner. It had booths that would seat up to four people, and a counter which had stools for about twelve. They were not busy, so he took a booth and ordered a donut and a glass of milk.

"I think you have a better chance of getting milk at the camp than you would here. How about a cup of coffee, and if you need cream, I got some canned milk?"

Looking up at the waitress, he saw a woman in her late thirties or early forties with a kind look. "That will be fine."

When the waitress sat his donut and coffee in front of him, she said, "We don't get many soldiers here in Middletown. Why are you so far off the beaten path?"

"I am going to the movies. I just wanted a taste of home. This is close. We have a place back home a lot like this. It is much smaller, but it has the same atmosphere. I understand you have great hamburgers. I may come back after the movie."

"We do have great hamburgers. I hope you do come back. By the way, where is home?"

"I am from Richmond, Kentucky. It is a small town and I had never been out of Richmond until I joined the army."

"Welcome to Middletown." She then turned and walked away. When he finished the coffee and doughnut, he looked at his bill. Five cents for the coffee and five cents for the doughnut. He placed a quarter on the counter and left.

Sitting down in the dark movie, he noticed the odor of popcorn, and the theater had a damp smell. The floor was a bit sticky. Someone had mopped the floor but had done a poor job. The theater had continuous showings. He got himself a coke and a bag of popcorn. When he took his seat the news reel was showing. He was surprised that they were still showing news about the taking of Paris. *I guess that is big news,* he thought to himself. He looked around the theater and saw that there were only about fifteen to twenty people to see the movie. When the movie started, he was about to leave the real world behind for a while. He almost laughed out loud several times during the movie. He really liked Ginger Rogers. She was more than a dancer. She was a good actress. She played the part of a young girl about his age, and she also played the part of a young woman.

Coming out of the movie, he could see a large clock at the top of some type of government building. The time was three forty-five or in army time fifteen forty-five. *I will never get used to army time. Too early to eat and way too early to catch the bus back to the camp.* Deciding to take a walk, he started walking away from the movie theater, and headed down the street. It wasn't long until he came to a park. Children were playing, and the sound they were making was that of a gaggle of geese.

He sat down to watch the children playing and enjoy the sun. After just a few minutes he closed his eyes and was just about to go to sleep.

Carman had noticed the young soldier lying back on the bench and didn't recognize him as the young man who had come to her diner earlier. As she got closer, she saw who he was. She thought of her brother, Wayne. Wayne had been in the army for four years. He had survived D-day and was now somewhere around Paris. For a moment she could see her brother stretched out on that park bench. *I hope that where ever you are, somebody will offer you some kindness and comfort.*

Looking at Jason she said, "I don't think going to sleep on the bench is too good of an idea. You might wake up and find that you have less money than you had before your nap."

Opening his eyes and looking up he could see a woman. She was the lady that had waited on him at the diner. "I was about to go to sleep. I was told that this was a good part of town. I will take your advice, and head back to the diner."

Giving him a smile, she said, "This is a good part of town, but down the street is a really poor area of the city. They don't have much, and they do what they can to survive. Some have been known to come to this area and take what they can. I don't think you can trust anyone. My name is Carman, Carman Reed. You are?"

"Jason."

"You are Jason from Kentucky. Walk with me Jason. You said that you wanted a good hamburger. I am heading back to the diner now. We don't get many soldiers in this part of town. Most of you go the other way. Why are you here, and about to go to sleep on a bench in the park? Most of the soldiers are looking for excitement, and you don't find any excitement in Middletown."

"If by excitement, you mean strip joints, I guess you are right. I was invited to join my friends at a place called the Merry-Go-Round, but I decided I would rather see a movie and have a good hamburger."

Carman gave Jason a big smile. She could see that he was younger than most soldiers, but wise enough not to go to a place like the Merry-Go-Round. "So, you don't like women. What did you say your name was? Oh yes, you said your name was Eunuch."

"My name is Jason." He then figured out that she was making fun of him. "I like women, but I have heard that soldiers who go to places like the Merry-Go-Round spend all their money buying women overpriced drinks and other things. I don't want to waste money. I have plans when this war ends."

"That seems very smart. I hope you are not offended by my crude remarks. I was just joking with you. May I ask what you plan to do after the war?"

He smiled. "You didn't offend me. I don't even know what a eunuch is."

Jason did not know why, but he wanted to talk about what he wanted to do after the war. After all he had no family, and no close friends. He needed to talk. "My father was a carpenter. He was very good, but we barely made a living. He had these plans of he and I becoming partners in the business. I never told him that was not what I wanted to do."

"What do you want to do?"

"I want to go to college. I want to design something big and then create it." He found that he was getting excited.

Carman pointed ahead. "We are almost back to the cafe." Jason had been talking so much that he never noticed that they were approaching the diner. "I am very good at drawing. I can just about draw anything. I can look at a building one time and remember every detail, and put it on paper. My teachers told me I was gifted. When I get home, I want to go to college. I want to become an architect, or maybe an engineer. That is going to take money. My father died just this year, and I have no family and we owned no property. When I sold everything we had, it was less than two hundred dollars. I put most of it in the bank and joined the army. I am sending half my money to my account. If I can survive this war, maybe I will be able to complete my dream."

Again, Carman's thoughts turned to Wayne. Wayne was older, but he was a lot like Jason. "How old are you Jason?" They were now at the diner and Carman opened the door and the two of them walked in. He did not give an answer. Jason was about five feet eight inches tall and still growing. He looked like a young man, but Carman could see the immaturity in him.

Jason suddenly realized where they were. "Do you have to go back to work?"

Smiling, Carman said, "Yes and no. My husband and I own this diner. We live upstairs. Come with me. I want you to meet him."

They walked to the back of the diner and Carman opened the door which led upstairs. When they reached the top of the stairs, Jason saw a man sitting in a wheelchair. The man turned his chair to face Jason and said, "Who do we have here?"

"Sir, my name is Jason. Your wife was kind enough to invite me into your home. It is good to meet you."

"You are training at the base. Soon you will be off to fight. Do you have any idea where you will be going?"

"No sir. They have not given us that information."

"Have a seat, we can listen to the radio together. You can rest up for a while."

Jason didn't want to stay, but Carman said, "Please have a seat and stay awhile. Eric does not get a lot of visitors. He was injured and does not get to leave this apartment very often. He will enjoy the company."

Jason took a seat in a large recliner. Carman turned on the radio. "I am going down to the diner and help with the evening rush. You two have a good visit."

Jason found that he enjoyed talking to Eric. He had worked in construction and was injured working on a pipeline when a ditch wall collapsed on him. The company gave him a settlement and he and Carman bought the diner. That was fifteen years ago. He could walk, but not very far, and it was a real struggle to go up or down the steps. After a while the conversation slowed down, and Jason drifted off to sleep. He was not in a deep sleep and could faintly hear the radio playing.

Suddenly he opened his eyes and standing in front of his chair was a girl about sixteen years of age. He didn't say anything, just stared at her. For a moment neither said anything. He looked to his right and Eric was not there.

"Daddy went to bed. He can't sit up too long. He gets tired. My name is Molly. Mother told me that your name is Jason."

Jason still didn't say anything. He just stared at Molly. She had long brown hair. She was wearing a short sleeved blue dress that clung to her body. She had a figure that was beyond her years, and he found that she was very attractive.

"Mother says you are going to eat with us. What makes you so special Jason? She has never invited any soldiers to join us for supper. Come to think of it, we don't hardly ever see any soldiers in this part of town. You must have made quite an impression on her." Molly walked over to the window and pulled the curtains open and the room came alive with the sunlight.

Jason tried not to stare at Molly. For the first time he looked around the room. He could see the wall was covered with a pale-yellow wallpaper. The living room and the dining room were combined into one room. There was and icebox against the wall, and he noticed there was no stove. There was a small table with four wooden chairs that did not match. Jason was finally able to find his voice. "I ate here earlier and later we ran across each other in the park. She is a kind woman. I don't want to impose. If there is a problem I can leave?"

"Heavens no. There is no problem. Like I told you we don't get hardly any soldiers here and most of the young men from this area are soon off to war. You are a breath of fresh air. Mom said that you are going to eat with us. Mom will probably just bring some food up from the diner. She said something about you wanting a good hamburger. You are in for a treat. We have the best hamburgers in the world."

Jason did not realize that Carman expected him to eat with her family. Molly was right. It was not long until Carman was calling Molly to help carry the food up the stairs. The food was placed on the dining room table. It was in boxes, but Carman and Molly got plates from the cabinets and placed the burgers on the plates. Molly also placed potatoes on the plates and a green salad completed the meal.

"I can't remember ever eating a better meal." Looking at Molly, he spoke again. "You were right. That was a great burger. What is your secret?"

Molly gave Jason a big smile. "It is no secret. We cook our burgers in a large iron skillet. I don't know why, but they seem to taste better cooked that way."

Carman got up from the table. "I have a treat. Peach cobbler. It is a good thing we live in Georgia. We have lots of peaches. Now sugar is another matter, but we are going to eat well tonight."

Carman could tell that Eric did not want to use his ration stamps except for the diner. "Don't fret, Eric. Fred Pearson came into the diner this afternoon and traded me two pounds of sugar for his supper and a free breakfast in the morning. He can't eat sugar."

When the meal was over, Eric suggested that they play a game of hearts.

"I don't know how to play, but I would love to learn."

It was during this game that Eric, Molly, and Carman learned just how special a young man Jason was. He learned the game very quickly, and could keep track of the cards in his head or logically figure out who was holding which cards. He ended up winning most of the games.

Molly looked at the time. "It is about 7:30. Do you want to go to the movies?"

"I would love to, but I went to see the 'Major and the Minor' this afternoon."

Molly smiled. "You went to the Strand. There is another movie theater around the corner at the end of the block. They are showing 'Tall in the Saddle.' It is a John Wayne movie. Do you like westerns?"

"Westerns are my favorites." He looked at Carman. "Is it okay if we go to the movies?" Just for a moment he wished that he had asked Eric and not Carman. Was he making Eric feel he was not the head of the household?

Even though Carman had just met Jason that day, she felt like he was a good person, and her daughter would be safe. After all, they were only going to be about a block away from the diner. Permission was given and in a short time they were seated in the back of the theater, and they had been lucky. The movie was just about to start. Unlike the matinée, this movie was just about full. As the movie started Molly took Jason's arm and put it around her shoulders. She looked at him and whispered, "I want to be cozy, but don't get any ideas."

It wasn't long until Molly had laid her head on his shoulder and had placed one hand on his thigh. He had never had such a feeling. He knew very little about women and wasn't sure if he was reading her signals wrong. Maybe there aren't any signals, and he laid his head over and touched hers. It was not long until the movie was completely forgotten, and they were locked in a passionate kiss. The kisses continued throughout the movie. She had continued to move her hand up and down his thigh and a couple of times had moved extremely close to finding that he was more than excited. His hands seemed to have a mind of their own, and for the first time he found the softness and delight of a woman's breast. Molly did not object to his bold moves, and when the movie ended, and the lights came on, he was embarrassed to stand up. He quickly regained his composure and took Molly by the hand to lead her from the theater. He glanced at the large clock as they walked hand in hand back toward the diner. It was getting late, and he would need to head back to the bus soon. There was a bench in front of the diner which was now closed, and they continued the kissing and petting until he finally said, "I got to get back to catch the bus. I want to see you again, but I am not sure when I will get another leave."

They were standing facing each other, and she looked down. "There is something I need to tell you."

Kissing her on the top of her head he said, "What is it?"

"I sort of have a boyfriend. He was out of town this weekend. He went to visit his grandparents. I didn't know I would have such strong feelings for you. If you want to see me again, call me. You can reach me by calling the diner." Looking up she gave him a light kiss on the lips and went inside.

It did not take a brisk walk to get back to the bus stop, so he took his time. Many thoughts were rolling over and over in his mind. What did she mean when she said, I sort of have a boyfriend? You either have a boyfriend or you don't. Do Molly and her boyfriend make out like they had in the movies? Would she break it off with him to continue to see him? Does she let him touch her like he had? Maybe he shouldn't call her. After all he was leaving.

When he got back to the bus stop, he found he was one of the first to arrive, and the bus was waiting. The time was 11:20 but by 11:30 the bus was full of young men laughing and talking and telling each other about the women they had encountered that evening. When the roll was called all were there except three.

"Where is Tony?" He turned to the soldier across from him and repeated the question. "Where is Tony?"

"In jail. He made a fool of himself."

"What happened? He seemed so level headed."

"First, he got loaded and we started watching strippers perform at the club. There was this big breasted dark-haired stripper that came out, and she was a beauty. Tony fell in love with her. He didn't want anybody else looking at her and said he was going to marry her. One thing led to another and the next thing that happened was bouncers are carrying him out. I think they called the police. I haven't seen him since."

The bus was just about to pull out when a police car pulled up with its lights flashing. The car stopped. Two policemen got out and opened the back door and there were three soldiers in handcuffs. One was Tony. All three were placed on the front seat of the bus, but the cuffs were not removed. They would spend the next week in the brig at the base. On Monday during roll call, Tony was back in the unit, but he would be spending his nights in the brig.

Jason and Tony were going back to the barracks when Tony said, "I should have gone with you. I didn't get the woman, I have a terrible hangover, don't remember much except waking up in jail. My money is gone, and I am on report and have some charges to answer to. How was your leave?"

Jason smiled. "It could not have gone better."

During the next couple of weeks, the training intensified. Jason was no longer a boy but a fighting soldier. He felt equal to the men around him. He was able to call Molly about three times and looked forward to seeing her on the coming weekend pass.

When the weekend came, he had supper with Molly, Eric and

Carman at the diner, and later he and Molly took a walk in the park. He was both disappointed and jealous when Molly told him she had not broken up with her boyfriend.

"Is he here in town? How are you going to explain me if he sees us?"

"I was going to tell him, I just couldn't find the right time or place."

"What if he comes to see you tonight? How are you going to explain me?"

"I told him I was spending time with my girlfriends tonight. Don't worry, I will break it off. Tonight, I want to be with you." She turned and faced him and kissed him, and then they held each other.

He could smell her perfume, and her kisses tasted like sweet milk. Her body was soft, and he could lose himself just being near her.

"What do you want to do? Do you want to go to a movie?"

He really didn't want to see a movie. He wanted a place where they could be together and somewhat alone.

"My mother's sister lives about three blocks from here. I sometimes spend time over there, and she works at night. We could be alone and get to know each other better."

It wasn't long until Molly was reaching above the door and retrieving a key. Jason felt funny being in the house alone with Molly, but he was also excited.

When they got inside, he kissed her, but she suddenly broke the kiss and stepped back. "We have lots of time. Let's see if my aunt has some of those great small cokes. Going to the icebox she found two and opened them and gave one to Jason. "How old are you, Jason?"

He was caught off guard by her question. He decided he should not tell her that he was fifteen. "I am seventeen. I graduated from high school last May."

"I am sixteen. I am a junior." She set her coke down and went over and turned on the radio. She and Jason took a seat on the couch. It wasn't long until they were kissing and holding each other.

Stopping for a moment, he somehow felt he should explain himself to her. "I have never been with a woman. Are you sure you want to be with me?"

Molly didn't answer. As he continued to hold her, he briefly was disappointed that she had not said she had not been with anyone either, but the excitement of the moment quickly made those thoughts go away.

Suddenly they heard a noise. Someone was opening the front door. They broke their embrace and stood up and went to the door. "Who's there?" Molly seemed concerned as she opened the door.

"It's me, Molly, Aunt Carolyn. "What are you doing here?"

"It was hot out, and Jason and I decided to try to get out of the heat and listen to the radio. We can't talk to each other or listen to the radio back at the diner because Daddy keeps questioning Jason about the army and the war. By the way, this is Jason Terry. He is from Kentucky and is here doing his basic training."

Carolyn gave Jason a quick look and said, "it is very nice to meet you. I don't think you can beat the heat in this apartment. It is as hot in here as it is outside." She then smiled. "Maybe you two were heating the place up."

"Aunt Carolyn, why are you not at work?"

"Didn't your mother tell you? I just got back on the day shift and I have the day off. I had just left the apartment to run down to talk to my friend. I see you helped yourself to one of my cokes. If you two are looking for something to do, the amusement park is back open. It may be hot, but it would be fun."

Jason perked up. "How far is it?"

"It is about ten blocks. You have several choices about how to get there. You could walk. Take a bus or you could take a taxi. The bus comes by about every hour, and it would only cost a dime."

An hour later, Jason and Molly were on the Ferris wheel. Jason had turned back into a little boy and was really enjoying himself. This was something he never got to do when he was living back in Richmond. He barely had enough time to catch the bus back to the barracks.

Two leaves later, Jason and Molly were seated on the bench near the diner. It was getting late, and Jason had to keep looking at his watch to make sure he had enough time to catch the bus. "I am just about to finish my basic training, and I think I might be sent overseas soon. I have no idea where I am going, and there is a chance I might not get another leave before I am shipped out. The guys at the barracks say sometimes they give a leave, and sometimes they don't."

"If they ship you out before we see each other again, how will I be able to contact you?"

"I am going to give you an address. You write to it, and it does not matter where I am. The army will forward it to me."

"I know you don't have much time, but do you want a cup of coffee before you go?" They went inside, and Carman and a couple of waitresses were serving a room full of hungry customers.

"Look who I found wandering the streets."

Jason smiled and quickly went to Carman and gave her a hug. Carman stepped away from Jason and said with a concerned voice, "Are you about to be shipped out? Surely not."

"I don't know when, but it will be soon." He turned and found that Molly had gone upstairs. He took a seat and told the waitress near the table to bring him a cup of coffee. He waited for the coffee and for Molly to return. He had just about finished his coffee when Molly came down the steps. She had changed clothes and had her hair pulled back into a pony tail.

"I feel a lot better. It was hot in the movies and it is hot in here. Let's go back to the bench."

When they took their seat on the bench, Jason took Molly by the hand. "Molly I am not quite sure how to say this. I know that we are both young and I think you care about me too. I want you to wait for me."

"Jason, what are you really asking me? Do you want to marry me?"

"I do, but not until I get back from wherever it is that I am going. I want you to wait. I don't think it will be a long wait. Our troops are moving toward Germany. The war in the Pacific is going well. Some say the war in Europe will be over by Christmas. It might be over before I am ever in it."

Molly turned her back to Jason. "I told you that I had a boyfriend when you first came to the diner. I still have not told him about us."

Jason was confused. Why had she not told him? He surprised

himself when he said, "It is okay. You can tell him now." He took her in his arms and kissed her.

She returned the kiss, and he felt she was his forever. "I will write, and I will wait. Maybe you will get another leave before you go. I will tell Ray this week."

Jason kissed her again and turned and made his way up the street. On the way back to the barracks he was somewhat confused. Why had Molly never told Ray about him? Then a dark cloud came over him. He had visions of Ray and Molly kissing and holding each other. On the bus ride back to the barracks he found himself gripping the hand rail on the seat in front of him.

"Hold on Jet," Tony said with a smile. "We take these leaves to unwind, not to get worked up. Are you okay?"

Jason looked at Tony, "I am okay." Then he lay back in the seat and closed his eyes.

The next morning during roll call Sergeant Carr informed them that they were shipping out the following Wednesday. On Tuesday the captain addressed the entire company and wished them well. He had been so busy that he had not even had a chance to think about Molly.

All the men were lined up in front of their bunks when the captain said, "Men you have been trained by the best and you have done well. We wish you the best. Buses will be here in the morning to take you to the coast. I know you will not like what I am going to tell you, but you will not be allowed to contact anyone off the base. I assure you this is necessary. Once you are on the ship and it is out to sea, you will be told were you are going. You will be able to write to your loved ones then, but again I caution you. Give no information about where you are going."

After the captain had left, Jason went over and sat down on Tony's bed. "I wonder where we are going?"

Tony laughed. "Jason, you are one smart cookie to be so damn dumb. We are going to the east coast to catch a ship. That means we are not going to the Pacific. We are either going to France or Italy."

Italy During the War

Jason had never been outside the United States. He was both scared and excited. He had only read about Italy, and now he was going there. He remembered that in his fourth-grade history book, there was a picture of the Leaning Tower of Pisa. He wondered if he would get to see it. He also wondered if he might die in Italy. He might even be buried there. He had no family and no close friends. If he were killed in Italy, there would be no one to claim his body. He thought of Molly. Should he write to her? Should he write to Mr. Elmer Hall and tell him that he wanted any money he had in his account sent to her, if something happened to him? After all, he had told her to wait for him and said they would get married when he got back. For some reason he felt angry. Why had she never told her boyfriend about him? That night he wrote a short letter to let her know he was doing okay and that he would write a longer letter and tell her as much as he could. Now he was on the deck of a large ship with a thousand other guys, going to war.

Crossing the ocean was not easy. He had never seen so much water. When they had left port the ocean was smooth, but a half day into the voyage, the boat was rocking back and forth. By nightfall he was sick, and it didn't pass. He was really scared, and the closer he got to Italy the more scared he became. He debarked from the ship at Anzio, and his company moved toward Rome. He was excited to see Rome and other places he had read about in his history books. They stayed two days in Rome. On the second day in Rome he got a letter from Molly.

Dear Jason,

I hope this letter finds you well and that you will forgive me for what I am going to tell you. I told you that I would tell Ray about us, but I can't. I want you to know that the time we spent together will always be special to me. I know that in the future that you will find someone who is much better for you than me. You are a good person, and I know when you get this letter you will write and ask me to reconsider and wait for you. Don't. When this war is over, and you come back to the United States, you might want to come and see me. Don't. I will be married by then. Ray and I are going to get married after I graduate from high school. Mom and Dad send you their greetings.

Please don't hate me,
Molly

Jason took the letter and tossed it into the campfire. "Shit." As he watched the letter burn and turn to black ash, he did not feel hurt. He was surprised. He had a feeling of relief.

The next day his company moved up the peninsula to a city name Caseno. The Germans had left the city but were fortified in the hills north of the city. Twice on the trip they were scraped by German planes. The first attack killed three men and wounded seven more. As they moved beyond Caseno, German artillery found their range. It did very little damage, but they scared the death out of Jason. His company made camp north of the city and dug in near a small river. It was here that his life changed forever. They dug a line of shallow trenches and waited.

Lying back in his trench, he heard someone say, "No smoking, pass it on."

"Gosh, I really need a smoke, but I don't won't to become a sniper target either." Tony was as nervous as he was.

Jason looked over at Tony. "I got some gum. Will that help?"

"Yeah. Toss the package over here."

After throwing his gum over to Tony, Jason heard voices and someone coming from behind them. Looking up, he could make out Sergeant Harris and Lieutenant Forbes.

"Jet, we need you to come with us."

Saying nothing, Jason and the two soldiers moved back away from the front lines to a tent that had been set up.

The lieutenant spoke first. "The sergeant and I are going to go on a scouting mission. There is a church ahead of us near the river. It is about a half a mile walk. We don't think the Germans are in the church, but we really don't know. There is a priest there we think we can trust. We hope he will know the strength of the Germans and maybe their location. Your job is to come with us and wait some distance back from the church. If we get the information, and we are also discovered, your job is to get any information about the Germans back to the major. Headquarters is some 800 yards from our camp. Get there as quick as you can. The major thinks that the Germans have moved out or are in small numbers."

Jason scratched his head. "If you don't come back, what information will I have to give to the major?"

"You will know that we have been killed or captured. That will mean the Germans are at the church or just beyond. What you will not know is their strength. If morning comes and we are not back, try to find out the German strength. If we don't get back and we are spotted before we can get back to our lines, Sergeant and myself will hold off the Germans, while you get the information to the major. If there is gun fire the men at the camp will hear it. They will not let you back in camp without a password. The password is check-mate. The church is going to be about nine hundred yards from our camp. We hope we don't need your speed. We hope we can get the information, and all come back together. Remember, if daylight comes and we have not come back, and you don't see any Germans, hold your position until about mid-morning and observe what you can and then come back to the camp. We hope to be in and out but who knows. It could be a trap and the priest could be a German."

Stopping about one hundred yards from the church, Jason took his place near a rock wall in the high grass and watched the sergeant and the lieutenant make their way to the church. In a few minutes they disappeared into the darkness and he was alone. His heart was pounding so hard you could hear it. He tried to relax but found that he could not. Every sound made him more scared. He just knew the Germans would find him and his life would come to an end. Just before morning he was getting sleepy. The lieutenant and the sergeant had not returned.

Coming Back to Richmond

The hospital ship made several stops and had to wait for escort ships to make sure they got safely through the Strait and out of the Mediterranean. It was near the end of November after he arrived in England that he was scheduled for surgery. He had to wait another week before the surgery could be done on his leg. He was scared. While on the medical ship he hadn't thought about the procedure. His leg was starting to heal, and although he could not walk, he was not in a lot of pain.

Early one morning a nurse came into his room. She was smiling. "Looks like today is your day. I am here to get you ready. It won't be long until your leg will be good as new."

"Could you get me something to eat? I haven't had breakfast."

"Jason, you were told last night you could not have anything to drink or eat until after you came out of surgery. I doubt you will want anything after that for a while." She came over to the edge of his bed. "Let me roll you over just a bit. I need to give you a shot in that cute butt of yours. This is going to pinch a little."

It was not long until he was feeling extremely sleepy. He was aware that the nurse was still in the room, but he closed his eyes and drifted in and out of consciousness. He was aware that he had been placed on a medical cart and was being wheeled down a hallway. He could see the overhead lights passing, and the next thing he knew a man was placing a mask that covered his mouth and nose, and then sleep came. He entered the magic world of dreams. In his dreams he was standing in front of a church. The church had a large steeple which contained three bells. In his dream the church just disappeared.

He was unaware that he was in surgery for nine hours. His first consciousness after the surgery was that he was in a shallow sleep. He could hear voices. Voices of nurses, or were they angels? He heard one clearly say, "I can't get a pulse." He heard another female voice say with some alarm. "Keep trying, I will get the doctor." His next memory was waking up in his hospital room with a terrible headache.

A nurse was standing by his bed. "Don't try to raise up. You must lie flat. If you raise up your head will hurt even worse than it is now. You must lie still for a couple of hours."

For a moment he had no idea where he was. The lying on his back seemed to last forever. When he was allowed to sit up, he found he was full of stomach gas. It was late in the night that a nurse came in with some soft food.

"I can't eat anything. My stomach feels like it is going to explode."

"I know how you feel, but believe me, the food will help take that gas down. You will soon feel better."

Taking food and starting to eat, he looked at the nurse. "What is your name?"

"My name is Helen, Helen Walters."

"You are not English, you are an American. Where are you from?"

"Can't jee tell." She stressed her accent. "I am from Georgia. I am from a little town just outside of Atlanta."

"I have never been to Atlanta, but I did my basic training in Georgia. You were right. The food is helping. I am starting to feel better."

Helen stood up and gave him a big smile. "I am going to leave now. You have had a very long day. I can give you something to help you sleep, but it is better if I don't. You were in a very deep sleep during the operation, and the nurses said that they had trouble getting you to wake up. Don't scare us like that anymore."

"I will trust you. I am still sleepy from whatever you gave me during the surgery."

"I will check on you tomorrow. The doctor is going to come by later. He has had a long day too, so he might not be here till in the morning."

It was well after sunrise when Doctor Redman came by. "How are you feeling? Are you in any pain?"

Jason had been asleep. "No, well maybe a little. My back hurts. I need to be able to move some. I can't even shift my weight."

"I am sorry about that. I will instruct the nurses to give you a massage and move you some. I don't want to move you too much. Your leg was in worse shape than we thought. I wish we could have operated sooner. We should have flown you back from the front. The bullet had hit the side of your femur. The bone was not completely broken, but a large part of the side of the bone was destroyed. We grafted another piece to strengthen the area and placed a steel plate alongside of the damaged area. For that reason, you are going to have to stay here longer than expected. It will take about four weeks for the graft. When we are sure you are healing, we will take the steel rod out. You should be able to sit up by the end of the week, and we will start your therapy then. By the first of the year, you should be walking, and then we will remove the plate. Do you have any questions?"

Jason didn't say anything for a moment. "Will I be able to go back to the front lines? I think I should rejoin my outfit if I can."

"I don't know about that. That should not be our concern at this point. I must be honest with you. There is a chance that what we have done will not work. If it does not, then we will have to see if we can just save your leg. Let's hope this goes well."

That night he could not sleep. His leg didn't hurt, but his back ached. About 2:00 he called the nurse, and she gave him a shot and he quickly went to sleep. He was able to sleep until about 7:00. Once he was awake, he was propped up a little and had his breakfast. About 10:00, Helen came in. She was smiling and seemed to glide about the room. "Good morning, Sunshine. How was your night?"

"Not bad. The shot I had about 2:00 helped."

"Doctor Redman has on your chart that you need a little tender love and care this morning. I am going to do two things for you this morning. First, I am going to give you a bath. While I am doing that, I am going to massage those sore areas of your back or what I can reach without moving you too much."

Helen quickly left the room, and it was not long until she returned with a pan of hot water and several washcloths. "Okay big boy. I am going to make you feel so much better." She quickly threw back his cover and kept him covered from the waist down. She removed his gown and said, "Just close your eyes and relax."

He could feel the warm wash cloth against his skin. The warm water felt so good. As she soaped his skin, it felt so good he closed his eyes and for some reason started to think of Molly. He wondered what had happened to her. Did she care about him at all? Was she just looking for excitement? She had to care about him. He let his thoughts drift. Maybe he would look her up after the war.

Nurse Helen continued her magic, carefully removing the soap suds from his chest and stomach before moving to other parts of his body. "There are some areas here that I think I will let you take care of." She looked at him, and he was sound asleep.

He spent several weeks of rehabilitation and was soon walking with a walker. One afternoon while sitting on the edge of his bed, the doctor knocked on the door and walked in. "Well, Jason, I have just looked at the last x-rays, and your leg is healing nicely. That's the good news."

Jason looked somewhat concerned. "What is the bad news?"

"It really is not that bad, some might think it is good news. We are ready to do the second operation. Your x-rays really look good. Once we remove the steel rod, your recovery should go quickly. I would say that in three weeks you will be able to walk with a cane, and in three more, hopefully you can throw the cane away."

Jason was propped up in his bed, and he could see out the window. The rain was coming down. It was not a hard rain, but a gentle mist, accompanied by a fog. He again looked at the calendar which was hanging on the wall. December 16, 1944. It was a special day in a not so special way. It was his birthday. He was now sixteen years old. *Shouldn't there be some rite of passage? No. He gave that up when his father lied about his age. He gave it up when he used that fake age to join the army.* He could hear the steady drops of rain falling from a window which was just a few feet from his bed. *Just another day.*

Suddenly there was a light knock on his door. Looking up, he saw nurse Helen. She came into the room pushing a wheelchair. "Hello, Sunshine. I get to be your date on this very special day. We are going to the recreational area. Do you want to go by this chair, or do you want to use your sticks?"

"What is so special about today?" *Surely, she did not know that today was his birthday.*

"Well it is special because I have the day off. I decided that I am going to take you to the recreational area and cheer you up. So, what is it going to be? Do you want to ride or walk?"

Anything is better than sitting in the bed all day. "I think I will ride. It is a long way to the recreational area."

Helen helped Jason slide from his bed over into the wheelchair. They were soon moving down the hallway. When they got to the recreational area the door was closed, and Helen pushed the swinging doors open and moved the chair inside.

Jason was surprised. The whole area was empty. Then the door to the kitchen opened, and several men and nurses came out holding a cake and singing Happy Birthday. Jason could not believe his eyes. They all gathered around his chair and continued to sing.

The party lasted for about two hours. At the end of the first hour people started to leave, and near the end of the second hour, Jason and Helen were seated at a table and Jason was eating his second piece of cake. He smiled at Helen and said, "I can't thank you enough. It is the best birthday I have ever had. This was my first birthday party."

"I am glad we were able to make this day special. Everyone should celebrate when they turn eighteen. You were a man when you came to this hospital, but this makes it official. I am going to leave the rest of your cake here for the staff that was on duty. I will take you back to your room now."

Helen took Jason back to his room. "I think I want to sit up for a while. What are you going to do?"

"I am on call. I am going back to my room and get some rest. I might be called to go back on duty. I will be back here tonight, and I will stop by and check on you."

Helen was good to her word. At 1900 hours she stopped by his room and came in and looked at his chart. "I see you are going back into surgery very soon. This should put you on the road to a quick recovery."

He was just about to say something when an announcement came over the speaker. "All nurses and doctors report to the briefing room." Helen quickly left the room.

Later that night, a young English nurse came into his room. "What is going on? There has been a lot of activity this afternoon."

"The Germans have attacked the Americans in the Ardennes. It sounds like it may be a major offensive. The Americans were caught off guard. It looks like there are going to be major casualties. Part of our staff is being mobilized to go to mobile units to help."

The next day, Jason found out that his operation was going on as scheduled, but nurse Helen was going to be transferred to France. He spent Christmas Day being prepped for surgery. The day after Christmas he was again in the operating room. He was lucky. Many of the planned surgeries where postponed because of the influx of injuries coming from the battle.

After the surgery, he was told by his doctor that the operation went extremely well, and he should be better than ever.

The doctor was right. Six weeks after the operation Jason was walking without a cane and had only a slight limp. He was no longer in the hospital, but staying in the local barracks. On Thursday he had an appointment at the hospital. After the x-ray he was in a small room waiting for the doctor. The wait seemed like forever.

Suddenly the door opened, and in walked the doctor. "Well Sergeant Terry, we are ready to dismiss you. Your leg is weak, too weak to return you to combat. So, we have to make a choice. We can send you home, or let you work on the base doing clerical work. The choice is yours."

Jason smiled. "Are you talking to the right patient? I am a private, not a sergeant."

"Yes, I am talking to the right patient. You have been promoted. The promotion has been back dated to the time you were wounded. I guess war heroes get some privileges."

"Wow. I guess I am making big bucks. I have not seen a pay check since I got wounded. How do I get those?"

"You need to check with the paymaster."

"I am somewhat relieved that I will not be back in combat. I want to stay in the army until the war is over. I would be glad to work in an office. I don't want to go back into combat. In fact, I don't remember ever being in battle. I really don't think I even want the medals. I did leave some friends in Italy and would like to see them again."

"It is my understanding that there was heavy fighting after you left Italy. Some of the boys may not have made it."

"Is there a way that I can find out who in my company might have been killed or wounded?"

Jason never got an answer to his question. A few days later he was assigned as a clerk to an infantry division that had a headquarters about twenty miles from the hospital. It was here that he would spend the next several months. In May, the war in Europe came to an end. Jason spent the next two months with the paperwork that was needed to move many soldiers to the Pacific and move others home. After the war he would find out that few of the soldiers that he helped transfer to the Pacific saw action.

Near the end of June, he was seated on a bench in a park. He had bought a drawing pad and some pencils and was going to draw some of the buildings that bordered the square. Just before he started, he looked up and saw a familiar face. "Nurse Helen, it is good to see you."

Looking down at Jason and with a big smile she said, "Jason, I wondered what happened to you!"

"I am working as a clerk in an infantry division."

"I thought that you might come by and see me. After all, we were so close," she giggled with a flirtation in her voice.

Jason had a perplexed look on his face. "I didn't know you were back from France. We were close?"

Helen laughed, "You don't remember that nice warm bath I gave you after your first surgery? You were supposed to help me, but you went to sleep." She could see that he was embarrassed and was turning red. "Don't worry, I had an orderly come in and finish the job. They are moving lots of men off this island. Where are you going next?"

Jason regained his composure. "I am not sure. I think my leg is as good as new. They might send me to the Pacific. Please, sit down."

Helen took a seat and they started to talk. Jason took out his drawing pad and started to sketch. They talked for over an hour. He found out that she was twenty-three years old. She was married, and her husband was currently in Berlin. He was a captain, and they had married just before the war started. He did not plan to leave the service, and she was going to join him in Berlin in about a month. During his stay in the hospital, he had not noticed how stunning she was. She had a sculptured face, and a good figure, but her beauty was more than that. He also found out that just about every man that she met wanted to take her out. Maybe she just felt safe sitting with him because the age difference was obvious.

"Jason, what are you going to do when this war is over? Be honest, how old are you?"

"To answer your last question first, I am sixteen. I lied about my age to get into the service. I have finished high school, and I hope to go to college. My mother died when I was four, and my father needed me to be in school. He needed free daycare, so he added a couple of years to my age. I have saved over half my money, and have been sending it back to a college fund I set up before I left. I think things will work out."

For some reason he needed to talk about Molly. He had not told anyone about her. "There is something else. While doing my basic training I met a girl. Her name was Molly Reed. I thought we loved each other, and she was going to wait for me, but after I arrived in Italy, I got a letter from her informing me she was not going to wait, and she had someone else. I think I might just look her up. I need some type of closure."

At first Helen didn't say anything. Then she spoke in a very tender voice. "Her letter was your closure. You were too young to make such a commitment. There are lots of girls like Molly. They get caught up in the excitement of the moment, and when the soldier has been shipped out, the excitement is gone. The real tragedy is that many times a quickie marriage takes place and all we have left is for a soldier to come home to a loveless marriage or an unfaithful wife. I know you want to know what happened, but I think you are better off never to see your Molly again."

"How long did you know your husband before you were married?"

Helen smiled. "We met in grade school."

Jason didn't say anything, but just closed his drawing book. He just sat there for a few moments. Then he spoke. "I think your husband is the luckiest guy in the world. I told you that my mother died when I was four. My father died last spring. I have no family left, and in one afternoon you have made me feel like you are a member of my family."

Helen was almost overcome with sadness for Jason. Instinctively she reached over and gave him a hug and to her surprise, he buried his head in her shoulder and started to cry. *How cruel war can be. We have taken a child and put him in combat. I fear he may be damaged forever.* She held him for several minutes and when he released her, he said, "I am sorry. I don't know what came over me."

Helen reached up and wiped the tears from her own eyes. "I think you are going to be just fine. You have a plan, a good plan. You are going to be okay."

Saying nothing, he opened his drawing pad and took out the drawing he had just completed and handed it to Helen. She looked at it and was speechless. He had drawn a picture of her.

"This is the best drawing I have ever seen. Do you really see me as beautiful as you have drawn me?"

"I think everybody who meets you sees you as an angel."

"You are beyond talented. Are you going to major in art when you get back to the United States?"

"No, I am going to become an engineer or an architect. I like math, and I think I am quite good at it. I hope you will send the drawing to your husband. I think he might like to have it."

They both got off the park bench at the same time and hugged each other. "There is a chance that we might not see each other again. If we don't, good luck, and I hope to read good things about what you have done in the future."

What Helen had said was true. They would never meet again. Near the end of July, he was called back to the United States. He had received a telegram inviting him to Washington, D.C., telling him he was going to receive the Congressional Medal of Honor.

This was an honor he did not want. He had no memory of doing anything that would merit such an honor. However, there were many witnesses that had confirmed his actions. They included a German soldier, Italian civilians and several American soldiers. He had refused to read the events of that day.

Just before he was to leave for the United States, he stopped by his headquarters and asked to see his commanding officer. General Tyler knew about the award and cleared his schedule to see him. "Sergeant Terry, it is an honor to see you. I received a communication about your honor. How can I help you?"

"I am leaving at the end of the week, and there are some things I don't understand. I have known that I was recommended for the honor before I left Italy. It was my understanding that these things take time, lots of time. Why is this happening so quickly?"

"Jason, I can call you Jason, I will be honest with you. You were put on the fast track to receive the award because the army wants and needs you to go on a bond drive. A Medal of Honor winner will help raise lots of money."

"So, I am being used."

"Yes and no. I have seen your records. You have earned that medal ten times over. You are going to receive the medal. You are just going to get it sooner than expected."

"I am not sure I can go on a bond drive. I would not know what to say. I don't even remember anything about being in combat. This is something I can't do."

General Tyler asked for Jason's records. "This will take some time. Do you want some coffee while we wait?"

The two men exchanged small talk while they waited. When the records arrived, General Tyler looked over them. He called for his secretary and asked for Dr. Allen. Dr. Allen was in the base hospital, which was only a couple of blocks away. In just a few minutes, the secretary came back and said, "He says he can't come right now."

"Call back and tell him that if he is not in my office in the next fifteen minutes, his office will be in the back building downstairs next to the latrine."

It was not long until Dr. Allen was coming into General Tyler's office. "Sorry, I had to move my schedule around. What do you need?"

"Dr. Allen, this is Sergeant Terry. I want you to give him an examination. I think you will find that he is suffering from shell-shock. You will find that he is no longer able to serve in our army and needs to be sent home. Put in the report that he still will be in Washington to receive his medal."

"You want me to make up a report to get this man out of the army."

"Look at the damn report. You are not making up anything. In my and your opinion he needs to avoid stress for a while."

On his way to Washington, Jason thought about the award. He would have to hear the events while standing in front of the president of the United States and many others. General Tyler was right. He needed to avoid stress. How could he get out of this?

On August 5, he received his discharge papers, and he went to Washington to receive his medal. He spent the night at a hotel which was in walking distance of the White House. The morning of the award he slept late. The ceremony was to take place at 1:00 pm. He was supposed to meet his guide, John Riddick. Two hours before the ceremony to get his instructions and protocol about the ceremony. After a late breakfast, he started walking toward the White House. He was surprised that there was so much activity going on. People were in groups, and many were talking and motioning with their hands. Some were even running. *Is Washington always like this?* When he arrived at the gate, he handed the guard at the gate his letter and pass.

The guard looked at the papers and then said, "The ceremony today has been postponed and has not been rescheduled."

Jason had not expected this. "Why? Is there a reason?"

"Have you not heard? We dropped an atomic bomb on Japan this morning. There is a chance that the war is going to be over soon. You will be contacted with information about a reschedule."

Jason felt relieved. He felt relieved that the war was coming to an end, and he felt relieved that he did not have to go through the ceremony. "Can you tell me where the bus station is located? I need to go home."

After he got directions, he made his way back to the hotel, packed his duffel bag, and at 3:00 am the next morning he was on his way back to Richmond.

The bus ride to Richmond was an adventure. It was hot. He tried to sleep but found he could not. The bus seemed to stop at every little town between Richmond and Washington, and he had to change buses five times. When they did pull into the bus station at Richmond it was night time. Jason secured his duffel bag and walked up a short hill to Main Street. On the corner of Main Street and Third Street was the Glyndon Hotel, a five-story hotel, which also had a restaurant. He was hungry, but he decided he needed to check in first. He was able to get a room for three dollars. He decided not to eat in the restaurant at the hotel, but at a drug store which had a diner and was right next to the hotel. His meal cost fifty cents. *Money is not going to last long at this rate.* The long ride from Washington had made him very tired so he went to bed around 10:30. Then it came. The same dream that haunted him again and again. In his dream he was standing in a field of tall grass. He was in a combat uniform. He was standing in front of a large church. The church was old and magnificent. Above the front door was a sign which said something in Italian. At the top of the church was a bell tower. The bells were not ringing, and he could clearly see three bells. Then all at once the church disappeared, and he woke up.

The next day he went to see Mr. Elmer Hall. The lady at the front desk asked, “Do you have an appointment?”

He looked at the young lady. She was giving him a big smile. “No, I don’t. I just got out of the army and back into town yesterday. Do I have to make an appointment?”

“Let me see.” She quickly glanced down at an appointment book on her desk and got up and disappeared through a door that was behind her desk. It was just a few moments until she returned and was followed by Elmer Hall.

“Jason, you look fine. I like the cut of that uniform. Are you out of the army or are you on your way to the Pacific?” He extended his hand to Jason.

Jason took his hand. "It is really good to see you, Mr. Hall. I am out. The war seems to be coming to an end, and I don't think they need me."

"Come into my office. I know you have questions."

Jason followed Mr. Hall into his office and took a seat in front of his desk without being asked. Mr. Hall took a seat and then pushed a button on his intercom. "Mildred, bring me the records for Jason E. Terry. I think he is the only Jason Terry in our records. I also want you to bring us a couple of cups of coffee." He then turned to Jason. "Where were you during the war, and did you see any combat?"

"I was in Italy. I did see combat. I was so scared I don't remember most of it."

"I am glad you got through it intact. You are intact, I assume."

"No, I won a purple heart."

"Where did you get it?"

"They gave it to me while I was in England."

Mr. Hall laughed. "That is not what I mean, and you know it. Where were you wounded?"

"In the leg. I got shot in the leg while I was in Italy. I have been in England recovering. My leg is strong, and I guess that I could have gone back into combat, but like I said, the war is coming to an end."

"What are you going to do now that you are back in Richmond? I can help get you a job. Your father was a great carpenter, and if you have any of his skills you will soon be in demand. When this war does end, we are going to have a building boom."

"I don't want to go back to work, or at least not full time. I want to go to college. A lot depends on how much money I have. I have already applied for the G.I. Bill. This would help pay my tuition and give me some money to live on. I am not sure how much. I think it will give me somewhere around twenty dollars a month. I am not sure. I am sure I can swing it. I may need some of the money here to start the first semester."

Just about that time an older woman came into the room. She was carrying a tray with two cups and a small bowl of sugar and a small pitcher of cream. She placed a large index card in front of Mr. Hall. Mr.

Hall picked up a cup of coffee and handed it to Jason. "Do you want sugar or cream?"

"No, black is just fine."

Mr. Hall picked up the card and looked at it as the lady left the room. "Well, you put one hundred and seventy-five into the account before you left. You have sent us three hundred and twenty dollars from your military pay, and with interest you have received another twelve dollars and fifty cents. It looks like you have five hundred and seven dollars. What do you want us to do?"

"I understand that the money is in a savings account. I need to transfer it to a checking account. Can you do this for me? I also have my last three checks from the army which I want to add to the account."

Mr. Hall again pushed the intercom button. "Mildred, come back in here please." He then said to Jason, "This will not take long."

About this time Mildred came back into the office. Mr. Hall handed her the card. "Add these checks to the balance, and then transfer the account balance into a checking account. When you get finished doing that bring me some counter checks. Ten will be enough until we get some printed."

It was not long until Jason was leaving the bank and started walking up the street. He did not want to spend another night in the hotel, but did not think he had any other choice. As he walked up Main Street, he decided he would walk out and visit where he used to live. It was only a little over a half mile. As he approached the street that led to his old home, he looked over to his right and saw the large old house that belonged to Mr. Winston. On impulse he crossed the street and walked down the path that led to the front door. The grass around the house was tall and had not been cut for a while. He walked up the steps and rang the bell. In a few moments a woman in her late fifties or early sixties opened the door.

"Is Mr. Winston here?" he asked.

"He is. May I ask who is calling?"

"My name is Jason Terry."

Before she could say anything, he heard a voice. "Let whoever it is in. We don't get that many visitors."

The lady opened the door and motioned for Jason to come on in. Sitting in a large overstuffed chair Mr. Winston said, "What can I do for you young man?"

"Mr. Winston, you probably don't remember me, but my father did some woodwork for you a few years back. He built you some cabinets and a table."

"Terry, yes, I remember. Damn fine work and I love that table. Sit down and talk to me for a while. I don't get out much anymore, and you can bring me up to date. I was sorry to hear about your father. He was a gifted man when it came to working with wood."

"Thank you. I don't think I could give you much information about Richmond. I just got into town yesterday. I think you know the war is coming to an end."

"I see you are in the army."

"No, I was in the army. I was discharged several days ago."

"Are you looking for a job? Is that why you came to visit?"

"No, I am not looking for a job. I want to go to college. I want to become an engineer. I want to design and build things. I am going to enroll at the local college and start the fall semester. School is going to start in a couple of weeks. I need a place to live."

Mr. Winston laughed. "You see this big house from the road, and you think I might have an extra room."

"No, that's not what I think. I remember that when my dad was working for you, we went into a small out building behind the house. It had a small apartment above the garage. I would like to rent it from you."

Mr. Winston again laughed. "How much do you think you could pay for my little apartment? You have seen it. It is not very big." Mr. Winston then laughed again. "I might want a lot of money."

Jason could sense that Mr. Winston had no interest in renting him the apartment, but then he surprised him. "As I recall, the apartment is a mess. I don't plan to pay you anything. I will fix up the apartment and move in. On Monday, Wednesday and half a day on Saturday, I will work on your yard, keep It mowed. The bushes and trees need trimming or cutting, and I saw your wooden fence that runs down each side of the property needs repair and painting. You will pay for materials and paint, and I will complete the repairs."

Mr. Winston smiled. He really liked this young man. He turned to the woman who had not left the room. "May, go get that set of keys that hangs near the back door and bring them here."

May was gone for only a moment. She handed Mr. Winston the keys. He fiddled with the keys for a moment and soon was taking one off. "Take this key and examine the apartment. If you think you can make the place livable, then come back and see me."

Jason took the key, and May showed him out the back door, and he made his way over to the shed. Using the key, he opened the padlock on the door, swung it open and walked inside. Inside the shed was a lawn mower, and other tools he could use to fix up the yard. On the right side of the shed was a set of steps which led to the apartment. As Mr. Winston had said, it was small. It also had a small table and a half size bed and a couple of lamps. It had running water and a very small bathroom. He took a seat on the bed and looked around the apartment. A small window gave him a limited view of the grounds. *This will do.*

In just a few moments he was back with Mr. Winston. "The apartment will do just fine. Today is Thursday. Tomorrow I am going to try to get registered for the fall semester. I will move in tomorrow afternoon. The place is a bit dusty, and I will need some cleaning supplies. I need a couple of sheets and a blanket or two. I also need some other clothing. I can't wear this army stuff anymore. I will do my shopping and get what I need after I take care of getting into school. I will see you tomorrow."

That night as Jason slept, again the dream came. He again was standing in a field of tall grass in front of a church. When he awoke, he was covered with sweat, and he had a headache. He got a drink of water and thought about the dream. What could it possibly mean?

The next day he enrolled for the fall semester. It took most of the morning, and he had to write his first check, and his second and his third. *I hope this G.I. Bill comes through. At this rate my money will not last too long.*

That afternoon he stopped by J.C. Penney and purchased some

sheets and blankets and some cleaning supplies. He was also able to find a secondhand clothing store and purchase some civilian and work clothing. That afternoon he cleaned the apartment and prepared to spend his first night in his new home. School would not start for a few days, so he decided to start his chores.

The next morning, Jake Winston was in the kitchen. May had made him a pot of coffee and fried a couple of eggs and sausages.

"Where do you want to eat, at the table or on the back porch?"

"Help me through the door? I want to eat on the porch." As he went onto the porch, he noticed the tall grass in the back of the property was lying flat. It had been cut. There was a small barn directly behind the house about twenty yards away. To the right of the barn he saw the young man with the scythe. With each swing, more grass and weeds fell to the ground.

This is going to be a good deal, he thought.

Going to College

Jason liked going to college. Majoring in engineering and preparing for architecture required a heavy load of math. The first semester he took two math classes, an English class, a science class, social studies and an elective art class. After about a month his art teacher was encouraging him to make art his major, but Jason stuck to his plan.

He enjoyed working and staying at the Winston home. His work on the yard was showing progress, but it would not be long until the weather turned cold and there would be little yard work to do. In October, he measured the fence along the side and back. There were over seventy-five planks that needed to be replaced, and the fence badly needed painting. Coming home from school on Thursday he went to see Mr. Winston.

"I am not sure you are going to like what I have to tell you about your fence."

"Damn Jason, just cut to the chase. What do we need?"

"You have seventy-five slats in your fence that need to be replaced. It would be a waste of paint to paint boards that are so rotten."

Mr. Winston smiled. "I guess that is the bad news. Do you have any good news?"

"Over half the fence is in good shape and only needs cleaning and painting."

Mr. Winston gave Jason a smile. "Do you have figures and measurements?"

He handed Mr. Winston a list of what was needed to repair the fence. "If this is going to cost a lot, we could do this a little at a time, or we could maybe set up some payments, so it won't be so much at one time."

"That will not be necessary. I'll take the figures and look at them. If I need money I will go to the bank. I believe that I am okay." He liked the idea that Jason wanted to look out for his money. It was a sign that he knew the value of the dollar and that Jason had grown up with very little.

When Jason came home after class on Friday, he saw the wood stacked up in front of the shed. There were wooden planks for the fence and several cans of paint and brushes. It looked a little like rain, so Jason opened the shed and carried all the wood inside. On Saturday morning it was raining so he spent the morning cutting the planks to the exact length and pre-drilling the holes for the nails. By noon he was finished, and he went upstairs and fixed himself something to eat and started to study.

By three o'clock he was tired, so he lay down on the bed and fell asleep. The dream came again. He was again standing in a field of golden grass that came almost up to his waist. He was looking at a large church. Looking up at the bell tower he could make out three bells, and beyond he could see the dark clouds. Then the church disappeared, and like always he came out of his sleep. He didn't know, why but this dream always disturbed him. It really was a very peaceful dream. Perhaps it was because the church always disappeared.

It took Jason several weeks to get the fence repaired and painted. Replacing the rotten boards and painting didn't take long. It was the scraping the old worn paint from the fence that took all the time. When he did finish, the air was turning cold. He went to talk to Mr. Winston about his job.

Knocking on the door, it was soon opened by May. Mr. Winston was seated in his big easy chair, listening to the radio. When he saw Jason, he reached over and turned the radio off. "They are getting ready to have trials in Germany. They are going to put twenty-four high ranking Nazis on trial. I wish they would just shoot them and be done with it. Did you come for a visit or do you need something? You did a nice job on that fence."

"I need to talk to you about my job. The weather is soon going to be too cold to do much work outside. I am going to start cutting and trimming the trees across the front next, but if rain and snow come, I don't think I can do much outside. Do you have any inside work you would like for me to do?"

"You have gotten far more done than you should have. I have been watching you. You always start before you are supposed to, and you work way beyond your quitting time. Why don't you slow down some, and wait for better weather in the spring?"

"I would not feel right doing that."

"Okay. I tell you what. This Saturday you can start cleaning out the barn. Have you been in the barn?"

Jason walked over to the fireplace which was burning and making pops and cracks. The warmth really felt good. He turned his back to the heat and said, "The barn is locked. I assumed what was in there was none of my business."

"May."

May was already walking toward the kitchen. "I will get him a key." It was not long until she came in with a set of keys. "I don't know which it is." She handed the set to Mr. Winston.

He quickly took a key from the ring of keys and handed it to Jason. "There is a hardware shop right in front of the courthouse. Next time you are in town have a couple of keys made. Have two made for the shed and two for the barn. That shouldn't cost too much. I will pay you back when you bring the extra keys to me."

As Jason was standing there, he noticed an old worn box that appeared to contain a chess set. "You have a chess set. May I see it?"

"Of course."

Jason opened the box, and it revealed a plastic Renaissance chess set. "I love this style. May I borrow it?"

"I have had that set a long time. There is a shop on Main Street that has mostly junk for sale. I got it there. I used to play years ago. I had a friend who would stop by, and we would play on Sunday afternoon. He has long since moved away from our fair town. Do you play?"

"I do. But that is not why I want to borrow it. I am taking an art class, and I want to incorporate a few chess pieces into my final piece. I will take good care of it." Jason had lied. He had no intention of using the set for his art class.

When Jason got back to the shed, he went to the workshop on the left side of the building. Digging through the wood pile, he found a couple of pieces of wood that were about six feet long. One was walnut and the other was maple. *These will do nicely.* A couple of weeks later and with permission to use the woodworking shop on the college campus and his carving skills, he had turned those meager pieces of wood into a wooden chess set. He was letting the varnish dry and had all the pieces sitting on a worktable when one of the teachers came by. "My, that is very good work. Is this something you would like to sell?"

Jason was so proud that someone wanted to buy his set. "No. It is going to be a gift."

When Thanksgiving Day came, he went to the hotel and had breakfast. He spent the rest of the day alone. He had been back in Richmond and had not renewed or developed any friendships. He had inquired about some of the boys he went to high school with. He had been younger than most of the boys at Madison High, and they had not created any lasting friendships. Three of the boys he had known had been killed during the war and a couple more had moved away.

Jason had spent most of his time the last couple of weeks working on the chess set and getting ready for first semester finals. He had done very little work, and he used the excuse that it was cold and raining. The barn would just have to wait until the semester came to an end. He was lying on his bed on a Saturday morning when he heard May calling his name.

"Jason are you up there?" she shouted.

He grabbed his Jacket and quickly went down the stairs and opened the door. "May, what do you need? Is everything alright?"

"Mr. Winston wants you to come by the house sometime this morning." She turned and started walking back toward the house.

I wonder if Mr. Winston is upset with me because I have not started cleaning the barn yet. No, that can't be it. He did tell me that I could cut back on my work schedule. I will just have to wait and see.

A few minutes later he was knocking on the door. May let him inside. Mr. Winston, like always, was sitting by the fire.

"Have a seat. Sit close to the fire. I know that it is cold out there."

Jason took a seat on the hearth. The heat on his back really felt good. The popping and cracking of the slightly green wood burning in the fireplace gave the room a nice odor.

Jason decided to go on the offense. "The weather has not been good, and the semester is coming to an end. I have not gotten to my chores for a couple of days."

"I didn't send for you to discuss work. I had a visit from Elmer Hall. He and his wife said that you had Thanksgiving breakfast at the hotel. They said you were there and were having breakfast by yourself."

Jason was puzzled. "Mr. Hall came out here to tell you that I had breakfast by myself? That is hardly newsworthy and not worth a trip out here to tell you that."

"Mr. Hall is my banker. He knows I have trouble getting about, so he brings my financial reports here every quarter. I was telling him about my new boarder, and what a great job you were doing, and he said he knew you and that he was also your banker. He just happened to say he saw you on Thanksgiving Day. He wasn't spying. Now I have a question. Where did you eat Thanksgiving dinner?"

"I had to study so I ate in the loft."

"Jason, I forgot that both your mother and father are dead and that you have no relatives. I should have invited you to have dinner with me. I am going to correct that at Christmas. I have called the Bennett Inn, and they are going to cater my dinner this year. They are going to have it here and ready at noon. I want you to share it with me."

Jason was caught completely off guard. "I don't know what to say, except I would be glad to come. No, I am excited to come. It's perfect." *This will be the perfect time to give Mr. Winston his chess set.*

"Well I know that you have some studying to do, so I won't keep you. I thank you for agreeing to come. It means a lot."

On Sunday, December 16 it snowed. He didn't think much about it being his birthday. His celebration consisted of staying in all day long and having cold pork and beans for lunch. On Monday, he had cabin fever, and he decided to brave the snow and walk to town. Near the end of Main Street was a movie theater. Looking at the marquee, he saw they were playing *Laura*. There was also some B western playing, He had no desire to see a cheap western, so he stood in the outer lobby waiting for the last possible minute to go in. As he waited, a young lady came into the theater. He knew her. Her name was Mary Westfall. She had been in his art class. When she saw him, she smiled, "I didn't know you were a local boy. I see you in class, but you seem to rarely talk to anyone."

"Yes, I am local, but I didn't know you lived here."

"I don't live here. I am from New York. Mom and Dad have decided to spent Christmas in Florida. I didn't want to go, and I didn't want to spend time in New York alone, so I stayed here. I have my own apartment just off campus and two blocks from Main. I was bored today so I decided to see a movie. I didn't go home because I didn't want to be alone, and now I find I am alone. Do you go to the movies a lot?"

"No. This is the first movie that I have seen since I got out of the army. I do like to read movie magazines."

"You surprise me. I would not have guessed that you were ever in the army. You seem too young. What movie magazines do you like? I read them all the time."

"I was discharged this summer. When I was in basic training there were always movie magazines lying around. The guys would make fun of me for reading them, so I had to start reading them when I was alone. I guess I liked Movie Star Parade the best."

She moved closer to him. "Tell me where you were stationed during the war."

Jason smiled. "It is a long story. The movie is about to start. You want to share a bag of popcorn?"

It was her turn to smile. "Why not."

He walked over to the concession stand. "Two cokes and a large bag of popcorn."

They did not exchange any conversation during the movie. The weather had kept most people away, so they chose seats in the middle of the theater. When the movie ended, they picked up their coats and headed to the lobby.

"Let me help you with your coat."

"Thanks, what did you think of the movie?" Mary started buttoning up her coat.

Jason reached up and scratched the top of his head. "I don't know. I am going to have to think about it. I am not a real big fan of Dana Andrews. This movie has been out for a couple of years. I am surprised they are still showing it as a first run movie. Don't get me wrong. I like the movie and I could fall in love with Gene Tierney."

"Are you going back to your apartment?"

At first, she was caught off guard and thought he was inviting himself over, but he continued to say, "There is a drugstore just up the hill that serves great hamburgers and hotdogs. We could stop and get a snack and talk about the movie."

She felt relieved. "I would like that. I would like that very much."

They did not talk as they walked up the hill. The weather had improved, and the sidewalks were filled with people doing their last-minute Christmas shopping. The snow packed roads were turning to slush, and they had to avoid walking too close to the road because cars were throwing a wet frozen concoction as they drove by. When they went inside the drug store it was very congested with Christmas shoppers. They were lucky. They found an empty booth in the back. It wasn't long until a slightly overweight woman was standing at their booth. Jason could tell that she was tired and wanted to go home, but she gave them a friendly smile and said, "What can I get for you?"

Jason looked at Mary. "I will have a Coney, no onions, an order of fries and a cherry coke."

"Bring me the same."

The woman scribbled out the order on her pad and quickly walked away. It was but a minute until she returned carrying the two cherry cokes. She placed them on the booth's table top and stared at Jason.

"You are Jason Terry, aren't you? What happened to you after your father died? You just disappeared." Then she paused. "I did not mean to be so blunt. I am sorry about your father. I really liked him. He did some good work for my husband and me. My name is Edith Cain. I was a friend of your mother."

"Thanks for the kind words about Dad. After Dad died, I joined the army. I have been back for about five months. I am now a student at the college. This is a fellow student, Mary Westfall."

Edith looked at Mary and nodded. "Jason, I know when you were born. You are not old enough to have joined the army."

Jason was getting uncomfortable with the conversation. He gave Edith a weak smile and simply said, "I am a good liar."

As Mary was listening to the conversation, she thought. Is *he a good liar about being in the army or is he a good liar about being able to convince the recruiters that he was old enough to be in the military? If he was not old enough to be in the army and lied his way in, I am older than he is.*

Edith left the table and went to wait on another booth. Jason quickly changed the conversation. "I think I like the movie. I guess I hate to admit that I like love stories. Three things I didn't like about the movie: Dana Andrews falls in love with Gene Tierney much to quickly. Clifton Webb over plays his part, and no one seems to care about the poor innocent woman who was killed in place of Gene Tierney, and as I said before, I could fall in love with Gene Tierney."

Mary was smiling and then gave out a laugh. "You are criticizing the movie because you said that Dana Andrews fell in love with Gene Tierney too quickly, but you see her in a ninety-minute movie and you are telling me that you fell in love with her also. The truth of the matter is, she is a beautiful woman, and I believe I could fall in love with her too."

Jason looked at Mary and smiled. *That is a strange remark coming from a woman. Can a woman fall in love with another woman?* He quickly dismissed the thought. It was not long until Edith Cain was placing the coneys and fries on the table. "Can I get you something?"

"Do you need anything Mary?" he said as Mary shook her head no.

Jason and Mary took their time eating and were really enjoying each other's company. He found out that she had a roommate and her parents had money. He also found out she did not date anyone. He found that this was strange. She was an attractive woman, could talk about anything, and he found out she was an honor student.

"What is the name of your roommate?"

"Her name is JoAnn. She is from Albany. She has gone home for Christmas and will not be back until next semester. I know what you are thinking. I could have spent the Christmas break with JoAnn. We are close, but the truth is, her parents don't like me, and they don't even know that we are roommates. Let's talk about something else."

Jason found this very bizarre. *How could anybody not like Mary?*

"I don't have any family and I am having Christmas dinner with my landlord. Why don't you join me as my guest? I am sure that Mr. Winston would not mind."

"I really don't have any plans for Christmas. I was just going to make my own dinner that day." She thought for a minute. "Are you sure it is okay?"

Jason got Mary's phone number and walked her home. At her apartment he told her he would phone her and give her the address, and if there was a problem he would let her know. When he told Mr. Winston about his guest, he was delighted. Everything was arranged, and on Christmas Day Jason joined Mr. Winston and waited for Mary, who was coming by taxi.

Mary arrived by taxi about eleven forty-five. Jason met her at the door. She came in and saw Mr. Winston, sitting in a wheelchair. She was caught off guard because Jason had not said anything about him being crippled. She quickly regained her composure and reached into a bag she was carrying. "When we go to dinners and parties in New York we sometimes bring wine. My problem is that I don't know anything about wine. My daddy always buys it. I picked out this wine because it is from a Kentucky winery and I think the bottle is very pretty. I don't have any idea how it will taste."

Everyone laughed as Mr. Winston said, "It will be fine, and I thank you so much for being so thoughtful. I know this wine, and it is very good. It is a good dessert wine. May, will you chill the wine, and we will have it with your fruit cake after the meal. Let's go into the dining room and eat."

Once they were seated, Mr. Winston gave a short prayer. "This is a very big table. It will hold twelve people. I don't think it has even had four people around it for many years. This table is made from wood that was from my father's house. The house is still there, and my father and mother lived there until my grandparents died. They had built a new section onto the back of the house and didn't want the wood to be destroyed. They brought the wood to this house, and I had a table made from it. Jason and his father made this table."

"Well, the truth is, my father made the table. All I did was sand it."

Mr. Wilson smiled and gave Jason a wink. "Well you did a good Job."

Instantly, Mary ran her fingers across the smooth table. "What kind of wood is this?"

Mr. Winston looked over at Jason and said, "Jason, you are the wood expert. Tell us what kind of wood this is."

"It is knotty chestnut. It is really getting hard to find."

It got quiet, and they started to eat. The silence was broken when Mr. Winston said, "This reminds me of the times when I was a boy, eating Christmas dinner with my family. They would often have my grandparents and maybe a couple of others. Thinking about it gives me a warm feeling. I know our group is small, but I have that same feeling today. Merry Christmas and thank you for coming."

The meal had all the Christmas favorites, ham, turkey and gravy, cranberry sauce, mashed potatoes, green beans, dressing, oyster casserole and dumplings. After the meal, Mr. Winston couldn't stop asking questions and really enjoyed Mary being there. It was getting late in the afternoon when Jason reached into the bag, he had brought with him and pulled out two packages. "I have gifts for my only friends in Richmond and for my new friend Mary."

Mr. Winston was somewhat taken aback. "Jason, I don't have anything for you."

"Yes, you have. You have provided me with a home, job, and given me the best Christmas dinner I have ever had. For this I thank you very much."

The first gift was for May. It was a set of wooden salt and pepper shakers. Jason had carved them into the shape of a snowman and a snowwoman. He had painted them, and they were a work of art. May was touched. "Jason these are wonderful. Where did you ever find them?"

"I didn't find them, I made them."

Mr. Winston opened his gift and saw a hand carved wooden chess set. "This is grand. Did you really make this too? Oh my, oh my, what a wonderful gift. We must play, and play often."

Mary's gift was a drawing. It was a pencil sketch of her standing in front of the movie theater. Mr. Winston was looking at it and said, "Jason, you are one of the most talented people I have ever met. Good things will come to you."

Mary was pleased, and said, "What did you say your major was? I thought you were a math major. You should be an art major."

Later, Mary called for a taxi, and when it arrived Jason and Mary stood on the porch and said their goodbyes. As Jason looked at her for some reason, he knew that they would never be anything more than good friends, and during the next four years Mary became his best friend. He found he could talk to her about anything. He also discovered that the reason she never dated anyone was because she and her roommate were more than roommates.

When Jason came back inside, he and Mr. Winston played chess on the new chess set. Jason found out that Mr. Winston really knew the game, and while Mr. Winston said that Jason let him win the first game, Jason knew that this was not true.

After Christmas, Jason started cleaning up the barn. Inside was a car covered with a large tarp. It was jacked up, sitting on wooden blocks, and the wheels were stored hanging up in the barn. Jason tinkered with the car in his spare time. He spent some of his own money to buy a battery and other things the car needed.

One Saturday afternoon, Mr. Winston was sitting in his big chair when he heard a car horn. "See who that is would you, May."

Going to the front door and looking out, she said. "It is Jason, and he is driving your old car."

"Help me up. I need to see what is going on." May helped Mr. Winston up and gave him his walker and he made his way to the front door. By this time Jason had left the car and was standing on the porch. Mr. Winston opened the door and said, "How did you get that thing running? It has been sitting in that barn for several years."

"It wasn't hard. May, get Mr. Winston's coat and help me get him to the car. We are going to take a ride."

May went to the back room and came out with a wheelchair. Mr. Winston took a seat in the chair and they rolled him down the ramp where he got into the front seat. May got into the back seat. He was excited as a young boy in a candy shop.

"Take me down Westover. I want to see Mom and Dad's old farm." He was excited to tell Jason about the farm, and who lived there when he was growing up. This became a routine for many Sundays to follow, and Jason even took him to a movie occasionally.

The years passed quickly. Mr. Winston was like a father to Jason, and he began to think of Jason as a son. It was true that he had helped Jason with a place to live during his college days, but Jason had done so much for him.

Mary and JoAnn would come by and the five of them would eat together. When a new drive-in restaurant came to town, the five of them tried it out. They were crowded in the car and they laughed so hard while trying to eat.

In his second year of college, Jason really concentrated on his math courses. In the spring semester he took a second art course, and Mary was again one of his classmates. They started studying together and often would sit on Mr. Winston's front porch when the weather would permit.

One late spring afternoon, Jason, Mary, JoAnn and Mr. Winston were all on the porch. Jason and Mary were studying together, JoAnn was reading a book, and Mr. Winston was asleep in his wheel chair. They were interrupted by a car coming up the drive.

Mr. Winston came out of his slumber. "Jason, that looks like a military vehicle." They all watched as the car came to a stop, and two men in uniforms got out of the car.

One of the men said in a loud voice. "We are looking for Sergeant Jason Terry."

Jason stood up. "That would be me." Then he recognized one of the two men. "Lieutenant Forbes, is that you?" He rushed down the steps to greet him. As Mary watched Jason rush down the steps, she thought to herself. *I guess this put to rest any doubts I have about Jason ever being in the army.*

"Jason, it is so good to see you. Hope you noticed that I am now Major Forbes? I stayed in the army."

"What brings you to Richmond? Please come up on the porch and meet my friends." After the introductions were made, Jason went inside and brought out two more chairs.

The two men took their seats. "Jason, this is Corporal Lonnie Goins. We are here on official business. I want you to know that I volunteered for this assignment."

Jason smiled and said, "I hope you are not here to draft me back into the army."

"Am I free to talk in front of your friends? If I am, you understand why I am here. You have been contacted by mail three times about your medal. We are not going to let it go. I have talked to the committee, and they have agreed for you to have a private ceremony. We are here to conduct that ceremony today. I came to see you while you were in the hospital in England, but you were in surgery. I talked to several people, and I know you don't remember the day you won this honor. Furthermore, I know you don't want to remember it. I am going to present you with this honor in private. I will not read the events of that day if you don't want me to. But I do have to say some things. Will that be alright?"

Jason didn't say anything at all. He just sat there. It was Mr. Winston who spoke. "Major Forbes. What award are we talking about here?"

"We are talking about the Congressional Medal of Honor."

Mr. Winston, Mary, and JoAnn were in total shock. Mr. Winston again spoke. "Jason, you are going to have to accept this honor. We will accept nothing less. You run over to your apartment and put on your uniform, and then get back over here."

For some reason, Jason did what he was told. While he was gone, Major Forbes told Jason's three friend's things about Jason that they had never known. They had no idea that he was wounded during the war or he was close to losing his leg. He had never talked about being in combat.

When Jason came back to the porch, the first thing he said was, "It still fits, but barely."

They were all standing when Major Forbes opened the case that held the medal. "Sergeant Jason E. Terry, it is my honor to present to you the highest award this nation can give, the Congressional Medal of Honor. This medal is being presented to you because you are credited with saving twenty-three Italian citizens, two companies of American soldiers, a priest, and a young girl that you hid from the Germans in a cave. I am one of the American soldiers you saved that day, and I wish I could thank you in a public ceremony. I thank you in this private one." He handed the medal to Jason and the two soldiers stood at attention and gave him a salute. He did not place it around his neck because he knew Jason would not want that.

Mary, JoAnn and Mr. Winston were in total silence. That silence was broken when Mary said, "Wow!"

Later that afternoon, Jason and Major Forbes had dinner together. When they got back to Mr. Winston's house they went in and Mary, JoAnn, Corporal Goins, and May were there. Somehow, they had ordered a cake and had made some punch. Just before Major Forbes and Corporal Goins left, Jason tapped his punch glass with his fork. "I want to thank you for being here and sharing this with me. I have done nothing that I can remember to deserve this honor. If you are my friends, and I know you are, you will keep this honor private, and we will never discuss it again."

After everyone had left and Jason was back in his apartment, he lay across the bed. His head was hurting. He didn't know why, but he felt like he wanted to cry. It was not long until sleep found him. *The tall grass was waving back and forth creating what looked like waves upon an amber ocean. Moving into the sea of grass, he spotted the church. He stopped. Suddenly a feeling of peace came over him.* The peace and the sleep came to an end when the church exploded. He opened his eyes and looked at the ceiling. Sitting up he could barely see anything in the room. His vision was blurred, and he had one of the worst headaches he had ever had.

New York Engineering

Jason graduated from college in three years. It was the fall of 1948, and he was offered an internship in a construction firm in New York. The firm was so impressed with him, he was working there full time within a year. Ken Abbott, who was the chief architect, took Jason under his wing, and it was not long until Jason was called upon time and time again. Ken Abbott had so much confidence in Jason that he could make suggestions or even make changes in his designs. Ken Abbott's specialty was creating dams. He would travel all over the world to start and oversee the company's projects. During the next five years, Jason became one of the most valued employees of the firm. He was making good money and even told Mr. Winston he could help him financially if he needed it. Mr. Winston said he was okay and for Jason to keep his money. Jason would call Mr. Winston about twice a month and about every two months he would write detailed letters about what he was doing.

Mary Westfall, who was from New York, remained his closest friend. They would see each other often. They would go out to eat and sometimes to a Broadway show. He dated other women, but only one time did something serious develop. There were only three things that remained constant in his life: Mary, Jake Winston, and a dream that seemed to come far too often.

Jason liked New York and was proud to make it his home. He would travel back to Richmond to check on Mr. Winston as often as he could. In each visit he could see the slow changes that were occurring in Mr. Winston's health. One summer afternoon they were sitting on the front porch when Jason said, "I am not trying to be nosey, but can I ask you what happened to your legs?"

"Jason, we are friends. You can call me Jake. I would like for you to do that. I guess you really don't know a lot about me. You have offered me money, and you think I am poor. I am not. I have enough to live on and enough to pay May. May has been with me a long time, but she is like me. She is getting old. Thinking back, at the turn of the century I was twenty years old. I had met Rachel Dobbs. She was the love of my life, and I think my parents loved her as much as I did. We were engaged to be married. About a month before the wedding she became ill. The doctors said it was consumption. We now call it TB. I wanted to go ahead and get married but she refused until she got better, but she never did. She died, and I never found anyone else. The truth is, I didn't want to find anyone. If there is a life after death, I hope she will be waiting for me there."

"I worked mostly for my dad when I was a young man. He had that farm that I showed you down on Frakes Road. Mom and Dad both died during the first world war. After their deaths I was somewhat lonely and began to drink, sometimes quite a lot. In 1919 Congress passed the Volstead Act and decided people in the United States could not drink. What a bunch of hypocrites. The only way to get something to drink was to buy illegal whiskey or something else. Anyway, I was with a bunch of my friends one night, and we were drinking. One of them had a drink called Jake. Its real name was Jamaican Ginger Extract. It was cheap, but not really. It caused paralysis of the legs and other problems, and some even died. I lost the use of my legs. I lost my ability to walk, and the Depression hit at the same time. I sold the farm, and I have been here ever since. I didn't sell the farm because I had to. I was crippled, and it was becoming very difficult to manage. The Depression hit in 1929. I was lucky. I saw it coming and had pulled out in time. Believe me, I have enough to live on. Do you mind taking me for a ride?"

After helping Jake into the car, Jake asked Jason to take him to the Richmond Cemetery where he pointed the way to a grave site. Jason looked at the marker on the grave. Rachel Dobbs, 1883-1900. "I own the lot next to Rachel's. When I die, this is where I want to be buried."

Not knowing what to say, Jason just laid his hand on Jake's shoulder and quietly said, "I will see that your wishes are carried out. Let's hope that is well into the future."

That night Jason took Jake to the hotel dining room for dinner. Jake was no longer melancholy and was joking with the waitresses and other patrons at the restaurant. Several commented that they were happy to see him.

After spending several days with Jake, Jason headed back to New York. After a couple of weeks back on the job, he decided he needed to see Mary. He picked up the phone and made the call. "How about dinner with me tonight if you don't have any plans."

"I don't. JoAnn has gone to visit her parents, and I was looking for something to do tonight. Where do you want to meet?"

"You feel like German? How about The Forest? We have never been disappointed there."

"Sounds great. Meet you there at 7:00."

The meal at The Forest was as good as ever. They both ordered the wiener schnitzel with German potato salad and a side of sour kraut. They both had a dark German beer which was served in a German stein. When they finished their meal, they decided against dessert in favor of a second beer.

"Mary, let me ask you a nosey question. What are you and JoAnn going to do? I love you very much and want you to be happy."

"We are happy, but when we get back to the apartment, I need a favor. I think some of the neighbors are starting to question our lifestyle. When we get back, you and I need to smooch a little and make sure the nosey neighbors see us. It might not throw them off, but it might."

When they got back to the lobby, they walked in holding hands and stopped at the elevator. He did not push the call button for the elevator. He put his arms around her waist and pulled her close to him. "I have had a very nice night." He then gently kissed her on the lips and gave her a big hug. He moved back and kissed her again. Several other people were approaching the elevator, and he did not release her. He gave her another hug and she whispered in his ear. "Nice show. See you when I can."

Maggie Black

Maggie was a beautiful child, and she grew up to be a beautiful woman. Her father was the manager of a large department store in Boston, and her mother was a teacher at Boston College. She had graduated from Boston College in the spring of 1951. After graduation she had taken a job at a large law firm and was working as a law clerk when she met Cam Black. He was thirty years her senior, but she was attracted to him, and they started dating not long after she took the job at the law firm. One year later they were married. This was Cam Black's second marriage, and he had three children with his first wife. Cam had a very nice home in one of the more affluent areas of Boston. Two of Cam's three children were older than Maggie, and the third was about her age. They treated Maggie well, but she could tell that they resented her and only came to their house to see their father. Cam had insisted that Maggie quit her job when they got married. He took her on a cruise for their honeymoon and everything seemed to go well. When they returned, Maggie found she didn't like just being a housewife. Cam gave her little attention, and his friends didn't accept her. Eight months after the marriage, Maggie packed her bags, left Cam a brief note and moved to New York. She started using her maiden name again and hoped that Cam would not be able to find her. When she arrived in New York, she took a job working as a receptionist on the ground floor of a large office complex. Her job was to answer the phone and direct people to the various offices that were in the building.

Merrick Construction, Engineering and Architecture occupied the entire eighth floor of the building. Maggie didn't get a lot of calls, but she was constantly directing people to the various offices. She had only been on the job about a month when a young man walked up to her desk. He gave her a quick smile and said, "My name is Jason Terry. I was to receive a package today, and it has not come to our offices. I was wondering if it might have been dropped off here?"

She returned his smile. "I just came on duty. Let me look." She turned around in her swivel chair, and leaning against a short cabinet was a large envelope. She picked it up and read the address. "Jason Terry, Merrick Construction, Engineering and Architecture. Yep, I got it right here." She turned in her chair to face Jason and handed him the package.

Jason glanced down at her name tag and said, "Thank you Miss Roth. Have you been working here long?"

"Only about a month. What do you do for Merrick's?"

"I check figures, and I am currently working with Ken Abbott. I check his projects, and sometimes will make a drawing of what the complete project will look like. Here, let me open the package and I will show you an example." Jason opened the package and pulled out his drawing.

"This is impressive, and I see a note saying, 'Project approved.' I guess that is what you wanted to see."

"It is, and I have to go. It was nice seeing you, and I hope to see you again."

Jason walked away and headed for the elevators. Maggie watched as he disappeared around the corner. *I wonder what he meant, by saying, 'I hope to see you again.' Does that mean that he might ask me out? He did call me miss, and all it says on my name tag and name plate is Maggie Roth. If he asks me out, what am I going to tell him? Maybe he is married, and I am jumping way ahead of myself.*

Over the next couple of weeks, she would see Jason coming and going, and when he noticed her, he would always smile and sometimes wave, but he never stopped to talk. One day she decided that she would eat just outside the building where there were several benches. There was also a low stone wall you could sit on that surrounded a fountain. This is where she chose to have her lunch. As she sipped a drink of her soft drink, she noticed Jason standing in front of a hot dog stand. He paid for his food and started walking her way.

"You are right to eat outside today. I don't eat out here enough. May I join you?"

"Yes, have a seat. Where do you usually eat?"

"I like a place down the street. You can get burgers and hot dogs, but they also have plate lunches. It is good, and for some reason never really crowded. Where do you eat when the weather will not let you come out here?

"There is an observation deck on the nineteenth floor. Sometimes I go up there. Do you ever go up there?"

"I do, it has a great view. Where are you from, Maggie Roth?"

Maggie gave Jason a big smile, "The question is where are you from? That is some accent you have. I am from Boston. I grew up there. My father is the manager of Goldin's Department store. So where are you from?"

"As you have already guessed, I am from the South. Not real far south. I am from Kentucky."

Maggie laughed out, "You can't be from Kentucky. You are in a suit every day, and if you were from Kentucky, you would be barefoot and married to your cousin."

He returned her smile. "I didn't know you were a Boston snob. Tell me why a Boston girl is working as a receptionist here in New York?"

She became serious. "Are you putting me down because you are from Kentucky and have a more important job than me? I didn't mean to insult you. I am sorry if I did."

Jason realized that he had made the wrong remark. "That didn't come out like I wanted it to. I am sorry I said that. If I could take it back I would. The truth of the matter is that I like you very much. I was just trying to find out as much about you as I could. I guess I just need to be blunt."

"What do you want to know about me? I will tell you what you need to know. I don't plan to be at this job long. I am between jobs. I have a degree from Boston College, and I was a legal secretary for a while for a firm in Boston. I was not fired from my job, but for reasons

I don't want to discuss I left Boston and came here. Anything else you need to know?"

Jason had finished his hot dog. He wadded up the paper wrap and threw it about fifteen feet into a nearby trash can. "That was luck. Most of the time I must go over and pick it up. I got to get back to the office, but I have one more question. Do you have a boyfriend?"

Two days later Maggie was sitting at her reception desk when up walked Jason. "Good morning Miss Maggie. Would you like to join me for lunch today?"

"Are you asking me on a date?"

Jason smiled and said, "No, I am asking you if you would join me for lunch today. You said that you had not been to Perkin's to eat, so I am asking you to join me there, and then I am going to ask you for a date."

"I would be happy to join you for lunch, but don't get your hopes up that I am going to agree to go on a date. My lunch break is at 11:30. Will that work for you?"

At 11:45, Jason and Maggie where taking their seats inside Perkin's. Once they were seated, Maggie asked, "What do you like to eat here?"

Jason pushed his menu aside. "I like the plate lunches here. They have chicken fried chicken with gravy and mash potatoes, green beans and fried cornbread. It is my favorite."

"No wonder you like this place, it is right out of the south. I think I am going to get a summer salad."

During the meal, they got to know each other better. She didn't know what she should say if he asked her out. But the question did come, and she liked him so very much. Despite feeling guilty for both Cam and Jason, she said yes.

He picked her up on Saturday night at 6:00. He had been surprised when she gave him her address that her apartment was in a very expensive part of town.

"Where are we going?" she asked as she greeted him at the door.

"I am taking you to eat, and believe it or not, I was able to find two tickets to *Guys and Dolls*. It starts at 8:00 so we have plenty of time.

As they sat in the back of the taxi on the way back to her apartment she said, "This has all been so great. The food was great, the play was great, thank you so much. I can't remember when I have had a better time." She turned and looked out the window. *I guess I made a mistake when I married Cam. Why did he stop taking me out to eat, and taking me to shows after we were married? Why did he seem so content to stay home?* She was brought back to consciousness when Jason asked, "I noticed a little bar just down the street. Would you like to stop and get something?"

She came out with a cute little giggle, "Are you going to try to get me drunk so you can have your way with me? No, I think I am ready to call it a night. It has been wonderful."

Jason walked her to the door and kissed her on the cheek and simply said, "I have a question. How can you afford to live in an apartment this nice?" She knew he would eventually ask that question. "This apartment belongs to my father. I pay nothing for it. I think this is where my father would bring his mistresses when he was out of town." She let out a little laugh, "The only thing true about that statement is this is my father's apartment. Good night."

During the next week they ate lunch together every day. Most of the time, it was a sandwich or hotdog from the food truck that was always parked in front of the building. They went out two more times. Once to take in a movie and once just to eat and walk in the park. As they were walking in the park, Jason stopped her and took her in his arms and kissed her. "I think you are the best thing that has happened to me since I got to New York. I am glad you are between jobs." He then kissed her again, and he could feel her respond to him. Maggie knew she should tell Jason that she was a married woman, and she was separated from her husband, but for some reason she did not.

The park was in walking distance to her apartment, and they stopped at her front door and kissed again. Then she released him and stepped back. "Jason, you are a wonderful man, but don't fall in love with me. It would not be good for either of us." Jason noticed she was not smiling as she turned and disappeared inside her door.

As Jason rode the taxi back to his apartment, he thought about what Maggie had said. *What did she mean? Don't fall in love with me, it would not be good for either of us.* He laid his head back and closed his eyes. *She is way too late to give me that warning.*

They continued to see each other for about two months. Sometimes she was open with him, and sometimes she seemed to keep her distance. They had been for a walk in the park, and Maggie was rather quiet that night. When they were back at her door, she opened it and took Jason by the hand and led him inside. She closed the door and came to him and kissed him. Moments later they were in her bed, and he was holding her gently in his arms. When they made love, she was almost aggressive, and he had never been so excited. That morning he awoke, and they were lying in each other's arms. Maggie woke up first, and she was surprised that she felt no guilt, but she did feel trapped. She had told Jason not to fall in love with her, and now she was falling in love with him. She had no idea of how she was going to solve her problem. She was married, and he did not know. She thought of Cam, and how she was going to have to go back to him and ask for a divorce. Would Jason want her when he found out that she was already married? Suddenly she pushed all her problems out of her head and threw her leg across Jason and straddled him. "Wake up big boy, it is Sunday, and we have the entire day to ourselves."

It was another month before everything started to unravel. Maggie had decided it was time to tell Jason that she was married and take her chances that he loved her enough to stay with her. He had asked her out the coming Saturday. She would tell him then.

Jason was in love, and he thought about Molly. It was not the same feeling. This was different. Molly had been an excitement in his life. He had not thought about what married life would be like with her. With Maggie, he could see a future. She would fit so nicely into his life.

It was Saturday, and they had a date that night. He had noticed that when he met her for lunch during that week, she had seemed different. On Thursday, he had gone to a jewelry store and purchased an engagement ring. He had made plans. They would go out and eat, and he would order a cake and have the waiter place the ring in the center of the cake. He was excited and could not wait to see her. He planned what he was going to say over and over in his mind. Now he was standing just outside her door giving it a gentle knock.

He was surprised when the door was opened, not by Maggie, but an older man. He was wearing a blue suit and was maybe in his late fifties or early sixties. His first thought was to look to see if he had knocked on the wrong door. He had not, and he stood there speechless.

The older man spoke first. "You must be Jason. My name is J.B. Roth. I am Maggie's father. Come in. I have much to tell you."

Jason said nothing but came into the apartment. "Is Maggie here?"

"No, she is not, and I find it difficult to know where to begin. I guess I will just come out with it. Maggie is married."

Jason felt as if he had been shot in the stomach. He felt sick. "This can't be true, I have been seeing her for months. I think she may be in love with me. What you say can't be true."

"It is true. Her husband's name is Cam Black, and he is a good man. Cam and Maggie were married a little over a year ago. He is much older than she is. They seemed happy to me. Several months ago, she came to me and said she had some things she needed to work out and asked if she could live in this apartment until she knew how she and Cam stood. She told me that she thought that Cam was having an affair right after they got married. Two weeks ago, I went to Cam, and we had a long talk. I found out the truth. Cam is sick. He has cancer. He is being treated, and the doctors tell him he has a fifty/fifty chance of getting better. I came here to give Maggie the information she needed to make her choice of what she wanted or needed to do. She has gone back to her husband. She left you a note." He handed it to Jason and said, "I am leaving. Lock the door when you leave."

Jason watched as J.B. Roth left and closed the door. Roth had made him feel small and tried to make him feel guilty, as if all of this was somehow his fault. Jason sat down and opened the letter and started to read.

My Dear Jason,

What cruel fates that brought us to this point in our lives. By now you know that I am a married woman. I also could tell by your actions of the last several weeks that you have fallen in love with me. I have fallen in love with you also, but I am not so sure you would even want me now. If you love me like I think you do, you will want to come to Boston and ask me to divorce my husband to be with you. I know this because during the last couple of months I have come to know you as a good and honorable man. If you come to Boston and ask me to leave my husband and marry you, the answer is no. It is no for two reasons. One is that you deserve so much more than me, and the second reason is, what kind of person would I be if I left my husband in his time of great need? My father has told you why I left Cam, and I find out that I really had no reason. I didn't plan on you, and I should not have said yes to that first date.

Forgive me,
Maggie Black

When Jason folded the letter and put it back inside the envelope, he felt tears roll down from his eyes. He knew that his life was over with Maggie by the way she had signed the letter. She had signed Maggie Black. If she had just signed Maggie or Maggie Roth, he might have had a chance. Now he knew he didn't. He took the ring from inside his coat and placed it on the small table in her living room. *Okay, Mr. Roth. When you come back to your apartment, you will see that Maggie was not just having an affair.*

The Death of the Old Man

In the six years that Jason had been a member of the Merrick firm, he had become one of the most important members of the staff. Even though he was technically under Ken Abbott, not very many projects had been approved without his review and recommendations. One project that had not been brought to him for review was the Argento River Dam Project. One day in late summer he was called to the main office. Jerry Merrick was the major stock owner and president of the firm. There were several other men in the room, and all took their seats at a large rectangular table that would seat about twelve people.

Merrick did not take a seat, but his secretary set up a large flip chart behind him. "Men, we have run into a problem in Italy with the Argento River Dam Project. We must make a decision. We can pull out of the project or see if it can be saved." Merrick pointed to the left side of the chart. "You can see in our seismograph tests that we figured that we would have to go down twenty feet before we would hit a solid bed of rock to support the dam. The construction site has reported that they have reached twenty-five feet and have only found loose rock. Also, it looks like the wall of the canyon will not support a plinth. Ken Abbott, who is on site, has done more tests, and it looks like the bedrock is not within our standards to create a safe dam. If we dig down further this project will lose money. On the right you can see the new measurements. Ken wants to make new readings at the alternate site. We have already invested a lot of money on the current site, and the alternate site is twenty miles upriver. The Italian government has not approved our second site. The dam was to help people in the valley and those who live in Caseno. The second site will not help that city. Ken Abbott is there, but I find it necessary to pull Ken from the project. We have another project in South America and I need him there. Jason, I want you to look over the project and report back to me. Today is Tuesday. Can you be ready by the end of the week?"

At the end of the week Jason was standing up in front of the group with a flip chart behind him. His presentation lasted for about an hour. When he finished, he said, "It looks like the dam is not where it is supposed to be. I see that we used an independent company to measure where that dam could be safely located. We may be able to save the project if we have not invested too much into the project already and we are sure that the original site is okay to construct the dam."

There was lots of chatter around the table. One of the board members in the back spoke up. "Are you saying we started the construction of this dam in the wrong place? Mr. Terry, why didn't you check the figures before the project committed so much money to the wrong construction site?"

Jason, who was taking down his flip charts, didn't even look up. "I wasn't asked to. The project never came across my desk. Any other questions?"

Jerry Merrick stood up. "Jason, I'm sending you to test and examine the current site. Let us know if we can build a dam and still make some money and produce a project that will benefit the people of the area."

Sitting on the plane two days later, Jason started wondering what it would be like to be in Italy again. He tried to push memories of the war from his mind, but he found he could not control his thoughts. He remembered coming ashore at Anzio. He thought about Rome. He might like to spend some time there. He didn't get to Pisa, and he wanted to. Try as he may, the only memory of anything related to combat kept forcing its way back into his thoughts. He was in the cave. His leg was bleeding, and there was some young girl with him. Suddenly he was snapped out of his thoughts by a voice on the intercom.

"Ladies and gentlemen, please fasten your seat belts and prepare your seats for landing. We will be in Rome in about fifteen minutes."

A day later, he was at the construction site. The construction boss was named Michael Costa. He was about thirty-five years old. He had a lean frame and dark brown hair. He was not from Italy, but he spoke both Italian and English.

When they first met, Jason was not sure if he liked him or not. He spoke his mind and pulled no punches. "So, you are the man who represents the company that has wasted my crew's time and your company's money. Welcome to Italy. I thought they would send a man of more experience. Do you even shave?"

At first, Jason said nothing. "Take me around to the original site. I need to see it."

"Do you want to see the site where we were supposed to build the dam, or the wrong site where we started?"

"Take me to where you started the construction and where the graphs were made."

Once the tour was made, they came back to the construction trailer. "Show me the seismograph readings that you made of the area to see where the bed rock started." Michael Costa pulled out the charts and gave them to Jason. "You take your time. Call me if you need me. I will not go far from the trailer."

Jason went over the figures several times before he sent for Costa, who was talking to several of his men. When he came in, Jason was sitting at a table, and he looked up at Costa. "These figures can't be right. Did Ken see these figures?"

"I think so. He said that the bedrock was another thirty-five feet down. That goes some twenty feet beyond our safe range and beyond any profit we would make. That would create a dam that is thirty feet higher than we need and place too much pressure on the canyon walls. It would be a waste of money to build a dam that would not hold."

"I know Ken Abbott and have worked with him many times. He would have sent these measurements back to our office to be checked and rechecked. Do you have his correspondences with our office on these figures?"

"They are in the top drawer of the file cabinet here." He pulled them out. The figures had been checked in the main office by a Glenn Whitamore.

"Who in the hell is Glenn Whitamore?"

Jason spent the night checking his measurements, and the next day was making arrangements to go back to the New York office. Three days later, he was in the office of Jerry Merrick and had requested that Glenn Whitamore also be there.

When they were all in the office, Jason was firm. He looked at Glenn Whitamore and said, "I have been here six years. How come I don't even know you?"

Mr. Merrick could sense where Jason was going with the conversation and spoke up. "Glenn is my sister's son. He graduated from MIT and came highly recommended."

"Who is he training under?"

Merrick was now getting somewhat angry. "He is assigned to me, and the reason you have not met him is that he has an office in the basement. He started just like you did. His primary job is to check project data. Get to the report from the site."

Jason still had anger in his voice when he started giving Mr. Merrick the report. "When I got to the site, I looked at Ken's figures. I know Ken, and he works fast and sometimes he makes mistakes, but he knows if he does, I or somebody in the office will catch the error. This time he made one. He had figured the bed rock was thirty-five more feet deep. It is not. It is only 12 feet further down. Before I left, I had the crew drill four holes and all hit solid rock in twelve feet or less. We can widen the base by just a little and keep the dam at the same height. It will not cost a great deal more to go down to it. I checked to see who checked the figures here, and it was signed off by one Glenn Whitamore. I have returned with the figures and rechecked them on the plane coming home. It will only cost us five percent more to continue the project at its present location."

Merrick looked at his nephew. "Did you recheck these figures sent by Mr. Abbott?"

Glenn Whitamore looked down at the floor. "Those came in while I was checking the Henderson project figures, and when I saw that it was Mr. Abbott's project, I assumed it was okay. Are you going to fire me?"

Merrick scoffed. "No, I am going to move you upstairs and make you an intern for a while. Some of this is my fault. I put a lot of pressure on Abbott to finish his part of the project, so I could move him to the South American site. Jason, I am sorry I sent you to Italy for this."

Jason quickly spoke up. "You don't need to apologize to me, and as far as assigning Glenn to someone as an intern, you can assign him to me."

Merrick looked at his watch. He handed the project package to his nephew. "Do the job you were supposed to do in the first place. Recheck these figures. Jason, we will take the project to the board Monday afternoon. Glenn, have those figures on my desk by 10:00 in the morning."

On Saturday Jason came into his office to start to do his planning for the Monday meeting. He figured he needed to update himself about the project, so he pulled as much information as he could get his hands on. By 2:00 he had gone through all the information, so he started to sketch out what the dam should look like when completed. By 5:00 he had added the color. He sent them down to have copies made. He was in luck, because Mr. Merrick had held the department over getting packets ready for the Monday afternoon meeting with the board.

On Monday afternoon he was standing in front of the board, with several charts on easels behind him. He went over everything including aerial photos of the area. When he finished, he asked, "Are there any questions?"

One board member spoke up. "We are quite impressed with your knowledge of the project. I was aware of your expertise on design, but you seem to have extensive knowledge of construction. Your information is most helpful. Are you sure we can do this project with only a five percent increase in cost?"

Before he could answer, Jerry Merrick spoke up. "I have the cost estimates from Mr. Terry, and they have been rechecked by Mr. Whitamore. I am confident the increase will only be five percent. I would like to thank Mr. Terry for his presentation and if he will excuse us, there are things we need to discuss even further."

Once Jason had left the meeting, Jerry Merrick said, "What do you think?"

Louis Taylor was the first to speak. "Jerry, now that Ken Abbott is on his way to South America, who are you going to put in charge of this project? Getting somebody up to speed is going to be a problem."

"William Sharp is who I was thinking of. We could send him to Italy, and he could catch up while working with the construction crew."

"Have you thought about Mr. Terry? He is impressive."

"Mr. Terry is very young. He has only been with us for six years and is a junior member of our staff. We pay him more that most of our young staff because of his value to the firm. I am not sure he will want to leave New York for the current salary we are paying him. I don't want to take a chance that he would leave our firm."

Louis Taylor scoffed. "Jerry, that is not a problem. Promote him."

The next day Jason was sitting at his desk making a drawing of what the South American dam was going to look like upon completion when his phone rang. "Mr. Terry, you have a call from Richmond. Will you take it?"

"Yes. Put it through."

"Jason, are you there? This is Elmer Hall."

Jason immediately knew there was a problem. He was doing most of his banking in New York, and he had only a token amount of money in Mr. Hall's bank. He knew that he would not be calling him about a banking matter. "Mr. Hall, is everything alright?"

"No Jason, everything is not alright. I am sorry to inform you that your friend Jake Winston passed away at about 3:00 this morning. Do you have time to talk at this moment?"

Jason fought back the tears and in a choking voice said, "Yes I can talk."

"Jake made all the arrangements for his funeral several years ago and named me to take care of things. I know he thought of you as a son and will want you here. If you can be here by Friday, I will set the date for the funeral that morning at 11:00. You will not have to do anything. I will take care of everything."

Jason arrived at Blue Grass Airport on Thursday and was met by Elmer Hall, who was standing at baggage claim. "Jason, it is so good to see you. I just wish it was under different circumstances.

Once they were on the twenty-five-mile trip to Richmond, Mr. Hall said, "I was not sure about where you wanted to stay. I know you often stayed at Jake's home. Do you have a key, and are you okay staying there?

"Just drop me off at the house. I will stay there. I need to make some calls. Is he at the funeral home downtown?"

"No, he is at the church just up the street. You can walk, but I don't mind picking you up."

"That's okay. I think I need to walk."

Jason decided not to spend the night in the house. He still had a key to his small apartment in the back, so he stayed there. He thought he should say something to May but decided not to. He wouldn't know what to say. He would see her at the funeral. Maybe words of comfort would come to him then. That night, Jason called Jerry Merrick.

"Mr. Merrick. I am sorry about not making the follow up meeting on the Italian Dam project but as you already know my good friend Jake Winston has passed away. We were close, and I need a few days or maybe even a couple of weeks."

"Take all the time you need. The project has been approved and I have contacted Michael Costa to start making the adjustments you have written into the project. I will see you when you get back."

When Jason arrived at the church, he was escorted to the front pew. He was the only person listed as family. It was then that he noticed May was not there. He got up and found Mr. Hall. "Where is May?"

"May is extremely ill. We have known this for some time. We have had nurses taking care of both Jake and her for the past couple of weeks. May went to the hospital about three days ago. She is not going to live. I don't think she will make it through the week."

At the cemetery, Jason thought about Jake and May. It was then the tears came, and he found he could not control himself. Mr. Hall came over and put his arms around him and held him for a few minutes. "He felt the same way about you. You made him so proud."

When Jason was back at the church, he walked down to the local taxi company, just a block away. He went to the hospital and was soon sitting next to May. She was asleep, and a young nurse came in. "Are you family?"

"I am family. I am not kin to May by blood, but she is family."

"I am so sorry. I have not seen you here before."

"I have been out of town. She was the housekeeper for Mr. Jake Winston. I have known her for almost eleven years. She has been so kind to me and Jake."

Jason sat in silence next to May's bed for about an hour. It was then that a doctor came into the room. "How is she doing?"

"She is resting quietly. She does not appear to be in any pain."

"She is on morphine. The nurse told me that you two were close."

"I stayed with her and Jake while I was going to college. She has fixed me many fine meals."

The doctor took May's pulse and said quietly, "Her pulse is weak. I don't think she is going to make it through the night. Are you going to stay with her?"

"Yes. Doctor, I don't think May had any family. Whatever her bills are, let me know and I will take care of everything."

"That will not be necessary. Her bills have all been paid by Elmer Hall."

The doctor was right. May passed on about midnight. Jason found out that Elmer Hall had already made all the arrangements and she was buried quietly three days later. After the funeral Elmer Hall came to Jason and asked him to come by his office the next day.

When he came to the office, Mr. Hall took him right in. "What are your plans, Jason? When do you plan to go back to New York?"

"I am not sure. Why do you ask?"

"I am the executor of Jake's estate. I am not going to officially read the will in front of a Judge for about a week, but I can tell you now, he has left the entire estate to you. I will take my five percent as the executor of the will, but everything else goes to you."

Jason did not know what to say. "Mr. Hall, you have done so much for Jake. I don't know what Jake's estate is worth, but five percent does not really seem like enough for all you have done. I can write you a check for a couple of thousand dollars if that will help."

Mr. Hall smiled. "Jake told me that you thought he didn't have much. He said you tried to give him money. Jake Winston's estate is worth well over twenty-five million dollars. I will get well over a million dollars of that estate. You will have to pay some taxes, but you should come out about twenty million to the good. You need to be here for several weeks, so we can get everything transferred to your name. His estate consists of stocks, bonds, property and cash. This is going to take some time."

Jason could not believe what he had just heard. He was going to be a millionaire. That afternoon he called Jerry Merrick and asked for a leave of absence.

"Jason, do you have a minute to talk?"

Jason shifted the phone to the other ear. "Yes, I have time. Is there a problem?"

"No, there is no problem. I am going to assign you to take over the project in Italy. You will not need to be there until the new foundation is surveyed and laid out. I know you are young, but you are ready for this. This will involve several things. First, you are going to be promoted to a project manager. You are going to get a six thousand dollar raise. There could be a bonus on the project if things go well. I will talk to Michael Costa and see when you will be needed. I will call you by the end of the week and let you know when you should be ready for the job. Don't worry about time. That foundation is going to take a while."

A couple of days later, Merrick called Jason and informed him that the government had decided to extend the road across the new dam, and all lost money would be recuperated. The project was going to be delayed for a couple of months and he could take all the time he needed.

He had at least three months to get the new estate in order.

Even though he now owned the big house, he continued to live in the studio apartment above the shed. During the next few weeks he met with Elmer Hall several times. He found he had cash, owned several businesses in the town and was even a partner with a couple more. About half his wealth was in various well-invested stable stocks. He really didn't even have to go back to work, but he loved what he did. He decided the money and the house were great, but he was going to go to Italy and finish the dam. Then he would decide what to do.

Jason lived in the studio apartment another day and then decided he would move to the big house. When he entered through the front door, memories of time with Jake Winston and May flashed through his mind.

It took a couple of days to get the house cleaned up and ready for him to live in. At first, he was not sure he would keep the house but then decided that he would. He was sitting in Jake's favorite chair when Elmer Hall knocked on the door. Opening the door, Jason said, "I am glad you have come by. I wanted to set up a meeting with you. Please come in. We can sit at the table in the dining room. Can I get you something to drink? I have restocked the house. I even have some wine."

"No, thank you. I can't stay long. I need you to sign a couple of things that I forgot the other day, and I need to give you an envelope."

Elmer Hall opened his briefcase and spread four documents on the table. "I can explain each of these to you, but they are standard for an estate of this size. With your signature I can take them before a judge and get things rolling. We will have to have a lawyer to help with all this. There will be a fee. I am sure a lawyer will charge by the hour, and I think I will use Green Williams, if that is okay with you."

Jason quickly signed each document and handed the pen back to Mr. Hall. "You said you have an envelope for me. What is it about?"

"It is a letter from Jake. His instructions are that you are to read this letter in private. I was not to give you this letter until after the funeral." He handed the letter to Jason and said, "I have to go. It may seem strange getting a letter from Jake, but I think there is something he wanted to say to you. If you need anything, just give my office a call."

After Elmer Hall had left, Jason sat down in the living room and opened the letter and started to read.

Jason,

Strange isn't it. You are reading a letter from me and me dead and in the ground. Do not weep for me. I am now with Rachel, and you are all alone in a big house. I have a feeling that you are not going to stop working, even though you are a very rich man. I hope you will keep the house, but if you decide not to, I understand. I am going to tell you something that no one else knows. My last name is not Winston. If you go downstairs, there is a cedar chest in the basement. It is in a room on the left at the end of the hall. Both the room and chest are locked. The key to the room is in the kitchen, and you know where the keys are hung next to the door. It won't take you long to find the right one. Once you open the door, look on top of the door. There is a hollowed-out area in the top of the door just big enough for the chest key to fit in. Once you open the chest, everything will be explained. If you remember you gave me all your medals from the war to keep for you. You will also find those along with the documentation inside this chest.

You are asking why so much intrigue. Once you read what is there you will understand, and I want you to destroy what you find there. I should have done this, but I guess I just wanted something to hold on to about who I really am.

I love you Jason,
Jake

Jason was somewhat excited when he opened the large cedar chest. Inside the chest there were several boxes. All were about the size of shoe boxes. He picked up the one that was marked 'Jason's Medals' and set it aside. There was a second box, marked Ross Conley. Jason opened it. Inside he found several items which included a photo, a gun belt and pistol, a newspaper clipping and a receipt. The photo was that of a young man. On the back it identified the man as Ross Conley. There was also a long letter which Jason started to read. Once he finished the letter all he could do was sit in disbelief.

The Story of the Old Man

Ross Conley looked out the door which gave a dusty view of his ranch. It had been a long dry hot summer, and the air was full of dust. Being late in the afternoon with the sun low in the sky, the sunlight coming through the dusty air created a strange amber light. From the back porch, he could look out on the spread. Twenty-two hundred and twenty acres of hell. His mother and father had tried to work the land with cattle and crops, but the fates had not been kind. Years of dry weather had created nothing but mounting debts and made orphans of him and his brother. If nature had been kind, the farm would have produced profits. It had a creek which ran from the hills into the middle of the farm. Now that creek was dry except for a few areas of standing stagnant water. They had had to make a choice. Use the water for the cattle or use it to irrigate the crops. Their decision had saved neither, and they had no crops and the cattle were slowly dying.

It would not be long until the ranch would be gone. Ross decided to take one last ride across the ranch. As he started to mount his horse, he had to brush away the hordes of flies. *Everything on this ranch is dying except the flies,* he thought. He rode down the edge of the mostly dried creek bed. A few cattle were drinking the stale water. The grass was just about gone and had been replaced with dust which was kicked into the air by the small whirlwinds which were common for this time of year. The cattle looked like skeletons that had cow hides draped over them. Ross was sure that when the bank took over, the cattle would be better off.

Ross had come to hate the banks. In his mind they were nothing more than big fat hogs that had sucked the life out of every poor person who lived in the southern part of the territory. The rich land owners in the north had not felt the effect of the years of drought. Their ranches bordered the river and had healthy cattle and good crops due to irrigation.

As he rode into the foothills, suddenly he saw a wagon among a group of trees. He reached down and released the strap that secured his side arm. As he got closer to the wagon, he could see a man lying up against the back wheel.

"Hey bud, what are you doing up here?"

As he moved closer, he could see that this poor man was suffering the fate of the dying animals of his ranch. He was covered with flies. His shirt was covered with dry blood. Sitting the poor man up against a wheel of the wagon, he went back to his horse and got his canteen. Water was precious. He had had to ride some fifteen miles to get drinking water for himself and his brother.

Taking his bandana, he quickly wiped the man's face and then gave him a drink of the water. "What in the hell are you doing out here? What happened to you?"

At first the man said nothing but took another drink of water. His voice was weak, "I was trying to get back east. I was attacked two weeks ago. I have been shot, and I have been robbed."

"Don't say anything more. I am going to build a small fire and create some smoke to get rid of the flies. Then I will see what I can do about that wound." A few minutes later the smoke had driven most of the flies away, and Ross was opening the stranger's shirt. When he saw the man's wound, he flinched. Looking the stranger in the eyes he said, "This is not good. It is not bleeding, but it is infected, really infected. You are going to need a doctor."

"I know my fate here. I am not going to make it to a doctor. Just sit with me. I am going to ask you to do something for me. It will be a lot."

Pouring more water over his bandana, he again wiped the stranger's face. "I will do what I can." *He knew this man was going to die, and all he could do was make him comfortable.*

"Give me another drink of water. You wouldn't happen to have a little whiskey in that bag on your horse, would you?"

"Just so happens that I do." He quickly went to his horse and opened his saddle bag and brought the whiskey back to the stranger.

Taking a drink of the whiskey, the stranger said, "My name is James Winston. I have been west looking for and found gold. I am engaged to be married. Martha would not come west, so I sold my mine and started back to Richmond, Kentucky. I sold my mine for twenty thousand, but I was attacked on the trail and shot and robbed and left for dead. I don't know how I got this far. I know that I am going to die, and I will never see Martha again. I have written her a letter. Can you see that she gets it? She has to move on with her life. Martha did not need the money that I got for the mine. Her parents come from wealth. The address is on the letter. Can you send it to her?"

Ross knew that he did not have to keep any promises he made to James. James would be lucky to make it through the night. As he took the letter from James's hand, James closed his eyes and was gone. Ross now had a wagon and a team of horses. He removed the leather billfold from James Winston's clothing and opened it. It contained no money, but did contain a picture of Martha. As Ross gazed upon the picture, he thought that James Winston was both lucky and unlucky. Martha was a gorgeous woman, and he was lucky that she had agreed to marry him. It seemed that luck had turned against him. Looking in the few possessions that James had, he found a pick and a shovel. He buried James at the foot of a large tree and said a few words of comfort for him. He attached his horse to the back of the wagon and drove it back to his barn. After he fed the horses and gave them some water he went back to the house.

The ranch really belonged to him and his brother. Ross was 18 years old, and his brother was only eighteen months younger. Ross was a little taller than his brother. He was a good six feet tall and very lean. He was lean from the years of working on their ranch which had produced nothing more than a mounting debt. His mother and father had both died the previous year. They died of hard work and influenza that was coupled with a hard winter.

Ross was sitting at the kitchen table, fighting the epidemic of flies, when he heard his brother returning from town. His brother tied his horse to a post that supported the front porch. He came into the house, and took a seat at the table with Ross.

"Damn flies. I think I am going to be glad to be gone from this hellhole. I got a couple of dollars. Do you want to go get drunk tonight?"

Turning to Ethan, Ross said, "The bank expects us to be out of here by the end of the month. We need to get a few more things ready. Save your money. It may stand between us and starvation."

"I know. What in the hell are we going to do?"

"I have got an idea. Let's rob a bank."

Ethan looked surprised. "You got to be kidding. We can't rob a bank."

"Hear me out. I have got a plan. About a month ago, Jesse James robbed a bank about seventy-five miles from here. We need to go about the same distance from here, but go the other direction, say Easton, and do the same thing."

Ethan walked over to the table and took a seat. "You are serious. Do you think we could get enough to save the ranch?"

"We can't save the ranch. If we suddenly came up with enough money to save the ranch, we would become suspects in the bank robbery. No, we can't save the ranch, but we can hope that we can get enough to start over somewhere else. We need to rob a bank, and let our bank foreclose on the ranch, and we will get out of here, and go somewhere else and start over."

Ethan gave Ross a big smile. "Let's say we rob a bank. Do you have a place in mind?"

"Yes. There is a small town about several hundred miles from here called Richmond. We could go there and reinvent ourselves."

"How did you come up with going to Richmond? Where in the hell is Richmond?"

"Richmond is a small town in Kentucky." He told Ethan his story of finding James Winston. "Winston asked me to take a letter to a woman named Martha. "I could send it, and we could go anywhere."

Ethan scoffed, "We won't be able to go anywhere. They will be looking for us the rest of our lives. I don't think I want to live and be looking over my shoulder for a Pinkerton's man."

Ross walked over and pulled out a chair. "I got an idea. During the robbery I want you to call me Jesse. If we do this right, they will blame the James gang."

"You have given this a lot of thought."

"I have. I have been to Easton. The bank has easy access. There is a small alley that is next to the bank. We could get into the bank almost without being seen."

For the next two days the two brothers planned their robbery. They decided that they would keep their guns unloaded. They did not want to take a chance that they might kill someone.

When all the plans were made, Ross looked at his brother, he knew that Ethan was worried. "Look on the bright side. If this fails, we could end up in prison, and at least we will have something to eat every day and a roof over our heads."

Ethan did not smile, "If this fails, we could end up lying dead on the streets of Easton, or hanging at the end of a rope in the town square."

The next day Ross and Ethan were walking down the streets at Easton. They had waited until the time seemed right. They pulled their hats down low. They didn't want anyone to see them on the streets. Everything was as Ross had said. There was a small alley between the bank and the dry good store. They could come into the town without being seen, tie their horses in the back and carry out their plan.

That night they camped in a group of trees that was about a mile just outside the town. They went over their plans again. "How much to you think we will get?"

"What did you say, Ethan? I was thinking about the final details of our plan."

Ethan repeated his question. "How much do you think we will get?"

"I really don't know. Maybe five or six thousand dollars. That would be more money than we would make in a lifetime on that dry parched hell hole. Let's get some sleep."

Ethan took a deep breath. "Who in the hell can sleep? I am so nervous that I am sick at my stomach."

The next day they waited until just about closing time. The bank closed at two p.m., and at one fifty-five they came down the alley. They pulled their bandanas up over their faces, and quickly stepped inside. Ethan put the closed sign in the window and pulled the shade as Ross shouted. "Everyone hit the floor." Pointing his gun at the tellers and bank president, he again shouted, "Put your hands in the air, and don't do anything foolish."

There were five people in the bank, and four of them went to the floor. A young woman did not fall to the floor but started to run for the door. Ethan grabbed her by the arm and slung her to the floor. "You move or say anything again, and I will shoot you right where you lay."

He felt sick, and he thought of his parents. *What am I doing*? he thought. He quickly regained a sense of what he was doing and handed the closest teller a bag. "Start putting money in this bag and don't stop until I tell you to."

The teller was scared and did what he was told. Within about a minute the bag was over half full of money. He grabbed the bag from the teller and stepped back out of the vault.

"Hurry, Jesse. We got to get out of here."

Ross looked at the bank president. "Where is the back door?"

The scared president pointed to a hallway next to the vault. Ethan and Ross rushed down the hallway and out the back door next to the building where their horses were tied. As they left the building, they heard the bank president shout for someone to get the sheriff. As they mounted their horses and rode down the back alley, they heard several gunshots, and Ross could hear a couple of bullets whiz by his head. They had previously looked at a wooded area not far outside the town, and they quickly made their way into the protective area of the trees. Ross slowed his horse and looked back toward the town. He saw no one coming after them, but he noticed the sky was turning dark. Rain would be welcome, he thought.

Riding deeper into the timber, they came to a creek. They guided their horses to the middle of the creek and headed up stream. The stream led them to the foothills, and to cover where Ross stopped his horse. "I think we are somewhat safe now. We will rest the horses a spell before we move on. When we are rested, we need to ride north for about thirty minutes and then to the east. We should be back on the ranch by late tomorrow afternoon. Let's hope those dark clouds produce a little water. It will help cover our tracks."

Ethan didn't answer. He was slumped forward on his horse. Ross could see blood running down his leg. "Where are you hit?" Ethan did not answer. Ross helped Ethan from his horse, and laid him on his stomach. "Where are you hit?"

"Somewhere in my back. I can't feel my legs."

Ross pulled the shirt up and examined Ethan's back. The bullet had struck him almost in the center near his backbone. Ross did not know what to do. He knew that if he did nothing Ethan was going to die, and if he took him to a doctor, they were going to go to prison.

Back in Easton, it took about thirty minutes for the sheriff to assemble a posse. By the time they had followed the trail to the wooded area, it had started to rain and rain hard. It was not long until any signs of the trail were gone.

Ross did not have to decide what to do about Ethan. He died about thirty minutes after Ross had helped him from his horse. He just sat there in the rain. The falling water mixed with his tears. He had a tremendous feeling of guilt. His plan to save Ethan from the failing ranch had cost Ethan his life.

The next morning the weather had cleared. He wrapped Ethan in a blanket and laid him across his horse. Staying off the main road and sticking to the back trails it took two days to get back to the ranch. It was the twenty-fourth of the month, and he had six days to turn over ownership to the bank. Stopping by the barn, he got a shovel and took Ethan to a secluded area of the farm where he had buried James Winston. He dug a second grave. He leveled the grave and covered both graves with brush.

When he finished, he kneeled next to the two graves, and started to say the Lord's Prayer. About halfway through, he stopped. Who am I to be talking to the lord? *He will not want to hear anything I have to say. I am a thief and murderer. I have robbed a bank and got my brother killed.*

When he got back to the house, he lay down on the floor, and cried, and he went to sleep.

The next day he went to the barn and started to prepare his wagon for the trip east. The buckboard had a tool box under the seat. Ross created a false bottom for the money. Going back to the house he emptied the bag of money and sorted the money into stacks. He had three hundred one hundred-dollar bills, and two hundred and fifty fifty-dollar bills. The rest was small bills. They had robbed the Bank of Easton of over forty thousand dollars. He quickly took the money to the wagon and hid it in the false bottom of the tool box. He filled the rest of the box with oats for his horses. He took the rest of the feed, and put it in the back of the wagon. Taking Ethan's clothing into the back yard of the house he burned them. The rest of his belongings he placed into the wagon, hooked up the horses and drove into town.

Stopping his buckboard in front of the bank, he saw his friend Lou coming out. "Did you hear about the bank robbery at Easton? The James Gang cleaned them out. They got nearly fifty thousand dollars."

"I could sure use some of that. I think you are aware of why I am here. I can't pay the ranch debts, so I am turning it over today."

"What are you going to do?"

"I am going to see if Mr. Bailey will buy my tools and what knots. I have a list of what I am leaving. If he will buy and give me a fair price, I am going to see how far east it will take me."

"Mr. Bailey is a fair man. He is getting a bargain in taking your farm. I am sure he will give you something. Where is Ethan?"

Ross thought to himself. *Bailey is really a fair man. He is getting a ranch for almost nothing.* "He rode ahead. We are going to meet in Redman."

Mr. Bailey gave Ross fifty dollars for his tools and other things that were left behind. Ross thought that the things he was leaving behind were worth much more, but he wanted to get on the road as quickly as possible. After he had signed all the papers, he decided not to go back to the farm. He headed his buckboard east and did not look back.

Not sure of what he was going to do, he just let the horses follow the dirt road heading east. He had not gone twenty miles until he was stopped by a posse looking for the bank robbers. A tall man wearing a vest that supported a star said, "Where is it that you are going, young man?"

"East, as far east as these animals will take me."

"Are you aware that the Bank of Easton was robbed a couple days ago? Have you seen two men on the road? I think one of them may be wounded. Not really sure."

"I have seen several men and some women on the road. I have not paid a lot of attention to them. I even dozed off to sleep a couple of times. Like I say, I have not noticed anything."

"What is your name, and where are you from?"

"My name is James. Most of my friends call me Jim. My name is James Winston."

"You need to get down from the wagon. We are going to search it. Don't be offended. We are searching everyone. It is possible you might even meet another posse, and they will search you also. Do you have any identification with you?"

Ross, who was now calling himself Jim, stepped down from the buckboard and reached into his back pocket and pulled out James Winston's identification. Two men climbed into the back of the wagon. They checked his clothes and his supplies. One of the men opened the tool box under the front seat, and reached down into the dry oats. Ross thought that his heart was going to jump out of his chest. Finding nothing and not finding the false bottom, the man closed the lid and fastened it back down. The posse thanked him for his cooperation and quickly rode away.

That night, he pulled the wagon into a small collection of trees to make camp for the night. Looking at the sky, he could tell it was going to rain, so he spread a tarp over the wagon and got under the wagon with his bedroll. It was that night he decided he really would go to Richmond. He would tell Martha about James Winston's fate and maybe stay. It was not long until the rain was coming down hard. *Where was this rain when he had the ranch? It had not rained forever, and now that the ranch was gone, and Ethan was dead, it has rained twice in the last week.*

Once he was in Kentucky, he stopped at a large town not too far from Richmond. There he went to the first of three local banks, and identified himself as James Winston, and opened the first of three accounts. He left five thousand in his tool box. He purchased a new set of clothes, and the next day rode on to Richmond. He rented a room at the hotel and spent the next couple of days finding out about the real James Winston. Luck was on his side because the real James Winston was not from Richmond. He couldn't find anyone who even knew him. It was Wednesday, and he had spent three days trying to find out about James. He was standing in front of the Glyndon Hotel when a carriage pulled up, and a lady who was sitting in the back, got up to get out. James walked over and took her hand and helped her down from the coach. He could tell it was Martha by her picture. When she was securely on the sidewalk, he released her and said, "James Winston at your service."

She did not even blink an eye and said, "Thank you. You must be a guest of this hotel. I am late. Some of the ladies and I are having lunch here today. I must go. Again, thank you very much." She quickly turned and went through the door.

That was strange, he thought. *She doesn't even know James Winston.*

Returning to his room, he stretched out on the bed. He was just about to doze off when there came a light knock on the door. Opening the door, he saw Martha standing there with her shawl draped over her arm, and he could see she was holding a small pistol.

"Quickly, step back into the room and don't say a word."

Once they were back in his room, she tossed the shawl over the back of a chair. This gave him full view of the gun. "I don't know what your game is, but I know you are not James Winston. I also know for the last couple of days you have been asking a lot of questions about him."

James turned his back on Martha and walked over to the window. "I know you are not going to shoot me, so put that thing away and let's talk." He left the window and pulled a chair over close to the chair where Martha had tossed her shawl. "Have a seat. How long can you stay? There are many things that you need to know."

Martha did not put the gun down and didn't take a seat. "You are not James. So, who are you?"

"We will get to that. James told me that you and he were going to get married. He is not even from this town. Were you two going to get married?"

"A couple of years ago, Father and I went to Louisville for a convention. It was there that I met James. He worked as a teller at a local bank. We saw each other a lot during the week. He fell in love with me and asked me to marry him after only a few days. For some reason I gave him my address, and he wrote me several letters, but I did not want to get married, so I told him my father would never accept a man with his station in life. The truth is, if I loved him, I would have married him regardless of how much money he had. He wrote me a letter telling me that he was going west to search for gold, and when he returned, he would be rich, and we could then be married. I liked him. I liked him a lot, and in time I might have come to love and marry him. He was just moving way too fast. I really thought that he would never return from his trip to search for gold. I guess I was right. I have not heard from him for over a year. I didn't know what happened to him."

"Well, he did find gold, and he became rich. He sold his mine and had started back to you when he was robbed. During the robbery, he was shot. He lived a couple of weeks before he died. He died as poor as when he left here."

"Did you rob and kill him? That makes no sense. Why would you come here?"

"My brother and I had a ranch, and one day I found James Winston dying in the hills. He told me about you and finding gold, and how he was robbed. He made me promise to find you and tell you what happened. So here I am."

Martha was confused. "This makes no sense. Why would you promise a dying man you would do this? I assume you have come a long way, and why would you take his name?"

"You are right. If I had killed him, I would not come here. After he died, I found a letter addressed to you, and he had your picture in his wallet. I did not have to do anything, but for reasons I cannot explain I needed a new start in life. The banks had just taken our ranch, and my brother died. I did some things I am not proud of to survive. So here I am. I am keeping my promise to James, and I am starting fresh."

"I guess you expect me to keep your secret. I really can't think of any reason why I should. From what you told me, I think you may be a wanted man and are hiding from the law."

"You do what you need to do. I want to stay here. I must settle down somewhere. I hope it can be here. What you do with this information is up to you."

After Martha had left, James decided he would take a wait-and-see approach to his situation. The next few weeks went well. He did not see Martha during this time, and no one came knocking on his door looking for him or asking questions. He took the five thousand dollars he had brought with him and opened an account at the local bank. It was there that he met Martha's father, who was the owner and manager. He did not let on like he knew her.

As the weeks went by, he found a large farm just outside of town for sale, and he bought it and moved into the large two-story brick house that sat upon a hill that overlooked the town of Richmond. The farm had four tenant houses, and soon he had tenants that were raising cattle, tobacco, hemp, and corn. He was lucky that he was able to make a profit the first year, and he started paying off the remaining debt on the mortgage of the farm. He did have more than enough money to pay off the mortgage, but he chose not to touch that money for a while.

The next year he started to learn about the stock market, and the first investments were small. Buying mineral rights on a hunch became one of his best investments. In just a few years he had invested in Oklahoma, Texas, and in Eastern Kentucky. It was not long until he was able to turn his forty thousand dollars in to a very large fortune.

William Caperton had watched James Winston's account grow and his wealth increase over the past five years. He knew that his personal wealth in Richmond was now about one hundred and fifty thousand dollars. He did not know that he had other bank accounts worth even more. He was looking for a partner in a local venture. He decided he would ask James Winston if he was interested. He invited him to come to his house for supper and to discuss a business project. The Capertons lived about a half mile from the center of Richmond on the west end of town. Their house sat on a large five-acre lot. The house had four stories with the first story almost underground. Near six o'clock he pulled his carriage up to the front of the house and climbed the steps to the second-floor porch and rang the bell on the large front door. An old black man opened the door and took his hat. Walking into the living room he saw Mr. Caperton's wife, and to his surprise, Martha. Mr. Caperton quickly got up and greeted him. "James Winston, may I introduce you to my wife, Emma, and our daughter, Martha."

Looking directly at Mrs. Caperton, he said, "It is so nice to meet you. Mrs. Caperton, we have seen each other around town." Turning toward Martha, he smiled, and with a hint of satire, said, "Mrs. Martha, I have been in Richmond for over five years, and we have not run across each other. How could that be?"

"Martha is not married. She is a miss." Mr. Caperton walked over and gave his daughter a hug.

Martha did not smile, she just said quite firmly, "I have not been here. I have been living with my aunt in New York. I like the big city life. Father tells me you are a Richmond success story. You have a large farm and are doing quite well."

"Oh, I don't know. I have had plenty of luck, and things have gone my way."

Martha smiled for the first time. "I bet you have your secrets too."

Here we go. Is she going to bring me down? If she is, why has she waited so long?

Mr. Caperton took his wife by the arm. "I think it is time to eat. Will you come with us?"

The dining room was large, and in the center of the room was a table that would seat eight. Four place settings were on one end. They had light conversation during the meal, and when they finished James and Mr. Caperton went to his study and discussed Mr. Caperton's business project. James told Mr. Caperton he would give it some thought and get back with him. As they left the study and returned to the living room, Mrs. Caperton and Martha were sitting on a couch. They both stood up.

"I want to thank you for the fine meal. It was so nice to be invited into your home." He took Mrs. Caperton's hand and gave it a light kiss. He then turned to Martha. "It was nice to meet you Martha. I hope we can see more of each other."

Martha extended her hand, and as he took it, she placed a note inside his hand. "I do think we will see each other again." She said this firmly and without any facial expression.

After leaving and returning to his home, he opened the note.

> *Mr. Whoever you are,*
>
> *I knew you were coming to the house tonight, and I was not sure if I should stay to meet you for a second time. I have thought a lot about you and your deception. I fear you have hurt people, and may hurt others. You need to give me a reason not to expose you. Meet me for lunch at noon tomorrow at the Glyndon Hotel. We need to meet in a public place.*

The next day James came into the hotel dining room to see Martha seated in a private booth near the back. He took his seat opposite her and didn't say anything. He simply picked up the menu and started to look at it.

Martha gently reached across the table and pushed the menu down, so she could see James's face. "Are you going to order lunch? Don't bother. We won't be here that long."

James gave no hint of his emotions. "No. I am going to order a drink and sit here and listen to what you have to say. Then I might tell you to go to hell, and then I am going back to work."

Martha scoffed. "I would doubt that you have ever worked. I think you might be a thief. If not, you are a liar, and I don't know why I didn't expose you five years ago."

"If you think I am such a bad guy, don't you fear I might do some harm to you? The way you describe me, you would not be the first person I have killed. You would only be the first woman."

For the first time, Martha was scared. She knew she had nothing to fear from James while they were sitting in the hotel dining room. But now she had concerns. "I think this was a mistake. I need to go. I won't say anything." She started to get up.

"Sit down!" he said in a firm voice. "You set up this meeting, and now we are going to see it through. If you are going to destroy me, at least you can know all the facts."

"I don't want to know anything." *If I don't know anything, maybe I will be safer*, she thought. "I really want to go," she whispered.

He opened his coat and she thought she saw a gun. "I have things you need to see, so you are not going anywhere."

Her heart was pounding, and she struggled to regain her composure. He could sense her concern and fear and started to talk. "My real name is Ross Conley. You are right. I am not a very good person. I lived on a ranch in the far western part of Oklahoma. I don't think hell could have been any drier or hotter. After my parents died, I lived there with my brother Ethan. What I told you about James Winston is true. The bank foreclosed on our ranch. I convinced my brother to help me rob a bank. We made it look like Jesse James pulled off the robbery. Ethan was shot during the robbery and died the same day. I had no idea of what to do, so I came here. I did keep my promise to James Winston. For some reason I thought you might need some closure. I am not proud of what I did. I robbed a bank. I got my brother killed. If you are going to turn me in, I am willing to take what is coming to me. I don't sleep well at nights."

Again, he opened his coat and Martha could see he did not have a gun. It was a large brown envelope. James took out the envelope and opened it and took out a receipt for fifty thousand dollars. He handed it to Martha. She looked at it. "What is this?"

"This will explain." He then handed her a newspaper clipping which had a headline which read, ***Bank Robbers Return Money.***

For the next two weeks James did not see Martha. He assumed that she had gone back to New York. One Thursday morning he had a meeting with Mr. Caperton. He was surprised that Martha was sitting in her father's office. "Why Miss Caperton, it is so nice to see you," he said in a mocking tone.

About that time a secretary came into the office. "I am sorry, but your father is not back from the lodge meetings. You know those men. They get started and can't find a stopping place. Martha, is there something you needed that I can help you with?"

"No, I just wanted to know if he wanted to have lunch."

James, saw his chance and said, "I have not had lunch, and I would love to have some company." The secretary left them alone, and Martha gave James a strange look. "I am not sure we have too much in common. I don't think either of us would enjoy lunch."

"Oh, I don't know. We really don't know each other. We have met twice. The first time you were pointing a gun at me, and the second time you were afraid I was going to kill you. I guess I really have not made a very good impression. Miss Martha Caperton, my name is, well you know my name. I would like to take you to lunch. Please do me the honor of joining me at the new restaurant that is just up the street?"

Martha wasn't sure why, but she agreed. It was early in the day, just a little after eleven, and the lunch crowd had not gotten there yet. They asked for a table in the back corner and took a seat. Once they had ordered, James said, "While I was with the real James Winston, I said to myself that he was both lucky and unlucky. He was unlucky because when I saw his wound, I knew he was going to die, but he was lucky that he fell in love with you."

"Are you trying to make me feel bad, because I didn't love him?"

"No, no, no. I did not mean that at all. A man would be lucky for just the chance to think you might fall in love with him. I didn't come to Richmond because when I saw your picture you were so attractive. I needed to be someone else. On the surface things seem, to be going well for me. By having money, I have been able to make money. I think I would be happier if my mother and father and brother had been able to make a go at the ranch life back in Oklahoma. My pa worked his whole life to make enough money to make a down payment on the ranch. I think it quit raining the day we moved on to that twenty-two hundred acres of purgatory. I am sorry. I didn't mean to get into this. Tell me about New York. I want to go there someday."

"It's okay to talk about your past. Your dark history is all I know about you. My father thinks you are some kind of genius. He thinks you have a sixth sense when it comes to knowing when to sell or invest." For the first time she gave him a smile. "Is this true?"

For the first time he really looked at her. Her smile gave her a completely different look and made her a completely different person. He could see her confidence. Her hair was pulled away from her face and gathered in the back. Her hair was dark brown, and her big brown eyes helped light up her face. Her skin was smooth, and he could tell that her clothing concealed a wonderful figure. He said nothing but just stared. He now knew why the real James had fallen in love with her.

He was brought out of his daze by her words. "Mr. Winston. Are you okay?"

He decided to tell her a small lie. "You just asked me a question, and I was trying to figure out a clever answer. The truth is I am just lucky. You know what I really like to do. I like to work on the farm. I love being outside. I would love to take you on a horse ride to see my farm. Do you like to ride horses? I have several, and they need riding."

Martha could see the excitement in his face. He had turned into a boy, and she surprised herself and said, "I love riding horses. I would love to go riding with you."

That weekend he picked her up and took her to his farm to a barn behind his large house. The horses had been saddled and were ready to go.

She got out of the carriage and walked over to the horses. "Is this going to be a private ride, or will we see people out on the farm?"

James did not understand the question. "Do you think I am trying to get you alone? I assure you, you will be safe with me. You are a good-looking woman, but I think I will be able to behave myself."

She laughed. "That's not what I mean. If we are not going to see any of the townspeople, I want to change this sidesaddle to a regular one. This outfit looks like a dress, but it is really pants. I want to feel free on the ride, but I don't want you or anybody else to think I am a loose woman."

"You will be safe. I will change the saddle."

When he finished changing the saddle he turned, and Martha had taken her hair down. It was hanging down past her shoulders. As he led her horse to her, he couldn't help but stare.

"What is it?" She knew that he was staring at her hair.

"I was just looking at you. I have not seen you with your hair down."

"Well, what do you think?'

"What I think might get me in trouble. Here, take your horse."

They rode side by side and carried on conversation as they rode. She found the more she knew about him the more she liked him. For the first time, she noticed how good looking he was. He was about six feet tall, and he was lean. His face was tan from being outside. When she first met him, he never smiled, and now he seemed to keep a smile on his face. They rode until they came to a small lake surrounded by trees. They let their horses wade out into the water to drink. When the horses were through drinking, they tied them to a tree and walked around the edge of the lake. "This is a beautiful lake and has some good fishing. It has some very large fish that are fun to catch. I have invited your father to come to fish, but he has never taken me up on it."

They walked a little further and found a place that had short grass. They stopped, and she sat down in the grass and leaned up against a tree.

"Are you going to go back to New York?"

"Oh, I don't know. I really have no reason to stay in Richmond. I love Mother and Father, but I like the excitement of the big city."

James left the tree and took a seat on the grass next to her. "What if I asked you to stay?"

"I would say that you have not only taken James Winston's name, it looks like you have become him. James, the other James, asked me to marry him after knowing me for only a week."

"Whoa, I am not asking you to marry me. I am asking you to stay in Richmond and get to know me, and for me to get to know you. When the other James asked you to marry him, he was broke. I am not broke, and I don't have any plans of getting married anytime soon. I just enjoy your company. After I have thought about it, maybe you should go back to New York. I could come and visit, and you could show me the little town."

Martha scoffed, "I don't think you can call New York a little town."

James got to his feet and took his hands and extended them to Martha. She reached and took his hands, and he pulled her to her feet. When she was standing in front of him, he bent down and lightly kissed her on the lips. "I have never had a woman friend. Right now, I need to get you back to town. If you do stay in Richmond, I would like to see you from time to time."

Martha didn't go back to New York. She stayed in Richmond and started working for her father. Her father was delighted and even more delighted when James would stop by his office, and he would take Martha out to lunch. For the next few months James and Martha saw each other from time to time. By the end of the year they were engaged to be married. After the honeymoon, she moved into James's house. A year later they would have their only child. A boy they named Jake.

Billy and Rachel

After a few days Jason set up a meeting with Mr. Hall. A day later he was sitting in Elmer Hall's office. "Mr. Hall, I think we now have just about everything in order. Is there anything I need to do to finish things up?"

"No. I have all the information I need, and once you get back to New York, your investment people can take care of things on that end. I understand you are going to keep the house."

"Yes, I am, but I don't want to leave the house sitting empty. Do you have somebody you could recommend that could be a caretaker at my home? I need someone to live there, a person that could be a good manager, hire people to take care of the grounds and stuff like that."

Mr. Hall thought for a moment. "Do you prefer a man or a woman?"

"I prefer a man, and I don't want anyone who is old. I want someone who is going to be with me for a while. That is why I don't want a woman. I don't want any talk when I want to get away from New York."

"I could recommend an old woman, but she might not be willing to live there very long. What about a black man. Do you have a problem with that?"

"Nope, I don't. I just want a reliable person. I don't care about the color of their skin."

"There is a man I know named Billy Ballew. Like you, he is a veteran. He comes from a good family. He has a high school education, and before the war he did quite a lot of work for me. I trust him."

"Is he working anywhere right now? Do I have to share him with another job?"

"Billy is not working anywhere. Like you, he was in the service and he was wounded. It has left him crippled. He walks with a bad limp. He was working for Ballard's Grocery store as a stock boy, but I understand they let him go a couple of weeks ago. He does not have a phone, but he lives at 107 B Street. It is about ten blocks from here."

"Do you know why Ballard's let him go?"

"I am really not sure. I know it would have been hard for Billy to carry boxes or to go up and down a ladder. I will give him a recommendation. He will do you a good job and he can do what you said you wanted."

"I think I will go out and see him. I think I might just walk out there right now."

Jason left Main Street and entered what was referred to as Colored Town. As he walked along the street, he noticed the poor conditions of the houses. When he arrived at 107 B Street, he found a house that had a weathered picket fence that needed repairs. The small house had a porch that ran the length of the front of the house. It was what was referred to as a shotgun house. It had four rooms. The first room was the living room, and sometimes doubled as a bedroom, the second room was a bedroom, followed by a kitchen, and the last room was a small bedroom. These four rooms where all in a single line to fit the narrow lot the house sat on. There was a young girl sitting on a swing on the front porch.

She was in her teen years and had light brown skin.

Before he could speak, she spoke first. "Are you lost, mister? I guess not. This town is too small to get lost in."

Jason had not been referred to as mister very often. "I would assume that you would be in school today." He was making a reference to her youth.

"Look at your watch, mister. It is after 3:00. School is out."

"I am looking for Billy Ballew. Would he be around?"

She did not answer, but instead shouted inside the house. "Billy! There is someone here to see you. Shall I send him in?"

Jason heard a voice from the other side of the screen door. "No, I am coming out. I was just getting ready to walk down to the store." When Billy came out, Jason looked at him. He was thin, about six-foot-tall and was walking with a limp. He was wearing a flight jacket, like pilots wore during the war. He looked at Jason. He did not smile, and said, "What can I do for you?"

"I have been talking to Mr. Elmer Hall. He says you might be able to come to work for me."

"Rachel, get off that swing."

Billy looked back at Jason. "Come up here and have a seat. What did you say your name was?"

"Jason Terry." He took his seat on the swing next to Billy while the young lady moved over and leaned against one of the posts that supported the porch.

Billy smiled, "The young lady who thinks she has to be a part of the conversation is my sister, Rachel. I would tell her to go inside, but she would just listen through the screen door."

Billy had a sense of humor, and he liked that. Jason could hear the love of his sister in his voice.

"What kind of work do you have? I am sure that Mr. Hall has informed you that I can't do a lot of jobs."

"Let me ask you a few questions before we start talking about the job. Do you own this house?"

Billy didn't understand why Mr. Terry was asking him if he owned his house, but he answered. "No, Rachel and I rent. I will be honest, I have not worked for about three weeks, and I have not paid the rent for this month, so we might just be put out before the month is over. I am going to see Mr. Hall in the morning to see if he will float me a small loan."

"My second question is, what did you do while you were in the army?"

"Well, it is not the army anymore. I was in the Army Aircorp. I flew escort missions for our bombers. I was shot down on one of those missions. That is how I messed up my leg."

"You were a Red Tail, a Tuskegee Airman?"

"I was. I flew twenty-two missions and I am an ace. Were you in the service?"

"I was. I was stationed in Italy."

"That is where I was. Wait a minute. I have heard that name. Jason Terry. Do I know you?"

"Terry is a very common name. I grew up here before I joined the army. I have been working in New York for the last six years. Let me get to the point of my visit. I own a large house on the west end of Richmond. I am not staying here much longer. I need someone to live there and be a caretaker of my home. That is why I asked you if you owned this house. You will need to live in my home. The reason I asked you what you did during the war was I needed to know if you could manage my affairs related to my home."

"What about my sister? Can she come too?"

Jason looked at her and smiled. "We can put her in the shed at the back of the house. It is not heated and sometimes the rain pours through the roof, but she will get used to it." He then almost laughed when he looked at the expression on Rachel's face. Then he did laugh. "The truth is, there is a shed in the back of the house that has a nice studio apartment. I lived there while I was in college. Rachel, you will have a choice. We can fix you a room in the house, or you can look at the studio apartment, and if you like it and want some privacy you can live there. It will be your choice. Shall we go look at it?"

Billy did not have a phone, so they walked down the hill to the store and called a cab from there. Billy and Rachel could not believe the home. It was big and private. On the way to the house he had been concerned about being black and living in a white area, but the grounds were completely private. He would not have to see anyone unless he wanted to. There was a guest bedroom on the first floor near the kitchen, and that is where Billy would live. There were four bedrooms upstairs and Rachel looked at each one. She decided the smallest bedroom at the top of the steps would suit her just fine. The master bedroom on the first floor was where Jason decided he would stay when he made his visits from New York. He really liked Billy and offered Billy one hundred and twenty-five dollars a week to run the household. He paid Rachel twenty dollars a week to keep the place clean. He knew for that time he was being generous, but they needed the money and he did not. Billy and Rachel moved in two days later. Jason had told them that he was going to be out of the country for at least two years, and he would decide if they were still needed after he returned. They all lived in the house for the next two weeks, and Jason found that he enjoyed Billy and Rachel. Billy took to his job like a natural. He was given an expense account. He was to check and pay all bills and see that other maintenance was taken care of, hire people to maintain the grounds. He knew he did not have to pay Rachel anything, but she went about dusting each day, did the dishes and made the beds. She was even a good cook. A few times he thought he might not even go back to New York.

Sitting in front of the fire, he was about to go to sleep when he heard Rachel come through the front door. She took a seat in front of the fireplace.

"I heard you tell Billy that you were in Italy. Billy was in Italy during the war, but he doesn't talk much about it. Will you tell me about Italy? You don't have to talk about the war, just tell what the people were like, and did you see some of the famous sites that we read about in our classes?"

"I was not there very long. We landed at Anzio. Anzio is just a little south of Rome. Rome had been declared an open city, and the Germans were gone when I got there. I got to see some of the ruins while I was in Rome. I was only there a couple of days, but I did get to see some of the famous fountains, the Forum, the Colosseum and a few other things. Have I told you that I am going back to Italy?"

"No, but Billy did. Did you learn how to speak Italian while you were there?"

"Gosh, I don't know three words. I am so glad you mentioned that. I am going to spend the time before I leave learning as much Italian as I can. I think I will go to the campus book store and see if I can find some material to study right now. Do you want to go?"

Rachel did not get up. "This is not New York; it is Kentucky. They will not let me in there. Thank you for asking."

Jason spent the rest of his time studying and learning the new language. He felt confident that he could master the language very quickly once he was in Italy.

A month later, he found himself back at his apartment in New York. The first thing he did when he got in from the airport was to call Mary. When she answered the phone, he said, "I am back. I have some sad news."

"Sad news. What is wrong?"

"You remember Jake Winston, the man I stayed with during college. He has passed away."

"Yes, I remember him. We had several holiday dinners with him on several occasions. I really liked him. He was so good to me."

"There is more. You will not believe the story I have to tell. What are you doing tonight?"

"Nothing. I can't wait to see you. You want to have dinner. You name the place and time, and is it okay if I bring JoAnn?"

"Yes, Billy Bob's, 8:00, and yes."

Jason did not tell anyone else about his inheritance. He reported to work the next day and had a meeting with Jerry Merrick.

Jerry Merrick was sitting at his desk when Jason came into his office. "Take a seat, Jason. We have much to discuss. Ken is in South America, and that project is going well. In Italy, the road has been completed, and we are ready to get the dam project moving again. That's your job. We have adjusted the schedule, and this project should take about two years. I want you there by the end of the week. Is this a problem?"

"No. I have been going over the figures and can foresee that we will have to make some modifications, but I cannot make any recommendations until I am there to assess the needed changes."

"There is a slight problem about where you are going to live. We have built a stipend into your pay, but you will have to make the arrangements once you are in Italy. You should be able to find something nice once you get there. The nearest town is about fifteen to twenty miles from the construction site. I am sure you can find something there."

Back to Italy

As the plane left Paris, Jason found all the travel of the last several weeks was beginning to catch up with him. When the plane leveled out, he drifted off to sleep. In his dream he could clearly see the church. This time the dream was different. He was walking toward the church, and it was surrounded by dark clouds. When he approached the front door, the church disappeared. This time he did not wake up. He was in a cave. The light coming from the opening lit up the cave, and he could see a young girl next to him. She looked up at him and said, "You could have saved her." She then disappeared. Looking down at his hands, he could see that they were covered with blood. He heard voices. Germans were coming into the cave. He reached for his gun.

Suddenly, someone was shaking his arm. "Mr. Terry, are you okay? You need to wake up. You were talking in your sleep." He opened his eyes and could see the flight attendant looking at him with a concerned look on her face.

"I am okay, I was having a bad dream. No, I was having a nightmare."

"Are you sure you are okay? Can I get you something?"

He thought for a moment. "Yes, yes you can. Do you have something for a headache?"

Jason spent several days reviewing the dam site and getting to know the work crew. He was disappointed that the construction crew had not de-watered the river valley. The weather was cold, and the rain in the mountains had caused the small river to overflow its banks.

Working with the crew, he was able to divert the river. He spent the first few weeks supervising the work crew on building a small earth dam upstream and constructing a tunnel to divert the water around the site where the dam was going to be built. They had been lucky. Being close to the coastal area, they didn't get much snow, but it stayed cold and damp. This took a month, and he was already behind schedule.

He spent his nights inside the office trailer sleeping on a mat. He had purchased a tent, and sometimes, if the weather would permit, he would build a small fire and sleep outside. March had been unusually warm, and he had been able to spend several nights outside. One night he was lying next to his fire and looking at the sky when he had an idea. *Why not buy a home while working in Italy?* He could be here two years or more, and it might be a good investment. He could hardly sleep just thinking about the possibility. The next morning after he reviewed the work arrangements for the day, he left for the town.

The town was not large. It had a population of about ten thousand people. In its center was a square with benches and a couple of restaurants with outside seating. The largest of the restaurants was Angelo's. It had both inside and outside seating. A large church was also in the center of the town, but there were also other churches scattered about. The town had a small hospital and a few government buildings. There was also a small river. A bridge crossed the river and was the main road back to Rome.

After asking about a million questions he found a local lawyer, Victor Del Carlo, who handled real estate and could speak English.

"What are you looking for? Our city is small, and there is not a great deal of houses on the market."

"I want something nice. I am looking for a place to live, but I am also looking for an investment. I will only be in Italy for about two years. I don't want to rent. I want to buy a house and then maybe make a little money when I sell."

Del Carlo was somewhat concerned about Jason's age. He didn't think a young man could afford much, but he didn't know. "How old are you, Mr. Terry?"

"I am twenty-four." Jason paused for a moment. "No, I have had a birthday since I came to Italy. I am twenty-five. I am project manager for the dam project north of here and I assure you, I have enough to buy a home."

Del Carlo put his hand to his chin, "How much do you have to invest?"

"I can assure you I can handle any home that you might have on the market."

Del Carlo laughed. *I will just put this young American in his place.* "There is a villa for sale just off the road that leads to your dam project. I am sure you have passed it several times, but you can barely see it because it is about a quarter of a mile off the road, and the bushes have grown rather tall. No one has lived there for about a year. It is very nice. It was built before the war. For some reason it was spared by the war, even though there was much fighting in the area. It also has about 150 acres of land around it. If I had the money, I would buy it."

Jason did not hesitate. "How much?"

"In American dollars, 90, 000. Do you have that kind of money? You would have to put all the money up front."

"I want to see it."

The villa was perfect. It had a living room, a small library, a great room with a fireplace, four bedrooms, a dining room and spacious kitchen, and a well-stocked wine cellar. There was a courtyard out back.

After the tour of the grounds and outbuildings Jason looked at Del Carlo and said, "How much did you say?"

Del Carlo smiled. "It is a steal at 90 thousand."

"I will give $85,000. I will pay all the money up front. If your seller agrees to this price, I can have the money in their hands within a week. I figure you are making 4% on the sale. That comes to $3,400. I will give you another 2% to represent me and handle all the details so I will have a clear title."

"I will make the offer. You did notice that the furniture was still in the home. It is for sale for another thousand. Are you interested?"

Two weeks later, Jason was living in his new villa.

The villa was not too far from the dam work site. It was only nine miles up the road. He was eight miles from the city.

One day while coming home, he saw a truck sitting in the drive that led up to the villa. He stopped and got out of his car. Two men and a woman were standing in front of the truck looking at a flat tire. His Italian was getting better each day, and in Italian he asked, "Qual è il problema?"

The taller and older of the two men spoke, "Non abbiamo alcun ricambio."

Jason struggled to find the next words but gave up and said, "Do any of you speak English? My Italian is not so good."

The taller and older man answered. "We all speak English. As I told you, we have a flat and have no spare."

Jason walked around to the front of the truck and looked at the flat tire on the driver's side of the vehicle. "Take the tire off the truck, and we will take it in to town to get it repaired. Where do you live? I could take your wife home, if it is along the way?"

"Aryana is not my wife. She is my sister. My name is Bonita, and Luke is my brother. We live about a mile up the road and over the hill. If you take them home, you and I can get the tire repaired."

It did not take long to reach the small house which was about 200 yards from the road.

On the way to have the tire repaired, Jason found out Bonita and his brother Luke scrapped out a living doing odd jobs. Aryana, who they called Ana, had lost her husband during the war. When they took the tire to town, they were told that it was beyond repair. Jason bought a new tire over the protest of Bonita. Once the tire was back on the old truck, Bonita thanked Jason, "I wish I had some money to pay you. I will pay you in time. You have been so kind."

"There is something you can do. My villa has not been lived in for a while. I would like to hire you and your brother to cut the bushes, help get the outside looking good. Tomorrow is Saturday, and I am not going to the work site until noon. Come by in the morning if you are interested."

The next day, Jason, Bonita and Luke started clearing the small brush that had grown up around the house. He found that the two brothers were very good workers, and both spoke English very well, but he tried to communicate in Italian. When he tried to talk to them in Italian, they spent the morning laughing at him as he struggled with the language. The brothers said that they wanted to work on Sunday, so he agreed, and he again worked right alongside them.

On Monday he was glad to go back to the construction site because, he needed to rest his aching muscles. The two brothers continued to work during the week. Jason allowed this because he could tell they needed the money. The next weekend, work on the villa was beginning to show. After three weeks he felt he knew the brothers and Ana enough that he invited them to have a meal with him at a local restaurant. They were impressed with how far his Italian had come in just a short time.

When they had finished their meal, Jason made his pitch. "I have an idea. We have made good progress on cleaning up around the villa. There is a barn right behind the villa. Behind the barn is an area that used to be a garden. What would you think about planting a garden and setting up a road side stand on the edge of the road? We also have lots of grapes that need to be attended to. Let's go into business. We don't have to sell wine, but I am sure we can sell the grapes. Ana, I need a housekeeper and cook. Would this be something you would be interested in?"

It was not long until they had their vegetable stand up and running. They were surprised that many people in the town would drive out to their stand. Ana was a good saleswoman. She expanded their market to the city to include a few restaurants and had a stand at the farmer's market on the weekends.

It wasn't long until he was living on a working farm, with Luke and Bonita as his partners in the new business venture. He like having Ana at the house. She was fun to talk to and was a wonderful cook.

The construction of the dam had reached another phase, and the river had been diverted. The project was behind schedule. It was not because of the work. The government was slow on issuing the needed permits. He had to go to Rome to persuade the officials to speed up the process. He called the office several times to get permission to bribe an official to keep things moving. The new revised completion plan was now two and a half years. The three weeks of delays were over, and the project was moving again.

During the summer months, the farm production was doing extremely well. He decided he would let Bonita and Luke take care of the farm, and he would concentrate on the dam.

It was dry and warm, and they were able to make up some of the time they had lost dealing with government delays. Working with Michael Costa was a delight, and Michael stopped by his villa often. Jason soon realized that he was not stopping to see him, but he was stopping to see Ana.

Jason desperately wanted to get the dam back on schedule, so during the fall months he worked the construction crews and himself long hours.

In November, the weather turned against them, and they were forced to slow down. He flew back to New York the second week of December and celebrated his birthday with Mary and JoAnn. He decided not to go to Richmond. With the help of Mary, he picked out some Christmas gifts for Billy and Rachel and gave them bonuses.

Back in Italy, Jason again found that January weather slowed the project down. He found he rarely went to town and left running the villa completely up to Ana, and the farm to Luke and Bonita. The two brothers were now starting to experiment with wine production, and for a while were losing money, but Jason saw that there was much potential in the endeavor. The year seemed to fly by.

He decided that he would spend Christmas in New York. He really wanted to see Billy and Rachel. He sent word for Billy and Rachel to come to New York to spend Christmas with him. This was one of the best things he could ever remember doing. Rachel was beside herself. He rented a limo and took them on a three-day tour of the city. Jason had the apartment decorated for Christmas, and they celebrated Christmas there.

Two days after Christmas he went with them to the airport, and they caught their flight back to Kentucky. After spending New Year's Day with Mary and JoAnn, Jason returned to Italy.

By late spring, the project was back on schedule. Michael came into his office and handed Jason a hard hat. "We are going to make some noise this morning. Do you want to watch?"

"Why not? I am not doing anything, and I will need the measurements of the wall as soon as you can clear away the loose rock. I hope this is the last time we have to do this."

A large area had to be blasted away to make way for the spillway and the future construction of a power station. Loose rock and rubble had to be removed from the valley wall and the river bed, which was now dry. Holes were drilled into the valley wall to make room for the explosives which would clear the unstable rock away. Jason, Michael, and several men took their places behind the protective barrier.

For some reason the blast did not go off, and as Jason raised his head up to see what was going on, the explosives detonated. A small stone was turned into a missile and bounced off the side of his hard hat with a tremendous force.

When Jason woke up, he was in a hospital room. A young woman was finishing putting a bandage on his head. He heard her say, "Good. You are awake. Do you know your name?"

"I am Jason Terry. I seem to be okay." His first thoughts were not about his injury. All that he could think about was another delay on the construction of the dam. He became angry. He knew better, and he knew the safety protocols about explosives. He forgot about his injury, and he wanted to get back to the work site. "Do you speak English?" He did not wait for an answer. He started using his Italian. "Did the doctor take any x-rays? I need to talk to him. I want to get out of here."

"In English," she said, "Your Italian could use a little work. The doctor did order x-rays, and as a result we are going to keep you overnight for observation." She continued to work on the bandage. "I told the man who brought you in that we would take care of you. He didn't want to leave, but he said he had to get back to his work site."

"What did the x-rays show? Are you allowed to tell me?"

"I can tell you. They were inconclusive. They might have shown a hairline fracture."

"Did I require stitches?"

"I am putting this bandage on your head to hold a pad which has a medication that will keep the pain down. You have a scrape, but no deep cut. Without this pad you are not going to feel well at all."

"Nurse, I don't think I need to stay here. Would you get me the doctor? I want to get out of here." He was being rude, and he didn't know why.

"One night will not hurt you, and it may save your life."

"That may be well and good, but I want to discuss it with a damn doctor. Now, will you go fetch him?" For some reason he was getting even more angry. "While you are getting the doctor, would you see if another nurse is available?"

About that time a nurse came to the door. "Dr. Acosta, are you almost finished here? We have a patient that needs to check out, and you have not signed the needed papers."

She had frustration in her voice. Speaking in Italian she spoke to the nurse and said, *"Asino ricco del America."*

Jason didn't like being left out of the conversation. "What did you just tell your nurse?"

Speaking in English, Dr. Acosta said, "I said we have a patient who knows much more than we do about what is good for him. If he wants to check out, let him do so, but make sure he signs the release papers, so we won't be responsible for him." She quickly left the room.

Jason looked at the nurse. "She said all that in just four words?"

The nurse looked at the dressing on Jason's head. "She just about had you finished. I see you made a good impression on our doctor. She is very good at what she does. If she said you needed to spend a night for observation, I would listen."

"We don't have many women doctors where I am from. I guess one night won't kill me."

"You are right. It won't kill you, and it might save your life."

Jason had a very restless, long night. He was not allowed to go to sleep, and the next morning the nurse told him that he could have breakfast in bed, or he could go across the square and have something at the local restaurant. He decided he wanted to get out, so he went to Angelo's and ordered toast and a cup of coffee. It was not long until he saw Dr. Acosta in the dining area carrying a cup of coffee. When she saw him, she came over and without asking took a seat. Her voice was firm. "I have reviewed your files this morning, and we are going to release you. I don't think you are going to listen to anything I have to say, but if I were you, I would not go back to work for a couple of days. You will have some pain, but that is only natural. If you get lightheaded when you stand or have blurred vision or anything out of the ordinary, you need to get back here. If you have someone to stay with you, that is what I recommend."

For some reason he did not say anything. He knew he should say he was sorry, but chose not to. He was somewhat intimidated by her. She was obviously smart and was very beautiful. She had dark brown eyes and long black hair. She was somewhat tall and slender. She picked up her coffee and walked away.

Under his breath he said, "Thank you, Dr. Acosta."

Jason did take the doctor's advice and did not go back to work for two days. He visited the two brothers who were busy on the farm. When he did go back to work, he found the work site almost abandoned. He had a message to call the main office. He placed the call and was soon talking to Jerry Merrick. "Jason, I am glad you called. Costa said you had been in an accident, but that you were okay. We are going to shut the project down for four months. The construction crew is needed elsewhere. You can come home, or you can stay there. I would prefer you stay there and keep an eye on things."

"I have got a personal project going on here, so I think I will just stay put. If you have things you need me to go over, just send them to me." *Four more months. That will put the project at three years. I could become an Italian citizen and just live here. It will give me time to get the farm up and running.*

Two days later, Jason was sitting in the waiting room of Dr. Acosta's office. When she came in, she said in English, "It is good to see you are doing well Mr. Triple A. Are you having any pain or problems?"

"Only with my doctor. I don't know what you meant by Triple A, but I know it was not a compliment by the tone of your voice. I am doing okay. The pack you put on my wound helped. I really felt no pain."

Dr. Acosta smiled. "Everything looks fine, I will not need to see you again. I have heard that the dam site has closed for a while. Are you going back to the States?"

"No, I got permission to stay here. I am going to become a farmer for a while." He stood up. What he wanted to say was, "I would like to take you to dinner and start over," but all he said was, "Thank you very much. I hope I don't need your services again."

He smiled and left her office and walked down the hall to the checkout desk. There was an older lady sitting there, and he asked, "What did the doctor mean when she called me Mr. Triple A?"

"You really don't want to know."

"Yes, I do, and I am not paying my bill until you tell me." He was smiling, and the lady smiled back.

"It means Arrogant American Asshole."

Jason really liked working with the two brothers and often thought that once the dam project was completed, he might consider staying in Italy for a while. When they finished work one afternoon, Bonita said, "Can we talk to you about something? You have been so kind, and we hate to ask, but we have found a trailer. It is not much, but we would like to know if we can set it behind the barn and live there. We have to leave where we are living now."

Jason agreed, and when the trailer was set behind the barn, the brothers were busy getting it level and fixing it up. Jason went inside and looked around. It had two bedrooms, a living room, a small bath, and kitchen. He had given the brothers permission to run water and electric lines from his villa to the trailer.

Ana was cleaning some dishes. "It looks like you are going to be crowded, but it seems nice. Ana, this may seem forward, but I wonder if you would like to use the bedroom upstairs in the villa. There is a bath right next to it. You could have all the privacy you want. I rarely go upstairs."

Ana did not even have to think. "If you are sure. I would like that very much."

The brothers agreed. They were happy to have their own bedrooms. Jason did have some concerns about Ana's reputation, but very few people knew about the arrangement, and those who did come by the villa thought that she lived in the trailer with her brothers.

The months passed quickly, and it was not long until the construction site reopened. Jason found that he was extremely busy with the dam, so he turned the farming operation over to the brothers. One Saturday he decided to have lunch in town. He liked Angelo's food, so he stopped for lunch. He was waiting for his food when Dr. Acosta came in. As she approached his table he said, "Well if it isn't Dr. Bubbles."

She scoffed. "What in the hell is that name supposed to mean?"

"It is because of your charming personality."

"Look, I have done nothing to you. What is your problem with me?"

"You started this. If you remember when I had my last checkup you referred to me as Mr. Triple A. Did you not think I would find out what you meant? Oh, I guess you intended for me to find out."

She did not wait to be asked to sit down. She pulled out a chair and took a seat. She started to say something rude and then stopped. She waited for a minute, and when her anger subsided, she said, "You are right, because you are an Arrogant American Asshole does not give me the right to be rude." She looked at him and he was laughing.

"I am sorry. I have not had such a conversation since I was in grade school. You are right. The way I treated you that day at the hospital, I am what you say. I really didn't intend to be. Let me start over. My name is Jason Edward Terry. I am from Richmond, Kentucky. I really thank you for what you did for me, and in my defense, I have never seen a female doctor. As you know I am here working on a dam project. I will be here for some time, and I hope when you see me again you will not think too harshly of me."

She had calmed down. Angelo had come out, and he said, "Are you okay Gabi?"

"I am. I am going to have lunch with my new friend. Bring me the special."

Jason was delighted that she called him friend. "Are you on duty? If not, I will order a bottle of wine."

"I am not on duty," She turned to Angelo. "Bring us a bottle of that wine that Tobia recommended."

As Angelo left the table, Jason said, "Who is Tobia?"

"Tobia Martin is my Fiancé."

He didn't say anything. He realized that this was her way of bringing into the conversation that she was not available. It was not long until Angelo brought and poured the wine.

"This is good. What does this Mr. Tobia Martin do for a living?"

She smiled. "He is a wine broker. He works out of Rome. I guess when we get married, I will have to find a hospital in Rome. I don't think that will be much of a problem. I got my education there."

"So, we are both destined to leave this fair city. It is sad. I really like living here."

"Where do you live? Do you have an apartment in the city?"

"No. I have purchased a villa on the road to the dam."

"I know that place. Oh my gosh, you are rich! How much do they pay you to build a dam?"

"It is an investment. I hope to make a profit when I go back to the United States. Even if I break even, I will come out ahead because of my housing stipend."

They stayed at Angelo's for over an hour. They found they enjoyed each other's company, and conversation was easy.

When they got up to leave, he said, "I don't have a lot of friends here, and I could use the conversation from time to time."

"I would like that. I am only on duty a half day on Fridays. If you are in town let my secretary know, and if I can I will come by. Since you are so rich, you must pay," she said with a laugh.

Jason made a point to be at Angelo's every Friday for the next four weeks in a row. Gabi met him during three of them. They talked about lots of things they had in common. They both seemed to avoid any talk of the war, even though he told her that he was in Italy during the war.

She helped him with his Italian. She told him about Rome and places he should see. He told her about Kentucky, and she especially enjoyed him telling about the history of the state. She really enjoyed him telling about New York and the wonderful plays he had seen.

During this time Jason continued to have his dream. He started to notice that each dream was followed by a headache, and they seemed to be getting more severe. One afternoon he was sitting in the great room of the villa, and Ana brought in a tray with coffee. "Get another cup and join me. I want to talk to you about something."

She quickly retrieved another cup. They sat on opposite ends of the couch, and she waited for him to speak.

"I don't know if you know it, but I was station here during the war. I was not here long because I was wounded and sent to England. I did not get to know anyone while I was here. I know you lost your husband during the war. If you don't mind talking about it, I would like to know about how the war affected you and your family. You would have to have been just a teenager during that time."

"The war started for us in 1939. It is strange, because that was also the year Dominic and I were married. I was seventeen years old. Dominic and I had grown up in a small village that was just south of Trento. I don't remember when I didn't know him. There was a church that had a school. We attended it, and that is where I got my education. Dominic joined the army. He thought he was being patriotic. In 1940 he was in the invasion of Greece. It was not really an invasion of Greece. Most of the fighting took place in Albania. Mussolini had told the people that the invasion would only last a couple of weeks. For some reason we thought that the invasion would be quick, and Dominic would be safe. As you know, the invasion didn't go well, and Hitler sent German troops to bail us out. Dominic was wounded in the first month of the fighting. When he returned home, he could barely walk. It took Dominic about a year to get over his wounds. I thought that the war was over for us, but Dominic joined the resistance movement."

"How did he get involved with the resistance?"

"In the summer of 1943, most of the people were against staying in the war. The Americans and British invaded Sicily and by August,

General Patton had taken Messina. Less than a month later, the British landed on the mainland and our government surrendered. That should have been the end of it. Mussolini was arrested and put in prison, but the Germans came to his rescue and set up a Nazi government in Northern Italy with Mussolini as the leader. Dominic hated the Nazis and joined a local resistance group and left me, and I never saw him again. I later found out that he had been killed, but he had fought with the resistance for about a year. What about your time in the war?"

"I am so sorry, but I know you must be proud that Dominic died making this country free. I don't remember much about being here. I do have a dream about a church, but I am not sure if the church even exists. If it is a memory. It is just about the only memory that I have. I have the same dream over and over, and sometimes the church disappears, and sometimes it explodes. I have no idea why I keep dreaming this over and over."

"Do you know where you were while you were here?"

"Not really. I know I came through Anzio and was in Rome. After that, it is fuzzy. I think my dream is trying to tell me something."

"I don't have any idea how I can help you. I am not from this area. I am not familiar with the churches or the countryside at all. I am Catholic, but I have not attended church since we came into this area. I know that you are a good artist. Why don't you make a drawing of it? That way we could see if we could find it. Maybe you could show it to some of the local townspeople. They might know about it."

"That is just it. I have no idea where it was. I was so scared when I was here. All I could think about was getting back home. If my dream is correct, that church no longer exists."

"Drawing it may help even though you might not be able to find it." Ana took Jason's coffee cup and left the room.

After Ana had left, he got his drawing pad and slowly made a sketch of the church. He spent most of the night drawing in every detail he could remember. When he finished, he thought for a moment and for some reason thought of his father. He had not worked in wood for a long time. The next day when he returned from the dam, he drove into town and went to a local wood shop, and bought a slab of very light maple.

When he got home, he took his drawing and started his carving. The wooden piece was thirty-six inches by twenty-four inches. During the next week, he created a very detailed relief. At the bottom, he carved the name of the church in Italian, Chiesa Delle Tre Campane, the Church of the Three Bells. When he looked at it, he was proud, and he felt good. For some reason he had a feeling that he wanted to give the relief to Gabi. He couldn't explain why he had this desire. Somehow, he felt that this would be something he should do. He wrapped it up and hid it in his bedroom.

That Friday he went to visit Gabi. When he went to her office, the secretary informed him that Gabi had gone to Rome. "I guess she has gone to visit her boyfriend," he said.

"Maybe, but she didn't say that. She told me she wanted to see her parents."

He was surprised. She never talked about her parents. "She told me that she was educated in Rome. I guess I should have known that is where she grew up. I have something for her. Would you give it to her when she returns?"

He left the wooden carving and went across the street and ordered his lunch. Angelo took the order. "I guess Gabi is not joining you today. That is a shame because I love the way she laughs when she is here with you."

"I have enjoyed our little afternoon meals. You have been a part of that. You are one great cook. How did you meet Gabi?"

"I have lived here my entire life. I have known her since she was a little girl."

"That is strange. I thought she was from Rome."

"Oh, she is from Rome, but she did live here for a while when she was a little girl."

When Jason had finished his meal, he went to the kitchen to see Angelo. "I have some vacation time coming. I think I want to go home for a while. I wanted to tell Gabi myself, but I am leaving right away. I need for you to tell her I will not be here for a couple of weeks."

Pushing the Envelope

Three days later Jason was in a taxi heading to Richmond. When he pulled into his home, he was surprised how well maintained the grounds were. He paid the taxi driver and went up and knocked on the door. Billy opened the door and at first extended his hand for a handshake, but when they grasped their hands together Billy pulled him into a hug. "It is really good to see you."

"It is really good to see you also Billy. How have you been? Is Rachel here?"

"No, she is at school. I wrote you and told you she got a scholarship to State. She is doing so well. She is very good with math. I think she might someday want to join your firm. She lives on campus, but when she found out you were coming home, she said she would be here. The bus is to arrive about five thirty. We don't have to pick her up. They drop her off right on the road in front of the house on the way into town."

For a while Billy and Jason talked about the town and people, they both knew. Then Billy got out his books, and the two spent about an hour going over records.

"You are doing a good job, Billy. Do I need to do anything more on my end?"

"No, everything is good."

Just about that time the door opened, and Rachel came bouncing in. "Mr. Terry," she screamed and came running to him and threw her arms around him. He had not expected such a response. After the hug, she hugged her brother.

"My life has changed so much since you came to visit us that day and hired Billy. I can't believe my life is going so well. I have now finished one year of college. I am on the Dean's list. You take time to write a letter once a month and send me such nice things to teach me about Italy. I don't think things could get much better."

"Billy, when I called you and told you I was coming home for a while, I bet you bought some extra food and planned to make me some good meals. Not tonight. I have not had a hamburger since I left New York. Let's go out and eat."

Everything got quiet. Then Billy spoke. "We could go to Corky's."

"I don't want to go to Corky's. I want to try something new. We could go to a drive-in restaurant. We won't go in. We will order from the car."

"We can't go. It doesn't matter if we stay in the car or not. They are not going to serve us. Why don't you go. You could bring us some hamburgers back."

"That's nonsense, Billy. There is a drive-in restaurant just up the road on the edge of town. It is less than a half mile from here. We will go there. We will eat in the car. It will be fun. Let's go. I saw the car in the drive."

"Let me let you in on a little secret, and if you don't want to be a part of it, it will be okay. We are going to call attention to ourselves. I am sure you will be alright. When we get there, you will be right. They will not serve us and ask, then tell, then demand we leave. We are not going to leave. If it looks like we are in any danger, we will high tail it out of there. If things go according to plan, you and Rachel will be alright."

Billy and Rachel got into the car without saying anything. Rachel was sitting in the back. "Mr. Terry, we love you for who you are, but everyone is not like you. I think at best they will ask us to leave and at worst they will call us names. Are you sure you want to witness this?"

Jason didn't answer. In less than five minutes he was sitting at a speaker. He ordered three hamburger boxes and three drinks. Then they sat and waited.

In just a few minutes a young lady came to the window of the car.

Jason could tell she was nervous. In a shaky voice she said, "I have to ask you to leave. This restaurant does not serve that kind."

"That kind of what," Jason flashed back.

"We don't serve black people here. I am so sorry. I am so sorry to have to ask this of you, but will you please leave? I am so sorry. I am just doing my job."

Jason leaned out his car window and said, "You can go back and tell the manager that we are not going to leave and please get our food ready."

The young lady quickly left, and in a few minutes the manager came to the car. He was holding a baseball bat, and he yelled at Jason, who was sitting behind the wheel. "Get the car moving you nigger lover."

Jason looked over into the backseat and could see that Rachel was scared. For a moment he thought about leaving, but changed his mind. He had to see this through. "I am not going anywhere, and if I get out of this car, I am going to take that bat and stick it up your ass."

"I have called the police. They will be here any minute. If you don't want to be arrested, then you need to get moving." By this time several people had gathered around the car. Jason could tell that the crowd was split by what they were saying. Some thought they should be served, and some did not.

A police car with its lights flashing pulled up, and two policemen got out. They went right to Jason's window and said, "You can leave now, or we will arrest you and take you to jail."

One of the policemen walked to the other side of the vehicle and looked inside. "Billy, I am sorry, but you know how it is."

Jason was very calm and in a soft voice said. "I am sorry that you were called to come here. May I ask what the charges might be?"

The policeman investigated the car and saw Rachel sitting in the back seat. He first looked at Rachel and then to Billy. "I am sorry Billy, if I owned this drive-in you would be welcome. But I don't, so please convince whoever this is to leave." He then looked at Jason, who was still in the driver's seat. "You are trespassing. You were asked to leave. Would you please step out of the car?"

"I will get out of the car for just a moment to talk to you and these good people, and then I shall leave." Jason got out of the car and addressed the policeman and talked loud enough for all the bystanders to hear. "In my car is Billy Ballew. He is a World War II veteran. He was a member of the famous Red Tails. I too was in the army. When I was in Georgia doing my basic training, there were German prisoners of war being housed there. They were treated better than we treated the black airmen who were training to help protect your freedom. Billy Ballew is credited with saving several planes and men during the war. He was shot down during the war and as a result is crippled for life. He is also my friend. Now let me tell you why I am not trespassing. If you will check, you will find that I own this property. Mr. Sims is two months behind in paying his rent, and I am here to tell him he has thirty days to clear the premises."

About that moment another car pulled up. An overweight man got out of the car and talked to the manager. The large man then came to Jason. "Are you Mr. Terry?" Jason nodded his head. The large man turned to the policemen and said they could go. Turning back to Jason, he said, "I am so sorry for this. I am Fred Sims and I own this restaurant. Please let me meet with you tomorrow or at your convenience. Please let me explain my side of all this."

Looking in the window at Billy, he said, "I know who you are. My son who was in the war has told me about what the Red Tails did." He looked in the back seat and saw Rachel. "If you and your wife want to replace your order, I will see that is quickly brought to you."

Jason was surprised. "I am going to call Mr. Elmer Hall in the morning. You need to call him after ten, and if he can meet with us. He will give you a time."

Several of the bystanders where still watching what was going on. Jason did not know why, but Billy got out of the car and faced the crowd. Then all at once they started clapping their hands and several were saying, "Thank you for your service."

They got their burgers and started home. Rachel leaned forward from the backseat. "I think I got my voice back." She reached up and patted Billy on the back. "That man thought that I was your wife. Billy, you could never get a wife as young and pretty as me."

That night they talked about the experience at the drive-in. Billy was very serious and said, "I am not so sure that we accomplished anything tonight, but I have to admit, I really liked so many people clapping for me."

The following Monday, Jason and Mr. Sims and Elmer Hall met in Mr. Hall's office. Mr. Hall started the conversation. "Mr. Sims has brought me up to date on what happened at the Big Burger. Jason, I wish you had called me before you went out there. I think if you had you might have handled this a different way."

Jason scoffed. "Are you telling me that it is right for a business to refuse to serve people because of the color of their skin?"

"No, I am not saying that, Jason. Let me talk, and then you can have your say. You hold all the cards here. You own the property, and Mr. Sims is in default. There are some things you don't know. I was with Mr. Sims when he rented the property from Jake. They discussed this very problem. Mr. Sims did want to open a restaurant for all. I am using Jake's words here. He told Mr. Sims that if he did, he would not be able to pay the rent. Jake said, 'The time will come, but that time is not now.' There is another restaurant on the other end of town called Corky's. Mr. Sims and John Orlando are the owners. The workers at Corky's and Big Burger are paid the same, and believe it or not the menus are just about the same. I know that separate but equal is not good, but right now it is all we've got. I have hopes that in the future things will change."

For a minute Jason said nothing. "I wonder if I went to Corky's this afternoon and ordered a hamburger if they would have asked me to leave and called me names."

Mr. Sims gave a weak smile. "No, they wouldn't. We have several white people from downtown who come to our outside order window and buy food. Not many go inside, but some do. It is not a great start on ending racial problems, but it is a start. I want you to give me another chance. If you do, I will open the drive-in speakers to include all. But you must know that I am risking your money as well as mine. If I start losing money, I may have to change back."

"Speaking of money, why are you behind in your lease payments?"

Mr. Hall spoke up. "I will answer that. I put them on hold because Mr. Sims needed the money. His wife Elaine has cancer and has undergone several operations in the last six months. She is very ill. I told him to get Elaine back on her feet, then he could pay the lease. I acted on your behalf. Did I make the wrong decision?"

"No, no you didn't. I am so sorry. I accept the terms of our new agreement. Mr. Hall, just mark the last payments he has missed as paid." He got up and shook Mr. Sims' hand and left the room.

Jason spent the rest of his vacation just spending time around his home. He would sit on the porch, read, and sometimes he would think of Gabi.

Jason's vacation was to end after the first week of December. When he called his office, he was told that the construction site was having winter weather, and they were going to shut down until the new year. He decided he would spend Christmas at home with the Ballews. At the end of the second week of December Rachel came home from college.

That Saturday morning, they were eating breakfast and Rachel said, "Mr. Terry, I know that next week is your birthday. Is there anything that you would like? Maybe something special?"

"Yes, there is. But first let me ask how old you are."

"You know how old I am. I am twenty."

"Next Thursday I am going to be twenty-seven. I am only seven years older than you. For my birthday, I want you to stop calling me Mr. Terry. It makes me feel old. My name is Jason."

Rachel gave him a big smile and said, "That will be cheap enough, Jason."

On Thursday, Jason's birthday was celebrated with just the three of them. Rachel had baked a cake, and after dessert, Jason said, "I got an idea. Let's go to the movies. I have not been to a movie since I left New York to go to Italy. Is there a newspaper here? I want to see what is playing and check the times."

About one hour later they were in line buying tickets to see "Calamity Jane."

When Jason got to the ticket booth he said, "Three adult tickets please."

"Are you buying tickets for the two people behind you?"

"I am."

"Your ticket is thirty cents and theirs is twenty-five cents each. That will be eighty cents please."

"Why does my ticket cost more than theirs?"

Rachel, who was standing behind Jason and listening to the conversation thought to herself. "Oh no, here we go again."

The ticket lady said, "They have to sit in the balcony. Costs less up there."

Jason handed the lady a dollar. "You misunderstand. We are all going to sit in the balcony. You owe me a quarter back in change."

Jason had remembered his first Christmas with Jake Winston and how wonderful it was. He had Christmas dinner catered. He bought a fruit cake from the local bakery. Rachel and Billy gave him a briefcase, and he had purchased a television set for the home. He gave Billy a silver Elgin pocket watch with a silver chain, and he gave Rachel a gold bracelet which he had purchased in Rome. Billy really liked his watch, but Rachel could barely contain herself.

"I can't wait to get back to school to show this off," she told Jason as she gave him a hug.

A week later Jason was on a plane heading back to Italy. Sitting on the plane he thought about Billy and Rachel. He started thinking about his life. Rachel would someday get married and leave. That would only leave Billy, and he couldn't see a life with just him and Billy in the great big house. Maybe he should just live in New York. He thought about Maggie. Just for a moment, he thought about what life could have been. He closed his eyes and drifted off to sleep.

The Other Boyfriend

The following Monday, Gabi returned to her office. Marie, her secretary, handed her a stack of mail and said, "The schedule looks light today. How was your visit in Rome? Did you see Tobia?"

"My visit was great, and yes I did see Tobia. We are thinking about getting married in August. If we set that date, then I will give my notice here at the end of July."

"Have you applied for a position in Rome?"

"I have not, but I don't think it will be a problem since they have offered me a position there before."

Marie with a big smile said, "By the way, your other boyfriend came by to see you on Friday for your afternoon get together. I told him you had gone to Rome to see your other boyfriend."

Gabi's face flushed. "He is not my other boyfriend! He is my friend. Do you think people who see us together will get the wrong idea?"

"They will get an idea. Only you will know if it is wrong. A man and a woman having lunch together every Friday could start people talking. Did you tell Tobia about Mr. Terry?"

Gabi laid down the stack of mail she had been holding. "No, no I have not."

"Then you see the problem. Even you have concerns about what people, and especially Tobia, will think."

"I am going to tell him that we will have to stop meeting. I will explain things to him. I will end the meetings this Friday."

"You are going to have to wait. He's gone back to the United States. I think he said something about vacation time. He is going to be gone for a couple of weeks. Who knows how the construction business works? He might not be back and then your problem will be solved."

Marie picked up the chart on her desk. Gabi's heart began to race, and she again felt flushed. Perhaps she did have feelings for him. "When is he coming back?" she tried to be casual.

Marie looked at the clock on the wall. "You have an appointment in thirty minutes. I don't know. He said he was going on vacation, but he left you a gift. That makes me think that he is not coming back. Your gift is leaning against the wall."

Gabi had not noticed it before. She walked over and picked it up. It had weight. "Is there a card with it?"

"No. There is no card. Perhaps there is one inside. Are you going to open it?"

"No, I think I will open it when I get back to my apartment."

At noon Gabi walked across the square to Angelo's. When Angelo came to her table he said, "Anything different today, or do you want the Monday special?"

"I'll take the special. Angelo, did Jason come by Friday?"

"Yes. I missed seeing you two together. I like your smiling and laughing. You two are good together."

"Did he tell you he was leaving?"

"He did. He said he missed his home, and that there were people he wanted to see. I can tell that you don't think he is going to come back, and you didn't get to say goodbye. He called his trip a vacation. I think he is coming back." Angelo then walked away and went back into the kitchen.

Gabi felt much better. She was going to tell him that the Friday afternoon lunch meetings were going to have to stop, but she wanted to tell him, not just quit showing up. After all, they had become friends.

That night Gabi sat looking at her gift. "Let's see what you have given me, Mr. Jason Terry." She carefully removed the paper. It was something large wrapped in a red velvet cloth. "No card," she said to herself. She unwrapped the cloth, and she froze. She could not believe what she was seeing. All she could do was stare at the wooden representation of the church. Time seemed to stop, and she thought about her grandmother and the times she had spent in the church. Her view of the wooden relief started to blur as tears filled her eyes. Who is this man, she thought? Where did he get this wooden relief? It was a work of art. It must have cost a fortune. Wiping her eyes to clear her vision, she looked down, and in a corner of the relief she saw the name "J. Terry" and a date.

The next two weeks passed slowly. The two weeks turned into four, and at the end of four he had still not returned. Each night she would go to sleep looking at the wooden relief of the church. *What am I going to do with it? I can't keep it. The relief is a treasure. It belongs to the people of Caseno.*

Gabi spent Christmas in Rome with the Borellis. Tobia had a long Christmas break, and they spent time planning their wedding. She had pushed Jason out of her mind.

Gabi returned to her office, on Monday after New Year's Day. As she came into her office, Marie said in a playful tone, "Your boyfriend, Mr. Terry, is back."

Gabi became angry. "Don't," she paused. "Don't say that again. Don't refer to him as my boyfriend. He is a friend, a friend I am going to lose because you and many others won't mind your own business."

Tears came into Marie's eyes. "I am sorry Gabi. I thought we were friends too. Friends joke with each other. I am really sorry."

Gabi's tone softened. "I am sorry too Marie. I should not have said what I said. You are my friend, and you are right. I do like him, but I am engaged, and I am not going to be here much longer. I don't want to lose what I have."

Jason was back, but he did not come to town that Friday to meet Gabi for lunch. In fact, he either was working at the dam site or on the farm all week and the weekend. Gabi wanted to see him. She wanted to thank him for the gift, and she had many questions. On Saturday afternoon she could contain herself no more. She got into her car and headed out to his villa.

Stopping her car in front of the villa, she got out and looked at the structure. More questions about Jason Terry came into her mind. There was nobody in Caseno that could afford to live in this villa.

Just for a moment she thought about what it would be like to live in such a magnificent place. There were only five steps which led up to the door of the villa, but she took each one slowly, giving herself time to change her mind about the visit. Standing in front of the door, she saw a door knocker shaped like a gargoyle. No, she was not going to be intimidated by this man. He had given her a gift, and she needed to explain why she could not keep it or give it back to him. Reaching out, she took the monster by the head and brought it down hard on its brass support three times. It was done. There would be no turning back.

It was a few minutes before Gabi heard someone unlock the door. When it opened, she was surprised. It was not Jason, but a woman about her age, or maybe a few years older.

"I am sorry I was late opening the door. Rarely does anyone come to visit, and if they do, they don't come to the front. May I help you?"

Gabi started to speak but found she had to clear her throat. "My name is Dr. Acosta. I am here to see Mr. Jason Terry. Is he home?"

"Yes, he is here. Please come in."

She barely heard the woman's answer. *Who is this woman? Is she his girlfriend or maybe his wife?*

Stepping inside the door, Gabi scanned the interior of the home. It seemed larger inside than it looked from the outside. She had never seen a home so enthralling. *Yes, he is a rich American.*

"Jason is out back with my brothers doing something in the barn. I don't really know what they are doing, and I don't ask. If you care to wait in the great room, I will send for him." The woman disappeared through a door that seemed to lead to a kitchen, and Gabi could hear voices. In just a few minutes she returned. "My name is Ana. Can I get you anything while you wait?"

"No, I am fine." As Gabi looked at Ana, she seemed familiar. "Do we know each other? I feel like we have met before."

Ana took a seat on the edge of the fireplace. "During spring and summer my brothers and I have a vegetable stand in the market one day during the week and on Saturday. Maybe you have seen me there."

"Maybe."

Ana could tell that Dr. Acosta was curious, and maybe to put her at ease, or maybe just to protect her reputation, she decided to tell exactly who she was. "I told you my name is Ana. My brothers and I work for Jason. My two brothers take care of the outside of the property, and I am Jason's housekeeper. Jason has let us grow a garden and sell the vegetables at the market." Then she decided to tell a small lie. "I come here twice a week to clean, although I am not needed that much. Sometimes I come extra days to prepare meals. That is why I am here this late. I am getting a meal ready. I might have to go back and forth a few times. When Jason gets here, I will leave you two alone and continue with the meal."

Hearing a noise, Gabi looked to her left to see Jason coming through the door.

"Why Doctor Bubbles, why are you here? Are you making a late house call?"

She smiled, because he had really stressed calling her a doctor. "No, I am here to thank you for the wonderful gift."

Ana stood up. "If you will excuse me, I need to finish the meal."

Jason motioned for Ana to stop. "Doctor, will you join us for dinner?" Before she could answer, Jason was talking to Ana. "We do have enough for one more?"

Ana smiled. "Yes, but you will have nothing for your noon meal tomorrow. I am only joking. Of course, there is plenty."

Gabi was surprised how casual Ana was with Mr. Terry. They treated each other like friends. She surprised herself and agreed to stay. "I would be glad to join you, and If I am going to be your dinner guest you can start calling me Gabi, and please stop with the Doctor Bubbles. We have been having lunch together for several weeks and you still call me Doctor, and I call you Mr. Terry. Jason, again my name is Gabi." After all, there was no need to put on a show in front of his friends. Just about everyone knew they had been having Friday lunches together.

Jason walked over and looked at the fireplace. "It has been rather cool today. I guess it is just this time of year. It is starting to get a little cool in here. I am going to get a fire going. I need to break the chill. Gabi, why have you come to see me? I know that I have not seen you since I got back from my vacation, but I was going to meet you for lunch this Friday."

"Two reasons. The first is not a pleasant one. People are starting to talk about us. I am getting married before the end of the summer. I have not told Tobia about you. I like being your friend, but I don't think Tobia and others understand our relationship."

"So, you are here to say you are sorry that we can't have lunch anymore?"

"No, that is not the only reason why I am here. I still think you are a rich, arrogant American, but after seeing your wooden relief of the church, I will add you are a very talented rich, arrogant American. That is the main reason I am here. I need to tell you two things. First, I cannot accept it, and second, I will not return it."

Jason was perplexed. "What is going on Doctor Bubbles? I mean Gabi. I am sorry, it may take some time to get used to calling you Gabi. You are going to have to explain."

"Don't get me wrong. The gift is wonderful. I need to ask some questions about the church. Do you have a photo of the church? If you do, I would like to buy it from you or at least borrow it so that I could make a copy."

"No, I don't have a photo."

"I can't believe you carved it with such detail from your memory. No one could remember anything in such detail."

"Gabi, you don't understand. This church doesn't exist. To my knowledge I have never seen this church."

"You are wrong. It did exist. You were stationed here during the war. You must have seen it when you were here."

Jason's voice became almost a whisper. "I was here during the war. I have very few memories of being here. Gabi, the truth is, I don't want to remember anything about the war. I remember some good things. We landed at Anzio, and the fighting there was over. I got a three-day pass to visit Rome. It was wonderful to see places that I had only read about. I remember leaving Rome, but I don't know even which direction we went. It could have been east or maybe north. I just don't know. I have a memory of being on a patrol and being left behind a stone wall. I have no memory beyond that. My records say I killed a lot of Germans. Who wants to remember that? I don't. I don't remember that church. Why is it so important to you?" Suddenly Jason found he no longer wanted to know anything about the church. He knew that Gabi knew about the church. He would let her explain about it and then he would move on and try to put it out of his memory.

"I know the priest of that church. My mother was a member. You had to have seen that church. You even gave the church its correct name. The Church of the Three Bells."

Jason turned and shifted in his seat. "You said it was not there anymore. What happened to it?"

Gabi started to have tears in her eyes. "It was destroyed during the war. I don't understand that you say you can't remember the church. How could you make such a detailed carving?"

"You are not going to believe this, but it comes to me in a dream. I am standing in a field of high grass, looking at the church from a distance. I have this dream quite often. That is all there is in my dream. I see the church and I wake up. I thought that if I made a drawing of the church, my dream would go away. It did not. When I finished the drawing, for some reason I thought of my father. He was a very talented carpenter. I decided to make a wooden relief to honor him. I really enjoyed making the carving, but for me, it only exists in my dreams. If you are not going to keep my gift and you are not going to return it, what are you going to do with it?"

"With your permission, I am going to donate it to a church. The priest of the church is Father Borrelli. He was the priest of the Church of Three Bells. After the war, a new church was built inside the city. He is the priest there, and I know that he and the members of the church would love to have this. Many of the former members of the Church of Three Bells attend the new church."

Jason smiled. "That will be fine."

Ana appeared at the door. "Everything is ready."

Jason got up and extended his hand to Gabi. "Please come with me."

To Gabi's surprise they were not eating in the dining room. Jason led her out to the back of the villa. "We have an outdoor kitchen back here. It is fun to eat out here, especially when it is hot inside. Ana can even prepare the meals out here."

"Well it is not hot out here now. It is winter time. How can we eat out here?"

"The outdoor kitchen is partially covered. Luke and Bonita have installed gas heaters above the table with radiators to reflect the heat down. We will stay quite warm if the wind is not blowing."

The table would seat about eight people. Two men were already seated at the table but got up when Gabi and Jason approached.

"Gabi, this is Bonita and Luke. This is Dr. Gabi Acosta. She prefers Gabi. If everyone will take a seat, I am going to go downstairs and get some of that cheap wine the previous owners left in the house. I think they took all the good stuff."

They all took their seats except for Ana. She was busy bringing food to the table.

Gabi was seated in front of the two brothers. She looked at them and said, "So, you are the two geniuses who installed the heaters, so we could eat out here. Jason came here from America. Where did he find you two?"

Bonita laughed. "You are blunt and to the point Gabi. He found us on the side of the road."

"That needs some explanation. I don't think you mean he found you on the side of the road."

Ana, who was carrying a large plate of bread to the table, smiled and said, "It's true. He found us on the side of the road. We had a flat tire, and we had gotten out of our truck to walk, when along comes Jason. He stopped and asked if he could help. He found out we were broke and couldn't even pay to repair a tire. He took me and Luke home, and took Bonita to get us a new tire. He hired the boys to clean up the grounds and me as a housekeeper. He is a wonderful man. Even though he did not know us, he paid us for the first week in advance."

About that time Jason came to the table with four bottles of wine.

Gabi almost giggled when she said, "I hope you don't plan on drinking all that. If we do, I don't think I will be able to drive home." Everyone laughed.

Jason set the bottles on the table. "You mean you are not Italian. You can't hold your wine."

During the meal, everyone was talking and laughing. Gabi had not had a feeling of being a part of a group since the war. She was so relaxed and peaceful. She had been so wrong about him. He was rich, but he didn't seem to be so. He was very comfortable eating and having conversation with his workers. He was not arrogant. She also could see that deep down he had some sadness in him. She found she wanted to know him even more. Then she thought of Tobia. What would he think of her being here having dinner with four strangers, who didn't seem like strangers at all, and one who she found herself attracted to?

When the meal was over, Bonita said to Ana, "Luke and I are going to the barn to load several bales of straw that we need to take into town tomorrow. We will pick you up in about thirty minutes. Will you be finished by then?"

Jason knew that Bonita was trying to protect Ana's reputation.

"I will, it will not take long." Ana started clearing the table and noticed that Jason and Gabi were both helping. This was not unusual for Jason, but she was surprised by Gabi.

When everything was cleared, Jason and Gabi walked back into the great room. "You know you were wrong about one thing." She took a seat on the couch.

Smiling he said, "Just one thing. You flatter me. What was I wrong about this time?"

"The wine was really good. We only drank three bottles. Could I take the other bottle with me?"

Before Jason could answer, Ana came into the room carrying a tray with coffee, some cream and sugar and two cups. Smiling she said, "Gabi, I know you only drank a couple glasses but if you are driving home, you might need this. I have had this wine before, and there is some kick to it."

She then turned to Jason. "Thank you for this evening. It has been delightful. Dr. Acosta, Gabi, you are wonderful."

"Thank you, Ana. Gabi is about to leave but I agree with you. She needs a cup of coffee before she leaves."

"Would you excuse me for just a moment?" Jason and Ana both left the room. While they were gone Gabi wandered around the room. Standing in front of a small table she noticed a letter. She did not pick it up but read the return address.

Rachel Ballew

403 West Main

Richmond, Kentucky

Maybe he does have a girl back home. I wonder if that is why he decided to go back there for his vacation.

Just about that time Jason came back into the room carrying a bottle of wine. "You said that you like this wine. Here is the extra bottle. This wine is good. We call it cheap wine because I didn't have to pay for it. There are many bottles with this label in the basement. I don't know why the previous owner left it, but I am glad he did."

Setting the wine on the table, Jason walked over and poured the coffee. It was Gabi who spoke first. "I told you more than once that I was engaged to be married."

"You did. Why do you bring it up? Do you think I have gotten you alone and that I am going to make a pass at you?"

"I would not want to explain to Tobia why I am alone in a villa with a man I barely know, but I like being here. I don't know when I have been so relaxed, especially around people I barely know."

"Just tell him you had to make a house call." He then smiled and said, "It has been a good night for me too. You don't have to tell him anything. No one is going to know you were here. I think the Aparos enjoyed the evening too."

"Do they eat with you often?"

"Yes, about once or twice every two weeks. Tonight, was special. As you know I went home for Christmas, and this was sort of a celebration of me coming back. That is why we ate outside."

"I think you understand why we can't be friends. It is impossible for a man and a woman to have a platonic relationship, especially when one of them is about to get married."

Jason took a sip of his coffee. "That may be true, but my best friend is female. When I am with her, I feel I can discuss anything. Her name is Mary. We met in college. She is from New York and is now an interior designer. I see her as often as I can."

"Are you in love with her? Do you want to marry her?"

"I am not in love with Mary, but I love her very much."

Gabi did not understand. "Is she in love with you?"

"Mary is in love, but not in love with me. She must keep her love a secret because most people would not accept it, and some people would even think that she is evil. She is a good person, and I have even helped her keep her secret. There are a few times I have taken her home, and we give each other some very passionate kisses just for show."

"Do she and her lover live together?"

"They do. They pass for roommates. Her name is JoAnn."

"I am not going to pretend that I understand that type of relationship, but I accept it. I guess love is love, and we really don't completely control who we fall in love with." Gabi felt she should end the conversation before it got complicated.

Gabi dropped her head as if ashamed to ask, but she asked anyway. "Are you married, or have you been married?"

Jason gave out a laugh. "I know you want to know more about me, so let's make a deal. I will answer one question tonight and you will do the same for me. If we meet again, then each of us will get another question. So, what is your one question?"

"The same as I asked before with one addition. I want to know if you are married, or have you ever been married, or is there a woman in your life?"

Does this woman have some interest in me? "Why do you ask me this?" He almost hoped she did have some interest in him.

She took another sip of her coffee. "I am sorry for asking something that is truly none of my business. Ana was right about the wine. It does go to your head. Let's not play this game anymore."

"Too late, you owe me a question."

"No, I don't owe you a question because you did not answer mine."

"I am not married. The second part of your question was, do I have a woman in my life? The answer is going to be in the past tense. There was not one, but two. I met Molly while I was stationed in Georgia doing my basic training during the war. I thought we were in love, and she wanted to get married. I convinced her to wait until after the war. A month after we shipped out, I got the famous Dear John letter. It would have been the same if we had gotten married. As I look back on it, Molly was my first love. I was only young teenager at the time. What does a teenager really know about love? If she had not broken my heart and waited for me, who knows how it would have played out."

"What do you mean a Dear John letter?"

"It is a letter breaking everything off. It is just like in the song. *I must let you know that my love for you has died just like the grass on the lawn, because tonight I wed another, Dear John."*

"That's awful. What did you do?"

"There is nothing I could have done. I was thousands of miles away. I never answered the letter. Aren't you asking more than one question? You are like a machine gun. You are in rapid fire with your questions."

Gabi ignored Jason's response. She looked at Jason and said, "Well at least she was not after your money."

Jason scoffed and thought to himself, *What money?*

"You said there were two women. Who was the other?"

"Her name was Maggie. We met at the building where we both worked, and after a romance that lasted several months, I find out she is married. It is more complicated than that, but I am going to leave it at that. It is time for my question. Why are you getting married?"

She was completely caught off guard by the question. "That is your question? You are asking me why I am getting married?"

"Yes, one simple question. Why are you getting married?"

"I met Tobia in Rome. I was there for a meeting to learn a new medical technique. I was there for two weeks. We met while I was eating lunch on the Spanish Steps. Romanic, no? We spent the entire two weeks together. We really liked each other, I found out he was from a good family that owned a distribution company and he was from money. He was well educated and extremely good looking. We started writing and seeing each other when we could. After about three months, he took me to see his family. I don't think they saw me as a doctor. I think they saw me as a young woman who came from a poor family and accepted me. It was on that visit that he asked me to marry him. I said yes. We have not yet set a date, but it is going to be this year. Perhaps it might be this summer."

Jason looked at her with a sad look on his face and at first said nothing. All she could do was stare back. *What is he thinking?*

"This is a dangerous game we are playing, and I have no desire to hurt you in any way."

She stopped him. "What do you mean?"

"If I were engaged to someone, and you asked me why I was getting married, I would have a very short answer. I would simply say, because I am in love. Nothing else would matter. Nowhere in your answer did you say, I am in love. All you told me was he offered you security."

Looking at Jason, Gabi felt as if she were going to cry. "I am not like you, Jason. Security is very important to me. Unlike you, I was not born rich. Life has been very difficult. I had to work hard and overcome a lot to be a doctor. Doctors in America make more than doctors make here. I have to go, I am going to Mass in the morning."

Jason was not sure what to say. He felt he had ended any chance of friendship they might have had. He decided to stay away from the question he had just asked and change the subject. "I didn't know you were Catholic."

"I didn't say I was Catholic. I only said I was going to Mass." She had regained her composure, and she gave him a weak smile.

He felt better. "I know we were limited to only one question, but why would you go to Mass if you are not a Catholic?"

"Ok, one more question. My grandmother was a Catholic, and my mother was Catholic, but my father was Jewish. My mother married a Jew at the worst possible time in history to do so."

He stood up and extended his hand to Gabi. She took it, and he pulled her to her feet. He picked up the bottle of wine and handed it to her. "It has been a wonderful evening, or at least it might have been if I had not been so blunt and kept my mouth shut."

"You did not ruin the evening. You made a good point about how I answered your question. I am still engaged to be married, and I still think you are a nice man."

They started walking toward the front door. They stopped at the door and Gabi said, "If you were engaged to be married, how would you have answered your question?"

He paused before he answered. "I would say that I am in love and I have found a person I want to spend my life with, a person who is going to become my best friend and be my partner in everything I do."

She smiled. "Please stop by at lunch time if you have some free time, and we will continue our questions."

"I thought we decided that we would not be having lunch anymore. Are we going to test the waters and see if people will let us be friends?"

"Maybe setting a meeting date to have lunch was not a good idea. Maybe we could just bump into each other every now and then. I don't know. We will just have to see."

He opened the door and walked her to her car. "I know the times for you have been bad, but your mother and father were like the play, *Abie's Irish Rose.*"

"They were what?"

"*Abie's Irish Rose.* It is a delightful play about a Jewish boy who marries a Catholic girl and all the problems they have because of their faith and their culture."

Gabi repeated the name of the play. "I will have to look it up." She then got into her car and drove away.

As Gabi drove away, Jason's thoughts turned to Maggie. She was someone he had wanted to spend his life with.

The Hard Truth

When Gabi got back to her apartment, she could not get Jason from her mind. At first, she was angry about what he had said, but he was right. She did want security. She had never had it. She had grown up with a Jewish father. She had lived in Rome during German occupation. She had to leave Rome and move to Caseno during this time. The death of her grandmother and going back to Rome and living with the Borrellis had all caused her to be insecure. Now she was in the medical profession, where there were very few female doctors. But Jason had been right. Did she really love Tobia? Could she really love anyone? Without changing her clothes, she lay across the bed and went to sleep.

The next morning, she went to Mass. Though she did not come to hear the Mass, she found herself caught up in Father Borrelli's message. Father Borrelli was her grandmother's priest. It was he who had taken her to Rome after she had been wounded during the war. He had checked on her often, and it was his brother who helped her get into the medical profession.

When Mass ended, and everyone had left the chapel, Father Borrelli came back in from outside after he had said goodbye to his flock. "Gabi, I didn't see you here during Mass. It is so good to see you. What brings you here this morning? I hope this becomes a regular thing for you."

Standing up, Gabi gave Father Borrelli a hug. "Maybe I will come more often, but today we need to talk."

He already had noticed the large package wrapped in brown paper lying next to her on the pew. "I have something for you," she said as she picked it up.

"Let's go to my office. It will be more private there. I do want to visit, and I don't want us to be disturbed. Come with me."

The office was quite large with one stained glass window giving the room a yellow light. It had a desk and two file cabinets. There were two wooden chairs in front of his desk, with a large blue couch against one wall. There was also a small table with a small lamp on it.

They took a seat on the couch. "What do you have for me?" He took the package, untied the string that held the brown paper in place and unwrapped it from the red velvet cloth to see the wooden carving. "Oh my, oh my, where did you get this?" He stood up and walked to the window holding the relief. He walked over to the small table and turned on the lamp to get a better view. "This is truly a work of art. Where did you get this? I was sure that the image of the Church of Three Bells was lost forever."

"There is an interesting story here, and I am hoping you can help me fill in the blanks, because I don't know the whole story. We have never talked about my grandmother's death, but I feel there is a connection between her death and the man who carved the wooden relief."

Father Borrelli leaned the carving against the wall. "You have never wanted to talk about your grandmother's death, and I am not sure you want to know all the events of that day. Tell me who made this wonderful carving. Does he have an old photo? He must have because of the magnificent detail he has captured."

"I asked the same question. He has no photo, and this is where the story gets strange. He has dreams about the church, or maybe a vision would be more accurate. He says the vision comes to him while he is asleep and that is all he sees. A vision of our church and then he wakes up."

"Where did you meet this man?"

"He is a patient of mine. He came to the hospital with a head injury. I got to know him, and he gave the carving to me as a gift for helping him."

"He is a patient, but can you tell me his name?"

"I can. If you look in the lower right-hand corner of the relief you can see his name. He lives north of the city. He is here working on the dam project. No, that does not tell you who he is. He designed the dam and is here supervising the construction. He was here during the war, but he will talk very little about it. He says this is a time in his life he does not want to remember. I think he won some medals during the war, but he takes no pride in them. He told me that there is no honor in killing." Gabi suddenly stopped talking and drifted off into thoughts about Jason.

Father Borrelli just let her sit there for a moment and then said, "I see that he signed J. Terry, but what is his complete name?"

"What Father? Did you say something? I am sorry, I got lost in thought for a minute."

"I said, what is his full name?"

"You can see that he signed his name J. Terry, but his first name is Jason. Like I said, he is here building a dam, but he must also be very rich. He has the villa north of town. I know that American companies pay well, but not enough to pay for this villa. It is something to see, and he employs three people to oversee his property."

Now it was Father Borrelli's turn to get lost in his thoughts. "Are you sure you want to know this story? First, what do you remember about that day?"

"I remember being at the church with my grandmother. You were with us. We heard the Germans coming and you hid Grandmother in the confessional, and I went into your office and got under the desk. I remember you told us we should not hide together because if they found one of us they might not find the other. You made us promise not to come out of hiding until you came and said it was safe. I remember while hiding, I heard several gun shots. I was scared. When you came and got me, and we went into the sanctuary, there were several people there. They were Jews. There were three American soldiers. I don't remember what they looked like, but they all had guns. As we started to leave the church, I saw a German soldier lying under a pew. There was blood. When we left the church, we got down on our stomachs and started to crawl toward the trees that were on the right side of the church. One of the soldiers was leading us, and the other two were behind us. About half way to the trees I thought of my grandmother. I thought she was still hiding in the confessional. I stood up to run back to get her. I don't remember anything else. My next memory was being in a hospital and you sitting beside me. It was then that you told me that my grandmother had been killed. One thing that I have thought about but never asked you about is why didn't someone go back and get my grandmother? Did you and the American soldiers abandon her? Was she killed when the church was destroyed?"

"That was some day. I have often wondered why you never asked about your grandmother. I always assumed you did not want to talk about it. I had no idea that you were blaming me, or perhaps the soldiers, for her death."

"It is not that way. I don't blame anyone. As you say, it was some day. It was a really bad day. No one can be blamed for what happens in a war where people are being shot and killed. I guess you thought it was too unsafe to go back and save my grandmother. I don't blame anyone for that. I am ready for you to tell me what happened after I was shot."

"I wish you had asked me about your grandmother a long time ago. I feel you and Mr. Terry are a lot alike. Neither of you wants to remember the war. You are right about one thing. I know the entire story, and if you are ready, I will tell you everything."

"I guess I am not that little girl you saved that day. I have grown up."

"I didn't save you. Our story starts after you were pulled out of that cave and I took you to Rome. I have got something I want to read to you." He got up and walked to one of his file cabinets. Opening the second drawer, he reached down and pulled out a letter. He walked back to the couch and took his seat. "This will pull everything together. Are you sure you are ready for this? This letter contains information that will change everything."

"What could it possibly change? I survived the war. My mother and father had already been killed by the Germans. My grandmother died when the church exploded. What could that letter contain that would change any of that?"

"Believe me it will." He then unfolded the letter and started to read.

Dear Father, Borrelli,

I am not sure if this letter will ever find you. I know you are well known in the city, so I am just sending it to you, general delivery. You were so kind after we made it back into the city. I am so sorry that the Germans destroyed the church. I hope you build it back or find you another. I am so sorry about the woman that was killed inside the church. She gave up her life to save the Jewish people that you were hiding. I wish we could give her a medal or something.

You asked me to give you information about the young man who saved us that day in the church. As you know, when we found him, he was wounded and had lost a lot of blood. There was some doubt about him making it. He was taken to a hospital ship, and I didn't see him again, or not for a while. He was taken to England. There he had surgery on his leg and was slated to return to the United States. When the fighting ended here, I was sent to England, and that is where we crossed paths again. I talked to his doctors at length and found out a lot about him. He was in surgery while I was there, and I didn't get to see him. After talking to the doctors, I looked up his records, and this is what I know. He does not remember anything about the day he became a hero. He doesn't want to remember, and even though he was going to be highly decorated, he did not think he wanted that honor. After the war, I was on my way home, so I stopped at Richmond where he was from and found some interesting things about him. His mother had died when he was four years old. His father was a carpenter. His father was a great carpenter but a poor business man. They were very poor, and his father lied about his age to get him into school early because he needed the school to take care of him. His father died the week he graduated from high school, and he joined the army because he needed the money and a place to live. The day he became a hero, he did some amazing things. As you remember, it was he who saved us from the Germans who were holding us captive inside the church. It was he who stayed with the young girl when she was shot, knowing his chances of making it back alive were small. Somehow, he was able to pull the young girl to the tree line and take out a German machine gun nest. He managed to save an entire company of American soldiers. When we found him, he and the young girl were passed out in the cave. His leg wound was severe, and I have no idea how he could have carried her up that hill. His pain must have been unbearable. Here is the remarkable thing. When he did all this, he was just fifteen years-old. I know you want to know his name. We could just call him hero. During the war, his fellow soldiers called him JET. His name was Jason Edward Terry.

Yours, Lieutenant Forbes

Gabi just sat there. She did not know what to say. Father Borrelli watched a tear roll down her cheek. "I could have told you this story a long time ago but chose not to. We did not want you to know how your grandmother died. The Germans had found your grandmother and captured the two American soldiers. We were bound to a chair and being questioned when Jason Terry slipped into the church. The Germans shot your grandmother. That is why she was not with us when we were in the dry creek bed. When he witnessed your grandmother being shot, he killed the Germans. Two of the American soldiers led us from the church. When you found out that your grandmother was not with us, you stood up and were shot. I never told you this story because I felt you would be filled with hate for the Germans, and that bitterness would keep you from becoming the fine person you have become. Forgive me if I was wrong."

Gabi just lay down on the couch and cried uncontrollably. Father Borrelli got up, got a small blanket and spread it over her and left her alone.

Gabi's Story

The American soldiers had found Gabi, along with Jason, in the cave, which was on a hill that overlooked the valley. They brought her back to a mobile hospital unit. She was given blood, her arm patched up, and she was lying on a cot just outside a hospital tent when Father Borrelli found her. Opening her eyes, she said, "Where am I, what happened?"

"You were found in a cave. You had been shot in your shoulder, but you are going to be alright."

"A cave. How did I get into a cave?"

"I don't know. There was an American soldier in the cave with you. Perhaps you can tell me what you remember."

"I remember that I was with you and several other people. There were some American soldiers, and we were leaving the church. I stood up to go find Grandmother." Suddenly Gabi panicked. "Where is Grandmother?" She tried to sit up but found she could not.

Father Borrelli gently pushed her back down on the cot. He chose his words carefully. He wanted to tell the truth, and he did not want to lie. "The church was destroyed by artillery, and your grandmother was inside." He did not tell Gabi that she had already been killed by the Germans.

The war had not been kind to Gabi. She had lost her father. He had been killed by the Germans because he was Jewish and was fighting with the resistance. Her mother had left her with her grandmother to go fight with the resistance and had never returned, and now she had lost her grandmother. Her tears began to flow, but she did manage to say to Father Borrelli, "What is going to happen to me?"

At first, he did not say anything, but waited for her to stop crying. "It was Lieutenant Forbes and his men that found you in the cave. It was he who was leading us out of the church. Everyone made it to safety. It was he who came to me and showed me where you were. He insisted that the army doctors take care of you. The world needs more people like Lieutenant Forbes."

"You did not answer my question. What is going to happen to me?"

"I am going to take you to Rome. My brother is a doctor, and he and his wife live there. I am going to ask him to help take care of you and get you back on your feet. I am told that you will be able to leave in a couple of days."

"What if I don't want to leave?"

"What are you going to do here? You are only fifteen years old. This town is scarred. If you stay here, you are going to become another casualty of the war."

"What are you going to do?"

"I told you. I am going to take you to Rome, but I have other reasons for going. I am going to seek an audience with the church. The war is coming to an end. The Germans are losing. The allied army has invaded France. The Germans are being beaten back. When the war ends this town is going to need another church. I am going to see that one is built and help ease the scars this community has."

"Let me stay with you? I can help."

"I don't know if this can happen. It is my dream, but there is a possibility that the church could send me somewhere else."

Three days later, Father Borrelli and Gabi were in the home of Dr. Borrelli. He was older than Father Borrelli. His wife was a kind grey-headed woman. They had no children and made over Gabi and made her feel special. Father Borrelli stayed for about three days, and then he was gone.

Dr. Borrelli continued to doctor Gabi's wound. Two weeks after she had arrived, he was changing the bandage. "Well, this is good, and maybe somewhat bad."

"Am I not healing right?"

"You are healing okay, and I am going to leave the bandage off.

There is a small pimple next to your wound. I know what it is. I have seen this before." He could tell she was getting concerned. "Don't worry so much. I have seen how you can move your arm, so there can't be much internal damage. Let me see." He reached into his bag, pulled out a small set of tweezers. "I am going to pop this pimple and I know what I am going to find. When he finished, he said, "Just as I thought. That German bullet must have nicked a bone. This is a bone splinter. Nothing to worry about, but tomorrow you are going with me to the hospital and we'll have a much closer look."

The next day Gabi and Dr. Borrelli went to the hospital. Gabi was sitting on a hospital table when Dr. Borrelli came in with an x-ray. "I was right. The bullet did hit your collar bone. There are a few bone fragments that will have to come out. It is not much of an operation. We won't even have to put you to sleep."

Gabi took the news in stride, and the operation took about an hour and a half. Her arm was back in a sling. The next day, she again went back to the hospital with Dr. Borrelli. She found she was fascinated with medical work. She watched the nurses and how they cared for the patient. It wasn't long until the sling was gone from her arm, and she was helping at the hospital. A month later she was changing bandages and helping with minor medical procedures.

One afternoon she was helping a young boy who had fallen and had scraped his leg in gravel. She was just about to finish when Dr. Borrelli came in and watched as she completed applying a bandage to the wound.

"You do good work. But I think I am going to make a change."

She quickly looked up. "I know that I am young, but I am soon going to be sixteen. I like working here. It makes me feel good." Then she smiled. "I also work cheap."

"Are you suggesting that we start paying you?"

"No, you and Mrs. Borrelli have been so kind. I like giving back. Don't make me stop."

"I am not going to make you stop. You are very good at what you do. In fact, I am going to give you even more to do. You are gifted, and I want you with me in the operating room. You will need to be trained.

I want you to start observation tomorrow. If this is what you want, Mrs. Borrelli, who was once a nurse, will teach you at home. Do you want to do this? By the way, you will get paid."

Gabi didn't say anything. She just gave Dr. Borrelli a big hug.

Time passed quickly for Gabi. She worked and studied hard, and in only one year she was a nurse and was assisting several doctors in performing operations in Rome. Mrs. Borrelli was a good teacher. She not only taught Gabi how to be a good nurse, she taught other subjects and insisted that she learn English. Two years later Gabi, received recommendations from several doctors that she be admitted to medical school. She had to leave the Borrellis to attend. On her first day of classes she was so scared she could hardly breathe. She was much younger than the other candidates, but it was not long until many of the students wanted to study with her. Her experiences in the operating rooms and working at the hospital with several doctors back in Rome had put her ahead of the other students. When she graduated, she was at the top of the class.

After she finished her medical training, she was offered a position as a doctor back in her home town. At first the people of the city did not accept her, but it wasn't long until she won them over and she settled into the job.

In the fall of 1955, she was called back to Rome for continuing education. She saw this as a vacation as well as another step in her medical career. She had often taken weekend trips to visit the Borrellis. She had begun to think of them as parents, and they treated her like a daughter. Dr. Borrelli talked about retiring and wanted Gabi to take his place. She had told him that for the time she was happy and was needed in Caseno.

During her four weeks stay in Rome she decided to visit the sites of the city. One afternoon she had finished her training for the day and was sitting on the Spanish Steps. She had purchased a sandwich and a bottle of wine and was just about to eat her lunch when she heard a voice coming from behind her. "Hello. I can see that you have very little knowledge about wine, and I would be glad to share mine for half of your sandwich."

Looking up she saw the shadow of a man, but she could not make him out because the sun was shining in her eyes. "Maybe I like this wine, and maybe I don't want to share my sandwich."

He came down the steps and sat down next to her. "If you taste what I have, you will see that I know what I am talking about. The wine you have has an Italian name, but it is produced in Spain. Not even a good region in Spain. Its only good quality is that it is cheap." He smiled and then added, "Are you a poor girl and can't afford good wine? My name is Tobia Martin, by the way."

He was extremely good looking. He was lean and about six feet tall and had an infectious smile. "Well, Mr. Tobia, I will have you know, I like cheap Spanish wine. I don't want to share my sandwich, and I didn't invite you to join me."

"Well, may I join you? I do have something you don't. I have two glasses. Did you plan to drink out of the bottle?"

"Why do you have wine and two glasses? Do you wander the streets of Rome looking for a woman to pick up that has a bottle of cheap wine?"

"It does look that way. I am a wine broker, and I am here to sample and buy wine. I am meeting with the Tuscany Winery to sample their wine for a possible market. I like this wine and took one of their gift baskets for myself. I would like to know what you think of it?"

Gabi was now meeting his smile. "I will have to admit that I know nothing about this wine. I bought it because I thought the bottle was attractive. It was wrapped in a basket weave, and it was sitting on the counter of the wine shop. My name is Gabi." She then paused. "My name is Dr. Gabi Acosta. Let me give your wine a try."

Gabi had to admit that the wine he had was very good, and she relaxed as she had a second glass.

"I don't get to meet many women doctors, in fact I don't get to meet any doctors in my line of work. Tell me, why is an unmarried lady sitting on these steps alone?"

"How do you know that I am not married?"

"You have no ring, and you are by yourself."

"I am a doctor. We don't wear jewelry."

"Well, are you married, and if you are not, do you have a boyfriend?"

Gabi gave a big smile. "No and no, I am not married, and I don't have a boyfriend."

"Well, if you are not married and you don't have a boyfriend, may I stay for a while?"

"I do like this wine and it does belong to you."

Tobia poured more wine. "Tell me Dr. Gabi, why are you sitting here on the Spanish Steps?"

It was this simple question that started a conversation that would last the entire afternoon. For some reason she wanted to tell him everything. She told him where she was from, about her mother and father and grandmother, all killed during the war. She talked about Father Borrelli and how the Borrellis had taken her in. She did not tell about being shot during the war and being saved by Father Borrelli.

"Gosh, I am doing most of the talking. Let me ask some questions about you. First, where did you grow up?"

"I grew up here in Rome. My mother and father still live here, and our business interests are based here and in Naples."

Gabi turned the bottle upside down. "All gone. It was very good. What about the war? How was your family affected?"

"We were not. I guess we were but not by the fighting. My father hated the Germans. We left Rome and stayed with my uncle in the United States and did not return until after the war."

"Do you speak English?"

"I do, and I also speak French. Our major markets are in the United States, England and France." He paused for a moment. "Tell me, Gabi Acosta, are you Jewish?"

She was caught off guard, and she almost snapped back. "If I am, does that make a difference to you?"

He could sense the anger. "Of course not. My last girlfriend was Jewish. I think my parents wanted us to get married."

"I assume that you are no longer together, or you would not be here with me. Why did you break up with her?"

"I didn't. She broke up with me. She said I was on the road too much, always gone. She said this was not what she wanted out of a relationship, especially if it was going to be long term, like marriage."

"Back to your question. My father was Jewish, but my mother was Catholic. I spent most of my childhood with my grandmother. I have never been in a Jewish synagogue. The only church I attended was with my grandmother. Shall we open my bottle of Spanish wine?"

"Why not?"

Tobia opened the bottle and poured a small amount into both glasses. After they had both tasted it, they each made an awful face and poured it out.

Standing up, Tobia extended his hand to Gabi and said, "We have not eaten that sandwich. Let's go to a restaurant and get something good to eat. I know just the place."

It was just a short walk, and soon they were seated in a small, well-decorated restaurant. They stayed and continued their conversation long after they had finished eating. He had a car not far from the restaurant and drove her back to the Borrellis. Stopping at the door, he said, "I don't know when I have had a better time. I really like you Doctor Gabi. I know you don't live in Rome, but I would like to see you again. How much longer are you going to be here?"

"I am going to be here another week."

Tobia boldly put his arms around Gabi's waist. "I know the boss rather well, and he will give me a few days off. When can I see you again?"

Gabi gave him a smile. "Your boss is your father. Are you taking advantage of the relationship?"

He pulled her a little closer and said, "You didn't answer my question. Can I see you again?" He leaned forward and kissed her lightly on the lips.

"Meet me at the Trevi Fountain tomorrow at four thirty." She stretched up on her tip toes and returned his kiss, opened the door and disappeared inside.

Headaches

Gabi went to sleep crying and slept for about two hours. When she opened her eyes, Father Borrelli was sitting in a chair next to her. "I noticed you were beginning to stir a few minutes ago, so I made some tea. Do you feel like talking?"

"I do. I have questions. First, thank you for taking care of me. Thank you for not telling me about my grandmother. I can handle that information now, and you were right. I could not have dealt with it when I was fifteen."

Father Borrelli poured two cups of tea and handed one to Gabi. "You have to make some decisions. Are you going to tell Jason Terry who you are, and are you going to bring back his memory that he has suppressed?"

Gabi took a sip of her tea. "Physician, heal thyself," She said under her breath. "I am not sure what I am going to do. The truth is, I really don't know what to do."

"He saw your grandmother shot. Like you, he was just a young boy. I think he feels somewhat guilty for not acting sooner, and that could explain why he refuses to remember. If he had gotten there one minute earlier, he could have saved your grandmother. He could not have known what the Germans were going to do. It is my understanding he was not supposed to even be there at all. If he had obeyed his orders, we would all have been killed. Me, you, the sergeant and lieutenant, not to mention the twenty-three Jews we were hiding. He also saved the better part of two companies of American soldiers. He should not feel guilty for anything, but somehow, I feel he feels guilty for every life that was lost, and that would include the Germans he killed. He is given credit for killing three Germans in the church, a sniper outside the church, another ten on the hill, and at least twenty-seven in the valley. I know he does not take any pride for that. What decent man would? If he someday remembers, what kind of man will he be?"

Gabi was still thinking about herself. "How come I never asked why I was in that cave?" She paused and then said, "I don't understand how I could just dismiss so many things. Why was he the one that carried me up the hill? Why did they leave such a young boy with me, knowing the chances were that we were both going to be killed? I have been blind."

"Slow down Gabi. I don't know why you have never asked these questions before. Maybe you have blocked them from your mind like he did. I told you I am going to tell you everything, and I am. When you were shot, the lieutenant wanted to leave you behind to save everyone else. I said I would stay with you, but I was needed to get the others to safety because I was the only one who spoke Italian. Jason Terry volunteered to stay with you. If he had not stayed, you would have been left at the mercy of the Germans."

"Good grief. How much can I owe one man?"

"You don't owe him anything. This all happened years ago. I am going to pay him back by paying everything forward. I have been doing that. You are a doctor. You also have been doing that."

"What are you going to do with his relief of the church?"

"I would like to have a ceremony and invite him to the church, but I don't think I will. I think it should be a medical decision to force a memory on him. You say he does not want to remember, and I will respect that. Do you know if he has any problems because of the suppressed memory?"

"I don't know. Ana his housekeeper told me that he has headaches when he has this dream. It could become a problem. I need to go." She quickly tossed the blanket aside stood up, and gave Father Borrelli a hug. "You have been a good friend. I will keep you informed about what happens with Jason."

After she left his office, he thought to himself. *She called him Jason and not Mr. Terry. Are they more than friends?*

The following week, Gabi could not keep Jason from her mind. That Friday she went to Angelo's, and there he sat. "Hey," he said, "Looks like we have bumped into each other."

She didn't say anything, but just took a seat at his table. She gave him a weak smile and picked up the menu.

"I can eat in silence if that is what you want. By the way, how is Toby?"

Her face lit up. "I don't think I would call him that to his face. He is very proud of being Italian and he would not want an American version of his name."

"Don't worry. I was in the army, and I think I can take care of myself." As soon as he said this, he wished he had not.

This gave Gabi the opening she wanted. "I know you don't like to talk about the war, but you were here. You do see a church in your dreams. Does that dream cause you any problems other than it's a dream that comes often?"

"Did you give the relief to the church?"

"I did, and Father Borrelli was excited beyond words. That does not answer my question."

He scoffed. "When I first started having the dream, it would come and go. I finally accepted that I would just have to get used to it. When I came here the second time and knew I was going to stay for an extended length of time, I had the dream on the plane. When I woke up, I had a headache. Now every time I have the dream and wake up, I have a headache."

"Are they getting worse?"

"Let's talk about something else."

"Are they getting worse?"

"Maybe, I don't know. I don't seem to be having the dreams as often, but maybe when I have the dream my headaches are worse." He then laughed. "Are you going to charge me for this consultation? If you are, I can't afford to eat with you."

She had the information she needed and let the conversation about the dreams drop. "Where did you grow up?"

He was glad to talk about something else. "I grew up in Richmond, which is in Kentucky. I went to elementary school, high school, and college there."

She knew that he grew up poor, so she pressed for more information. "You would think that a man that grew up rich would have gone to one of the big schools in the east. Why didn't you?"

"When we first met, you called me Mr. Triple A. You just assumed that I am rich. I don't see myself as rich, or arrogant, or even an asshole. I am just an American. You just assume I am rich because I have a nice villa. I could assume you are rich because you are a doctor. Most of the doctors I know in America seem to have money, or at least more than the average person."

"Oh, you are rich. You could not even touch the price of the villa unless you had a pile of money. By the way, who is Rachel?"

"Good grief, Gabi. Have you turned into Sam Spade? What in the hell is going on? How do you know about Rachel?"

"Who is Sam Spade?"

"Sam Spade is a fictional private investigator. Why are you asking about Rachel? How do you even know about her?"

"When I was at your home, I saw a letter from her on the end table. I thought she might be your girlfriend and you didn't want to share that information with me. You said there were only two women in your life, and as I recall neither of them was named Rachel."

He was now getting a little mad. "Why do you even care? You are getting married. I have made no advances toward you. I like you a lot, so I think I will humor you. The game is on. If you asked me a question, I get one in return. So, you already owe me some questions. I would say at least a half dozen. Rachel lives with me back in Richmond."

"You have a mistress?"

He laughed and began to relax. He now had her on her heels and decided he would have some fun. "Yep, Rachel lives in my home. You are going to owe me a really large bunch of questions."

She could see that he was having fun with her. "Tell me about Rachel."

"Rachel is one of the most stunning young ladies you have ever seen. She is tall. I would say she is at least five seven, maybe five eight. Her features are outstanding. She is smart, and I really like her a lot. I have a very large home back in Richmond…"

Gabi interrupted. "You have a large villa here. How large is your home in Richmond?"

Jason laughed out loud. "Do your questions have no end? It has six rooms on the first floor. There are five rooms upstairs, and four in the basement. It also has a small fourth floor with several small rooms there. It sits on a four-acre lot, which includes a large barn and a shed which has an apartment above it. Behind the main property is about two hundred acres of farm land."

Gabi interrupted. "Good grief, that's worth more than the villa, and you tell me you are not rich."

"I am rich, but I was not born that way. You asked about Rachel. Are you going to let me finish?"

"Go ahead."

"Working in New York, I can't live in Richmond. I plan to go back there someday."

"What does this have to do with Rachel?"

He paused and just stared at Gabi.

"I am sorry. I will not interrupt again. Go on."

"I needed somebody to take care of my home and property. I hired a man to do this. His name is Billy Ballew. Rachel is his sister. She did not have a place to live so she came with Billy. Billy and Rachel are good people. Rachel is currently a student at Kentucky State. I saw both when I was back in the States a few weeks ago, and yes, when Rachel comes in from college, she has a room in my home."

Gabi sat there and didn't say anything. Angelo came up and said, "I am sorry I was late getting to you. Are you ready to order?"

Once the orders were placed, Jason said, "I guess it is my turn to ask my questions. How come you can speak English?"

Again, she was caught off guard by his question. "I thought your question would be more personal."

"No. I think we need to reel in this conversation. Your English is quite good, by the way."

"When I was training to be a doctor I stayed with a doctor and his wife. They both insisted that I learn English. My question. You have a talent with carving wood. Are you an artist? What I mean is, can you also draw or paint pictures?"

He did not like to brag, but this time he did. "I can draw and paint. I am very good at it. I wish I had time to do more. My father was a carpenter. I learned a lot of my woodworking skills from him, but I think my art really comes from my mother. Would you like for me to do a drawing or perhaps a painting of you? I could do a drawing and then turn it into a painting. It could be a wedding gift for Toby."

She frowned. "I told you not to call him that. You two are someday going to meet. I want you to like each other. As for your question, I would like that." She gave him a smile. "Do you think you could capture the real me?"

"Maybe not, because for some reason, I don't think you have shown me who the real Gabi Acosta is."

They continued light conversation for the rest of the meal and then said their goodbyes.

They didn't see each other again the following weekend. On the Monday when Gabi came to her office, she was greeted with a strange message. "We had an emergency call last night from Mr. Terry's villa. A woman named Ana Marina called and reported that Mr. Terry was having a heart attack. We were just about to send an emergency team there, when a second call came and said everything was alright and not to come. Do you think we should check on him?"

"I am not sure. I may drop by there this afternoon. When is my last appointment?"

"You have nothing after three. I will keep you free after that."

Gabi was worried and could not get Jason out of her mind. About three-thirty she found herself knocking on the villa door. In a few minutes Ana opened the door.

"Is Jason here? I have come to check on him."

"No, he went to the construction site. I tried to get him to go in for a checkup, but he said he was fine."

"I see that you called the hospital at about three this morning. Were you with him when he had his attack?" Just for a moment, she thought that Ana and Jason might be lovers. She quickly dismissed the idea. *Why should she care?*

Ana did not want to say that she had a room inside the villa. She wondered how she could tell Doctor Acosta that she heard Jason crying out from her room. She knew that Doctor Acosta would assume that they were sleeping together. She did not say anything.

Ana was right. Doctor Acosta did assume they were sleeping together and confirmed it when she said, "Look Ana, I don't care about you and Jason's personal life. I care about his health. I need to know what happened."

"What you are assuming is wrong. Jason and I do not sleep together. I have a room upstairs. We keep it a secret to protect me from what people would think. There is a set of steps just outside my room that leads down to the kitchen. Most of the time I only see Jason at dinner time. I was asleep in my room last night when I heard Jason crying out. He was not talking in his sleep. He was shouting. He was saying things, like, I could have saved her, and he was shouting it over and over. I knocked on his door, and he did not respond, so I went into his room. I could tell he had a shortness of breath and was really laboring to breathe. I put my hand on his chest and could feel his heart was pounding hard and fast. I could not get him to wake up, so I called the hospital. When I went back to his room, he was sitting on the edge of his bed. I asked him how he was doing, and he said he thought he was going to throw up. I told him I had called the hospital, and he insisted that I call back and tell you not to come. I stayed with him for a while. When I was sure he was okay, I left him alone. I did not go back to bed. I stayed on the couch to be close if he needed me. This morning he got up and said he felt fine. He ate a light breakfast and left for the dam site."

"Don't tell him I came by. If you can, get him to come in for a checkup. If you can't I will find some excuse to see him."

A couple of days passed, and Jason had not come in. Gabi decided that she might need some help. In the afternoon she placed a called to Rome. When she reached the right office, a man answered.

"Doctor Borelli, is that you?"

He recognized her voice. "Gabi, you must be making a professional call. You referred to me as Doctor. What can I do for you?"

"I have a patient. I think he had a panic attack. The reason I think this is because he has suppressed memories. He also has a recurring dream. His dream is followed by headaches that appear to be getting more severe. Have you ever dealt with anything like this before?"

"I have. After the war I had several cases like this. All were different, but the one thing they had in common were the panic attacks. I have found that patients that I have treated suffer from high levels of stress, including high blood pressure, some have increased incidence of diabetes and heart disease. Many will suffer from what looks like panic attacks. If left untreated, the patient may suffer a heart attack which may lead to death. I assume you are referring to Jason Terry."

She paused for a moment. "How did you know about Mr. Terry?"

"My brother Danti is here. He has told me all about Mr. Terry. He is a remarkable man. Here is what I know. Suppressing a memory for this long after the war is rare. I am surprised that he has not had problems before. He may have, and you just don't know about them. The panic attack may be his first, but I would guess it is the first of many to come. They will become more severe, and he will not be able to function. That is a best-case scenario. The severe panic attacks could produce a stroke, which might cripple or kill him."

"What do you suggest we do?"

"You need to bring his suppressed memories to his consciousness. It will not be easy, because there is a chance if you tell him what he needs to do, he will reject it. If he were my patient and he was agreeable I would place him under hypnosis. Do you think he would agree to this?"

"No, I really don't. I will try to find a way to talk to him about it. Thanks for the information. I will be there in a couple of weeks. We need to talk about the wedding. I will see you soon."

Jason did not come to her office, and Gabi waited a couple of days until the weekend. Driving to the dam site she pulled over on the gravel road and looked at the concrete monster rising above the valley floor. *This project is coming along faster than I thought. He will soon be gone,* she thought to herself. She sat there in her car high above the site and watched the trucks and men moving material that would soon be holding back millions of cubic feet of water. Water that would create cheaper electric power for the valley and for Caseno.

How am I going to approach him, she thought as she put the car in gear and started down the steep grade to the valley floor. Once she reached the base of the valley floor, she could see Jason and several other men holding charts and pointing toward the dam. When he saw her get out of the car, he walked toward her. "Doctor Bubbles, what brings you all the way out here? Perhaps you are lost."

"No, not lost. Making a house call. Is there somewhere we can talk?"

"Let's go inside my trailer. We can talk there."

Stepping inside the trailer, Gabi noticed the many charts scattered about the room and on small tables. "How do you find anything when you need it? This place is a mess."

"It is more organized than you think. We just had a meeting, and we had the charts out. Michael will put these back this afternoon." He quickly removed several charts from the small table and took a chart off a chair and said, "Have a seat. I know why you are here. I am going to listen to what you have to say before I throw you out of my little office." He then gave a laugh.

Gabi was serious and took a seat at the table. She noticed a pot of coffee on the counter that went across one side of the trailer. "Can I have a cup of that coffee? I didn't sleep well last night, and maybe a little caffeine will help get me going."

Jason went to the counter, got a clean cup and poured her a cup of coffee. "Do you want cream or sugar?"

"No, just black will do. Jason, why didn't you come to my office for a checkup? I know that Ana talked to you about it."

"I had a bad spell, but I am doing better. I am trying to relax and not worry about the job. I think I was putting myself under a lot of pressure. I worked a lot, and we now have the project back under control. I am fine."

"I have talked to a doctor back in Rome. He is a man doctor, and I know you think men doctors are better. I told him about your dreams and your headaches. He believes you had a panic attack or something maybe worse. You could be on the verge of having a heart attack or perhaps even a stroke. He believes your panic attack is caused by some suppressed memories. He can help you if you will go to Rome to see him."

Jason was now serious. "How does he think he can help me?"

"He can place you under hypnosis and find out about your memories that you have forgotten. It may be hard to face, but he believes if you go on, you are going to get worse, much worse. He even thinks it could become life threatening."

Jason pulled up a chair, took a seat across from Gabi, and reached out and patted her on the hand. "It really means a lot that you came all the way out here. If we were back in the United States and you were not engaged to good ole Toby, the wine man, I might be asking you out. We are not back in the United States. You are engaged, and my construction will be finished before your wedding. With all that said, I am not going to do anything about what you called a panic attack. There is no way I am going to let some strange Italian doctor poke around inside my head, and I am going to enjoy what time I have left in this country. The weather report calls for heavy rain for the next week. One reason we are working so hard is we are shutting down and making things safe because we expect a lot of rain, and we must make sure our temporary spillways can handle it. Gabi go back to Caseno. Let this go." He then laughed, "You can send me a bill for the house call."

Gabi knew before she left Caseno that this would be Jason's response. "Okay Jason. I will leave you alone about this." Thinking to herself, she decided to go to her second plan. "You said that you will be gone before my wedding. Remember what you said. Are you going to paint my picture?"

"Yes, I would like that very much. Where would you want to meet?"

"I would like to go down by the river outside of Caseno. There is a large field of grass. It has a golden cast, and if the light is right it is spectacular."

"If the rains come, we will have to wait about a week. If the river gets out of its banks, we might have to wait or do the painting somewhere else."

She stood up and extended her hand to him. They said their goodbyes, and soon she was on her way back to Caseno.

Jason was right about the rain. The following Monday it was coming down hard, and by Wednesday there was no sign it was going to let up. On Friday morning she got a call from Jason.

"My good doctor, Ana and the boys are here, and I am getting bored with their company. Why don't you see if you can come by the villa, and I will start on your painting? I will start with a pencil sketch. How about it?"

Gabi didn't even give it any thought. At five o'clock she was standing in front of his front door with an umbrella in one hand, and with her other hand using the monster to let them know she was there.

Ana opened the door. "My, you look soaked. Come inside and take off your raincoat and I will get you a towel to dry your hair. Jason is in the back. I will let him know you are here." Ana was gone just a minute and returned with a large gray towel. Gabi wiped the raindrops from her hands and face, and then dried her hair the best she could. She found that she was also cold and was shivering just a bit. "Go on into the great room. There is a fire, and it will warm you up and dry your hair." She quickly went into the den, and took a seat next to the fire.

When Jason came through the doorway which led from the kitchen to the great room he stopped. She was seated on the edge of the fireplace and could not see him. She was drying her hair, and he had never noticed how black and beautiful her hair was. The light coming from the fire gave her an orange glow and accented her beauty. The rain had given her long hair which had always been straight a light curl. She turned, and he could now see her face. *I am not sure a painting could possibly do her justice,* he thought to himself. Her dark eyes were round, and when she saw him, she smiled, and that smile lit up her entire face. She tossed the towel to the side and stood up. "This is what I have chosen to wear for my painting." She stood up, and did a turn. She had chosen a full red and white skirt with a pattern of flowers scattered throughout. Her blouse was full, with a square opening at the top. It showed a lot of skin, and he couldn't help but stare.

"You look fine," he said. "Once you get dry, we will get started. I hope it doesn't get too hot in here. The house felt a little cool and damp, so I lit the fire."

"I am glad you did. It really feels good. The rain has made me so cold."

"Do you want some wine?"

"Yes, I do. Do you have any of that cheap stuff we had with our meal the last time I was here?"

"I do, I will get it."

Just about that time Ana came back into the room. She walked over to Gabi and picked up the towel from the floor.

"I was going to get that. I am sorry that you had to pick up my towel."

"It is not a problem. I will take it to the washroom. You are through with it, aren't you?" She then turned to Jason and said, "Luke sent word that he needs to see you in the barn behind the house. Your raincoat is hanging next to the back door, and I put the large umbrella with it."

"Your brother's timing could not be worse." He looked at Gabi and said, "I will be back in just a minute, and then we will get started." He then quickly left the room.

Once he left the room Ana came to Gabi, "Luke and I made up the story. I needed to spend some time alone with you. Jason has had two more spells of what you are calling panic attacks. The last one was bad. What are we going to do?"

"I went to see him at the dam site and tried to get him to seek help. He refused."

"So, there is nothing we can do. I fear he is going to die."

Gabi could see the tears in Ana's eyes. "Don't give up. I have a plan, and me being here is part of that plan. I am going to start doing things that I hope will bring his memory back. Just trust me and hope for the best."

When Jason returned, he went downstairs to the wine room and retrieved two bottles of wine. When he came into the great room, he was carrying one bottle of wine and two glasses. "Are you ready to get started?"

"I am, but do you think just one bottle of wine will get me through this? I need something to make me relax."

Jason went to the couch that was in front of the fireplace and pulled it around, so it was not facing the fire. "There is another bottle in the kitchen. Take a seat on this end of the couch, and place your left arm on the arm rest." She did as he instructed. He walked over to a floor lamp, turned it on, and placed it behind the couch. He turned on a second-floor lamp and positioned it to her front. The two lamps, and the glow from the fire created a work of art in Jason's mind. "You look absolutely stunning."

"I bet you say that to everyone you have created a painting of." She smiled and was slightly blushing.

Jason didn't say anything and continued to draw. Just for a moment he thought of nurse Helen and remembered telling her how beautiful she was. He wondered where she was and how great it would be to find your soulmate so early in life.

Gabi didn't say anything but just let Jason continue his work. She could see he was deep in thought because he stopped drawing for a few moments.

Jason pulled up a small stool, and was just about eight feet from Gabi, and he just stared for a moment. "Something is not right." He got up and walked over to her. "I am going to have to touch you for a moment. Is that okay?"

She nodded as he reached down and slid the top of her blouse slightly off her shoulders. He said nothing as he observed the scars on her left shoulder. Without thinking, he reached down and let his finger trace over the scar. "You have a scar on your left shoulder. Is there a story behind it? In the final painting I can leave it, or I can remove it. It is quite small and does not look bad."

"I want you to leave it. It is very much a part of me."

"How did you get it? You have two scars. One on the front, and one on the back. It looks like a bullet wound."

This was the conversation Gabi wanted from Jason. "It is a bullet wound."

Jason went back to his stool and started drawing. He continued his drawing, looking up and then back to his drawing pad. "How did you get it?"

"I was shot during the war. I was only fifteen. A German shot me. I had to have surgery. I really don't know much about it."

Jason stop drawing and just stared into space. He said nothing for a long while. Gabi did not break the silence. Then he spoke. "I was shot during the war. I was shot while I was here in Italy. I don't remember much about it either." He continued to draw.

"Where were you shot?"

He did not answer. He continued to draw. She asked the question a second time.

Again, he did not answer. He continued to draw. Several minutes passed and Gabi let him continue without saying a word.

After several minutes he spoke. "I was shot in the leg. Like you I had to have surgery. In fact, I had to have two surgeries. At one time I thought I was going to lose my leg, but now it is good as new." He got up and moved the stool closer to her. He didn't explain but took his seat and continued to draw.

When she looked at him, she could see his eyes on her breast. She felt uncomfortable, and he noticed she was getting embarrassed. "I am drawing your…" he paused. "I am drawing your chest and cleavage. You have to be the most gorgeous woman in Italy."

She was turning red with embarrassment. She smiled. "Just don't enjoy yourself too much. Are you about done?"

"It is going to take a few more minutes."

Gabi picked up her glass of wine. "I think this wine is going to my head. I am feeling just a little light headed."

When he finished his drawing, he closed his drawing pad and said, "The first part is finished. I may want to do another drawing, but I will see if we got what we needed." He walked over to the window and looked out. The rain was really coming down. "I hope this lets up before you have to go back to town."

"Me too. Are you going to show me the drawing?"

"No, not yet. You will just have to wait. You can just relax by the fire. Ana is fixing supper."

Gabi was surprised that Jason did not ask her more about her scar and how she got it. It was like he just pushed it out of his mind. She looked at Jason, and he was somewhat flushed. "Are you okay?"

"I just have a slight headache. It will pass." He walked over to the small table which was out of place and picked up his glass of wine. "I got so caught up in the drawing that I have neglected my cheap wine. Do you need any more wine? I think it will be a little while before supper."

"What is supper?"

"Supper is what we call dinner in the South. Ana is fixing dinner. She told me that we are having spaghetti with meatballs, a salad and baked garlic bread. It is going to be a while. If you will excuse me for a moment, I need to go to my room and put the drawing supplies away. I am afraid if I leave them here, you will peek."

The truth of the matter was that his headache was killing him. He needed something to relieve the pain. When he got to his room, he took two pills and took a seat on the edge of his bed. He waited for about ten minutes before he returned. When he returned to the great room, he saw Gabi stretched out on the couch. She had consumed almost the entire bottle of wine while he was drawing her. He could tell she was about to go to sleep, so he said nothing and joined Ana in the kitchen. While he was talking to Ana the phone rang. Ana took the call, and all he could hear her say was, "Okay, okay, I will let everybody know. You take care, and I will see you later in the week."

"Who was that?"

"That was Michael. He was in town, and he said that when he started out here, he found the road is washed out. I guess we will have one less for dinner."

During the meal, Gabi continued her assault of questions trying to force Jason to remember the war. The pills and wine had just about masked his headache, and he was feeling better.

"Jason when you were here during the war, how did a boy from the southern part of the United States handle the Italian food?"

Jason smiled. "I didn't eat it. Most of the people I came in contact with didn't have enough food to share. The army supplied us with food." He then paused. "The truth is, I was always too scared to eat. It is strange as I look back on it. I joined the army for security, and while I was in the army was the most insecure time of my life. Can we talk about something else?"

Ana glanced over toward Gabi. She knew what she was trying to do.

"I don't know. Jason, I think it sometimes helps to think about what happened to us during the war. I like to remember my husband, and I am proud that he chose to fight against the Germans. I think Italy is a better place because he did. I want him to be remembered. As everyone knows I am seeing Michael. We are growing very fond of each other, but I don't think I will ever stop loving my husband. Michael lets me talk about my time before and during the war."

Gabi had stopped eating. "The war took from me my father, my mother and my grandmother. I have just found out that my grandmother was a hero and saved several people. The Germans tried to kill me. Had it not been for the American soldiers, Father Borrelli, Doctor Alonso Borrelli and his wife, I would hate to think what my life would be like."

Jason was becoming very uncomfortable, and he barely heard what Gabi had just said. His head was starting to hurt again, and he said very quietly, "I know the war is full of heroes, but I am not one of them. I was here during the war, and the only thing I remember is that most of the time I was so scared that I felt like I was going to throw up or shit in my pants. I am sorry. I should not have said that."

Gabi knew part of the story about Jason but could not tell it. "Jason, how old were you when you came to Italy during the war?"

"Fifteen. I was fifteen. My army records will say I was seventeen, but I was fifteen." He looked down and said, "I have a headache. I am going to go sit by the fire."

Jason got up and left the room. Ana pointed at Gabi. "I will finish up here. Go be with him."

When Gabi came into the great room Jason was sitting on one end of the couch. "I have some pills that will help with your headache. If you want, I will give you one. They are in my purse. I must warn you though, they don't go well with alcohol. They will put you to sleep, but maybe that is not a bad thing."

"My head really hurts. I have already taken a couple of over-the-counter pills. Maybe going to sleep is what I need. Get me one."

Gabi retrieved her purse and gave Jason a couple of the pills. Once Jason had taken the pills, she sat down next to him and laid her head on his chest. "Don't get any funny ideas. I don't have my stethoscope with me, and I want to listen to your heart."

Jason really liked her sitting next to him. *I wonder if she could ever fall in love with me.*

It was not long until he was sound asleep.

Ana finished the dishes and her brothers left. She came into the room which was only lit by the fireplace. She could see Gabi laying there with her head on Jason's shoulder. "How is he doing?"

"Okay, I think. His breathing is deep and regular. His heart is beating at a normal rate, but it sounds like it is beating rather hard. I have just been sitting here trying to figure out what's going on in that head of his."

"You are trapped here for tonight. If it stops raining, Bonita and Luke will go help repair the road."

"Where are your brothers? Have they already left? I enjoy their company. They are fun."

"They said that they may have to get up early to go help repair the road, and they wanted to get some rest." She then looked at Jason who was in a very deep sleep. "Are you going to stay with him during the night?"

"No. He is doing okay. We will not try to move him. We will just cover him with a blanket. He should sleep all night. Do you have a spare bedroom I could use?"

"I am going to put you in the bedroom next to mine. I will also get you something to sleep in. It is a little early for bed. Do you want to talk for a while?"

"I do. That would be nice. I got the impression that we were expecting someone else for dinner. I heard you say the name Michael. Who is Michael?"

"He is the construction boss at the dam. A while back he and Jason had a meeting here at the house. I think he may have fallen in love with me because he started coming by for no reason at all to see Jason. A couple of months ago he took me to dinner. We have been seeing each other ever since."

"I assume that he has been picking you up and dropping you off in the back. Does he know of your living arrangements?"

"He does, and he has no problem with it."

Ana left for a few minutes, and when she returned, she was carrying a tray with two cups of coffee. She had also changed into a sleeping outfit. "I have something for you to sleep in. Why don't you change? You will be a whole lot more comfortable."

After Gabi had changed, she came back into the room. She took her cup of coffee and took a sip. "You understand that even though Jason and I are friends, I really don't know that much about him. The one thing that I have learned is that he really cares about people. I have found out that he grew up poor. Do you know how he ended up so rich?"

Ana looked confounded. "I have no idea. I just know he seems to have more money than a king but acts like a pauper in the way he lives and treats people. Take away this villa and he is just one of us."

"When we first met, he treated me rudely. He was nothing like he is now. I guess it was that severe bump on his head. I called him Mr. Triple A."

"I know. He has told me. Did you know he is from a very small town in the state of Kentucky?"

"I think Jason is just a little boy in some ways. He came here as a boy, fought in a war, was shot, and was damaged far beyond belief. He must have seen many people die during the war, and that is something a young boy should not see."

Ana leaned over and gave Gabi a hug. "You care a great deal for him, don't you?"

"Another place, another time, who knows. I know he is leaving in just a few weeks, and he is going to be gone a long time. I am getting married very soon. One thing I do know. Jason Edward Terry is always going to be a part of my life."

The two women talked until midnight. By the time they went to bed they were acting like two sisters. The next morning it had stopped raining, and by noon the road had been made passable. Jason slept all morning, and Gabi checked on him several times before she left. She felt that rest would be the best thing for him.

When Gabi got back to Caseno, she decided she would go see Father Borrelli. He was in his office when she arrived at the church. Once they had exchanged greetings, she sat down and said, "Father, if I were a Catholic, I think I would need to go to confession."

"Well, you are as much Catholic as you are anything else. What is on your mind that makes you think you need to go to confession?"

"My problem is that I am engaged to Tobia Martin. It will not be much longer until we are married. The problem is that I think that I might be falling in love with another man."

"You are talking about Jason Terry. What makes you think you are falling in love with him? Have you two been intimate?"

"No, of course not. I just have such strong feelings for him. When we first met, I could barely stand him. I even called him Mr. Triple A. To me he was nothing but an arrogant American asshole."

Father Borrelli laughed. "That's rather strong coming from you. What changed?"

"I have gotten to know him. He is kind, he really cares about people. He is rich, but he was born poor, poor as me. Like me he was damaged by the war. I think he might love me."

"You left out the most important thing. He saved your life during the war. Maybe that is what you should concentrate on. Maybe it is not love you feel, but a powerful gratitude. He has an advantage over you. If he is falling in love with you it is not because of some misguided sense of gratitude, or maybe a misguided sense of guilt. He gets to see you for who you are. You don't have the same advantage. Have you been able to help him remember his role in the war? If you can bring his memory around, I sure would like to thank him for saving me."

Gabi stood up and walked over to the door, "I think I may be more confused now than I was before I came to see you. I still love Tobia. Maybe what you say is true. How am I ever going to know? I know that I was attracted to him before I knew he was the soldier in the cave. I have not been able to restore his memory. He will not seek professional help, and my efforts to stimulate his memory are not working."

"Maybe you should take him to the church site. I go there quite often. The ruins are there. Take him to the river, and then find some excuse to walk to the site."

On Friday Jason was sitting at Angelo's with the hope that Gabi would stop by. Looking across the square he spotted her, but she was not alone. She was with a man, a man he had never seen before. As they approached the restaurant, he could see they were laughing and talking. Coming up to his table as he stood up as Gabi said, "Jason this is Tobia. I have told you about him. Tobia, this is Jason. He is here constructing a dam."

Tobia took Jason by the hand, "So you are Jason. Gabi has told me so much about you. I would like to visit the dam site sometime to see how it is coming."

"Please join me, I have not ordered yet. Once we have eaten, if you want, I will be glad to give you a tour."

"I would love to, but I am only going to be here this afternoon, and I would like to spend it with Gabi. Once we have eaten, we need to go back to her apartment and discuss wedding plans. I need to be on the road by four o'clock."

The three ordered lunch and talked about construction, New York, and other topics until Tobia turned to Gabi and said, "We have to get going. It is already near two o'clock and I have to be back on the road."

Jason stood up and took Tobia by the hand. "It was nice to meet you. I hope to see you again."

"You will be coming to the wedding?"

Jason took the bill for the meal from Tobia's hand. "I will get that. I am not sure if I will be here. The project is coming to an end. The construction could take another year, but my part is just about finished. I talked to the main office yesterday, and they are planning to move me to another site."

Gabi's heart sank. She knew Jason was leaving, but just hearing him say it made her feel somewhat sick at her stomach. She would have very little time to try to force Jason to confront his demons.

Jason watched as Gabi and Tobia started back across the square to the hospital, when he saw them stop. Gabi said something to Tobia, and then started walking back toward him. When she was back at the table, she said, "Why didn't you tell me you were leaving so soon?"

"I have told you I am leaving. I told you when you came to the trailer. I mentioned it at the villa the other night, and I just did again. Have you not been listening to me at all? The reason I came to town today was to say a more formal goodbye because we might not get to see each other again."

"Toby, I mean Tobia is going back to Rome this afternoon. Can we meet later? We need to talk."

"I have to go back to the villa. I am leaving, and I must make some arrangements about the villa with Ana, Bonita, and Luke. Do you want to come by, or do you want to meet back here?"

"I will come by the villa. I will be there about five o'clock." She turned and ran back to where Tobia was waiting. She took his arm, and they disappeared into the hospital.

As Jason drove back to the villa, his thoughts were on Gabi. *Why did she want to see him? Maybe he should have said he was too busy to see her. Maybe he should just avoid her. Leaving her was going to be hard enough.*

He forced his thoughts to the problem at hand. He was going to keep the villa at least for a while. He would form a partnership with the Aparos to continue the wine and vegetable production. Ana would stay on as his housekeeper, and he would try to get back three or four times a year. If things didn't work out, he would sell the whole place.

Later that afternoon as Gabi drove to the villa, she was thinking of how she could try to get Jason to remember the war. She was worried that if she didn't succeed, he might face dire consequences. By the time she got to the villa she had made her plan. Parking in front of the villa she again knocked on the door. To her surprise no one came, and she again called upon the iron gargoyle to summon the occupants of the house. Again, the mythical creature failed to bring anyone to the front door. She decided she would go to the back, and as she approached the back of the house, she could hear voices coming from the barn. The large sliding doors were open, and as she went inside, she could see Jason, Ana, Luke, and Bonita sitting on bales of straw and talking and laughing. It was Ana that saw her first and came to greet her.

"Please join us. We are just talking about the villa and farm. Jason is going to keep everything, and we are going to take care of it for him. We are all just so excited."

Gabi came over and took a seat on a bale of straw next to Bonita. "Making plans, are we? I am sorry that I am not really all that excited about losing a friend, but I am happy for you." Turning to Jason she said. "Do you have any idea as to when you will be leaving?"

"The main office has given me three weeks to close down things here. When I get back to the United States, I am going to spend two weeks at the New York office being brought up to speed with the new project, and I am going to take a leave for a month to take care of things back in Richmond."

Gabi looked at Jason and again tried to link her conversation to the war. She remembered the letter that Father Borrelli had read to her and that Jason's nickname was Jet. "Well, Mr. Jet, where is this new project going to be?"

Jason looked back at Gabi and seemed for a moment to drift away in his thoughts. For a moment, he said nothing and then he replied in a very soft voice, "South America, I am going to South America." He then seemed to drift away again. Everyone just sat there waiting for him to come out of his daze. He then spoke again. "Why did you call me Jet?"

"I assume you would prefer Jet over Mr. Triple A."

Ana laughed but was unsure why. Even though she knew the answer she said, "What is Mr. Triple A?

Jason scoffed. "Gabi is quite good with nicknames. Mr. Triple A is my name she gave me when we first met. It stands for arrogant American asshole." Everyone laughed.

"Gabi, where did you come up with the name Jet?"

"I just used your initials, Jason Edward Terry."

Again, Jason got quiet. "That is what some of my army buddies called me. Jet. I have not been called that for a long time."

Ana stood up. "I have things I have to do in the house." Turning to her brothers, she said, "What are you two boys going to do?"

Bonita stood up. "We need to clean the vegetables for the market in the morning. I thought that it might rain, but I hope it holds until after we sell our vegetables tomorrow."

It was not long until Jason and Gabi were in the barn alone. "Jason, I know that we will not be able to see each other much for the next several weeks. I must get ready for a wedding, and you are getting ready to leave. Feel free to say no, but I was wondering if I could take you on a picnic tomorrow? It will give you a chance to finish my painting. I am not going to let you out of your commitment."

"Okay, but you heard what Bonita said. He thinks it is going to rain."

"If it does, we will go to plan B."

"What is plan B?"

"Don't know yet, but remember, you still have not completed my painting."

Late on Saturday morning, Gabi pulled up to the front of the villa. Jason was standing out front wearing a dark blue t-shirt and a pair of blue jeans. She got out of her car wearing a yellow sun dress, which had spaghetti straps that exposed her shoulders and bare arms.

"You look nice. I see you decided to change your outfit for the painting. This is good. I like this too. I hope you packed a lot of good food, because I am hungry. Ana has made a few things for us. She has a pie. I don't know what kind. There is also a pasta salad, and I have several bottles of that wine you like so much. Maybe we can drink it all before I leave Italy."

He did not tell her he had not had breakfast. He had had a bad night. The dream had returned followed by an extremely bad headache and a seizure. Ana was not there. She had made him the picnic dishes the afternoon before, and had left that night to visit relatives in the north. At one time he had thought of calling Gabi and taking a rain check but had started to feel better, and now there was no sign of his illness. He had told her that she looked nice but wished he had not. He had decided he would not flirt with her. After all he was leaving, and she was getting married.

"Where did you get the jeep?" she asked.

"Like the car it belongs to the company. I wasn't sure how rough the area around the river would be, so I decided to swap the car to this. I think we will be alright. We have had a lot of rain, but the river goes down as fast as it goes up. I am sure we will find a good spot with water at its normal level. I have already loaded my art supplies, and we need to load what you have, and we will be off."

Going down the drive to the villa, he stopped at the main road. "Which way, right or left?"

"Right, and then take the first road to the left. It is a small road, and it is in disrepair. I talked to Father Borrelli, and he said we might get tossed around a little going down the hill. I am glad you have this jeep. I really don't know how shabby it is going to get. I haven't been down the road for a very long time. I do know that it is passable because Father Borrelli told me that he still comes down here to do some fishing. Once you make the turn it will be about a mile over the hill, and will lead straight to the river." She thought that she had made a mistake by saying Father Borrelli came to this area, but he did not seem to question it.

Going down the hill was a rollercoaster ride. "I should have tied things down. God almighty this is almost impassable. I don't think we could get a car down this hill."

"I think there used to be a better way to get to the river, but that road closed a long time ago."

About half way down the hill, he stopped the jeep. "Are you okay? It looks like it might not be so bad ahead of us." He looked at the narrow road ahead. It had two tire paths with only patches of gravel. Grass was about three feet high and had grown up between the tire paths. To the right and left of the road, the fields had been cleared for farming, but next to the road were trees growing up and forming a canopy over the road. The air was fresh, and he could smell the river. Taking the jeep down the last bit of hill, the river came in to view. It was not a big river. Back home he would have called it a creek. It was about forty feet across and not very deep. In most cases it would not be over three feet deep. Despite the heavy rains of the previous week, the river appeared to be back at its normal level. Going over the bank and down to the edge of the water he spotted a sandbar and eased the jeep to a stop. Tall trees lined both sides of the bank and created a nice shade.

"I think we should just stay here."

"Looks good to me," she said as she hopped out of the jeep tossed her shoes aside and waded into the shallow water.

As she played in the water, he looked upstream and saw large rocks that created a natural dam. Water was cascading through and around some of the rocks. *This is perfec*t, he thought. He went back to the jeep and retrieved his art supplies.

"Gabi, there is a path that leads to those large rocks which are in the center of the river. I will help you so why don't we sketch you sitting on that large rock in the middle. There is water coming around on each side of the rock, and it is perfect."

Once she was posed on the rock, he started his sketch. He was about twenty feet from her. Her yellow sun dress was lit up by the sun, and the way the light was creating highlights in her hair, he thought he had never seen anything so dazzling. For a moment the sky seemed perfect and he thought that they might avoid the rain.

"Jason, I am going to be nosey. I know you are rich, but you don't act like you are. Who are you really?"

He laughed. "How are rich people supposed to act?'

She remembered the letter that Father Borrelli had read. "You have not always been rich, have you?"

He quickly avoided the question. "Being rich is a state of mind. I have money, the company pays me well. That is not what makes a person rich. Being happy makes you rich. Having a good family and friends make you rich. Having a job that gives you satisfaction makes you rich. So yes, I am rich. The problem is, I am leaving in a couple of weeks, and that will make me less rich. Going back to the United States and leaving friends behind is going to be hard, but this place will always be important to me. That is one reason I am keeping the villa. I hope to make many trips back. I may come back and even go to Rome and look up you and old toad frog."

"If you don't quit making up names for Tobia I am going to come off this rock and throw you into the middle of this river. Can we take a break? I am ready to eat."

Taking her basket from the jeep she spread a blanket on the ground. It was large enough for them to stretch out and put the food between them. She too had brought wine but got his bottles instead. She placed the bread, a pasta salad, ham panini and chicken on the blanket. "We might not need the bread, but I brought it any way."

He smiled at her and for some reason broke his own rule about flirting. "Do you bring all your boyfriends to this sandbar?"

She gave him a smile. "I have not been here for years. I had forgotten how magnificent it is."

He was surprised that she did not correct his statement about being one of her boyfriends. He continued to eat, and continued their light conversation. When they finished the meal and packed up the jeep he said, "I don't know if you have noticed, but the sky is getting quite dark. It is going to rain, and we don't need to be on the creek if it does. Back home a creek of this size could get out of control in a hurry. I don't think this one is any different. The hills that surround this river are rather steep and could cause flash flooding."

"Before we go, I have something I want you to see. It will not take long." She took him by the hand. "There used to be a rock wall near here. Let's see if we can find it."

They walked up the creek bank, and it wasn't long until they were making their way along a rock fence which was about four feet tall. The grass near the fence was short and walking was easy, but the grass which was out of the shade that grew about twenty feet from the rock wall, was tall, almost coming up to their waist. They had gone about fifty yards up the fence row when Jason stopped and let go of Gabi's hand. Looking to his left he could see the ruins of a church. All that was left was the outline of the floor, and a few walls that stood about ten to twenty feet high. He said nothing but started walking toward the church. Once he reached what was left of the front door, he had a quick vision. It was just a flash, but he was crawling through the open door. After the flash passed, he walked through the door and to the right. He seemed to forget that he was with Gabi. Another vision. He could plainly see four people tied up and sitting in chairs. There was a woman, a priest, and two soldiers. He stopped walking and watched his vision unfold. A German pulled out his gun and shot the old woman in the back of her head.

Gabi was just behind him following his every step as he let out a scream saying "no, no, no." He turned and walked past her out of the ruins of the church and went back to the rock fence and fell to his knees. Gabi sat down beside him. "Move over and sit against that tree. I will help you." She took him by the arm, and he stood up and walked over to a tree and sat down. He wrapped his arms around his knees and laid his head over on them. He closed his eyes and watched the visions of his past unfold.

Gabi was not sure what to do. As Jason sat there, she felt a drop of rain on her face. Looking toward the ruins of the church, she could see it was raining quite hard, but they were somewhat protected by the tree. She knew this would only be temporary, but she also knew that there was no way to move Jason until he recovered from the shock of seeing the church. All she could do was sit with him and become soaked with the rain.

Jason Remembers

Jason had his orders. He was to wait for Lieutenant Forbes and Sergeant Harris. But if they did not return, he was to leave them and report back to the major. The night had been long, and he was scared. He was scared the enemy might find him, but he was more scared for Lieutenant Forbes and Sergeant Harris. He would wait for morning, and if they had not returned, he would head back to the camp. It was the longest night of his life. He heard every sound, and several times he thought he could hear footsteps. It was extremely dark, but he could still make out the outline of the church against the night sky.

As the sun came up Jason could see the church. The light was coming from the left side of the cathedral, and for a moment he wished he had his drawing pad. He just stared. He was impressed with how spectacular the church was. He was about seventy-five yards in front of the church, and Lieutenant Forbes and Sergeant Harris had not returned. His thoughts ran wild, and he had never been so scared. He knew he had orders to leave, but something was telling him he should check inside the church. Picking up his M1 rifle, he decided to sneak toward the church to see if he could see what was going on inside. The grass was high and rocking back and forth in the wind. It probably had not been cut during the entire war. A small dry creek circled from the right and came in front of the church. It was dry and offered some cover.

When Jason came to the front of the church, he noticed that the door was slightly ajar. He stayed on his stomach and used his M1 rifle to push the door a little further open and stuck his head slightly inside. He was low and could see nothing. He could hear men talking. Sometimes they were speaking English and other times German. He raised up just enough to see over the last pew. Lieutenant Forbes and Sergeant Harris were sitting in chairs along with a woman and a priest. They were tied. There were four Germans with them, and two of them had handguns pointed at the captives. Going back to his stomach, he slid along the floor to the right and slowly made his way toward the front of the church. Near the front was a large support pillar. Reaching it, he stood up. He felt sick at his stomach. He stood there for a moment unseen with his back to the column. *You can do this, this is what you trained for. You are the best shot in the company. Your rifle is semi-automatic. You can get off four shots before they can react.* He waited for what seemed to be about two minutes. Peeping around the column, he heard one of the Germans say something to the other three, and he started walking toward his column. The tallest German took his pistol and pointed it to the back of the woman's head and pulled the trigger. Jason was horrified. It was like it was in slow motion as the bullet passed completely through her head and came out the front, scattering her brains all over the front pew. *If only I had not waited. I could have saved her.* The one German continued walking toward his column. Surely the German could hear the loud beating of his heart. He would wait no more. He reached down and took out his bayonet from his side, and as the German became even with the column, he plunged it deep into his stomach. He then stepped out from behind the column, and as the German fell, he raised his rifle and took three shots. They were true. He quickly bent down and took his bayonet from the German's stomach and rushed to the other three captives. Taking his pocket knife, he cut their bindings, and then he saw the poor woman slumped forward. A large bloody hole was in the back of her head and half of her forehead was gone. He fell on his knees and began to throw up.

"Get control," he heard Sargent Harris say. "This is not over yet."

Looking up he could barely see. His eyes were filled with tears. He stood up. "Do you think other Germans heard the shots?"

"Not likely," the lieutenant said, "And boy I am glad you didn't obey my orders. We need to get out of here." The lieutenant and sergeant picked up their weapons, which the Germans had left on the floor.

"Wait," said the priest. "I have people hiding in the basement. There are twenty-three Jews that the church was trying to protect." He was gone for just a moment, and soon they were surrounded by an assortment of men and women. Some were young, and some were old. "There is one more in my office. I don't want her to see the lady the Germans shot. It was her grandmother. She is just a child. Move her grandmother to the fourth pew, and cover her with the rug. I don't want her to see her grandmother like this." Jason and the sergeant moved the lady and did what the priest requested. The priest was soon back with a young girl of about fourteen or fifteen years of age. Jason could tell she was as scared as he was.

The lieutenant addressed the group, and the priest repeated what he said in Italian. "We don't know how many Germans are out there. There is a dried-up creek bed just outside the church. We will try to get to it and slip into the trees which are about three hundred yards to the left and to the front of this church. We cannot stay here. I think we heard the Germans say they were going to blow it up. They don't want us to be able use the church's height for any advantage. We have got to move quickly."

Jason spoke up. "We can't go out the front. I heard German voices coming from down by the river. They will be able to see us if they are watching the front of the church."

The lieutenant went to the front door. "I can see five Germans standing near the rock fence. They are about seventy-five yards away. They don't seem to be alarmed by Jason's shots. Jason, you were lucky to get in here without being seen. If we can get to that dry creek, they will not be able to see us. The church will block their view."

Sergeant Harris peeped out the door which was slightly open. "The three of us could open fire from this door. They would be caught off guard. They would be taken out before they could react."

Lieutenant Forbes looked out the door a second time. "No, that won't work. We see five, but there must be more that we don't see. If there are more Germans, we would not be able to make it to the tree line before they opened fire on us. We will have to find another way."

The priest spoke up. "We can go out the side door. That dry creek bed is only about twenty yards from the door. If we stay low, we can get to it and make our way out of here."

He was right, and in just a few minutes they were sliding on their bellies up the creek bed trying to get beyond the end of the rock wall and into the trees. The lieutenant was leading the way, while Sergeant Harris, Jason, and the priest were at the back.

They were about half way to the trees when the young girl said something to the priest. She quickly stood up. She turned to go back to the church when a shot rang out, and a German sniper bullet went through her left shoulder. She fell to the ground. She looked at her shoulder, then to the priest and then passed out.

The sergeant quickly took her dress off her shoulder and examined the wound. "The bullet has gone all the way through. She has a wound front and back. If the bullet hit a bone it is bad. What made her do such a fool thing?"

The priest moved closer to help with the young girl. "She realized that her grandmother might still be in the church. She was going to run back to get her."

Sergeant Harris continued to administer first aid to the girl. He reached for his first aid supplies and took sulfa powder and sprinkled it over both wounds. "It does not appear to be bleeding all that much, so if someone has a large belt, we will strap her arm to her side and maybe we can move her." By this time Lieutenant Forbes had slid his way back to where the girl was. About that time another bullet came just over their heads.

Jason looked at the young girl who was still passed out. He thought about what the sergeant has said. *There does not appear to be much bleeding. What is much bleeding?* Her front was completely covered with blood."

"Up front the grass is much shorter. This sniper is going to pick us off one by one. Jason, you are listed as a sharp shooter. We are going to find out just how good you are. Put a full clip in your rifle and slide up the bank, but keep low. Just before you are visible to the sniper, I am going to distract him and hope he will take a shot. You might not be able to see where the shot comes from, but if you can't, use the sound to guess where he is, and take as many shots as you got into that area."

Jason slid up the bank and the lieutenant took a scarf from one of the women. He took his knife and cut several long blades of grass and wrapped the scarf around them. Moving down the creek bed about five yards, he slowly raised up the grass wrapped by the scarf and quickly brought it back down. "Be ready Jason." He moved about another yard and raised the scarf again. This time a bullet came right through the scarf.

Luck was with them as soon as the shot was made by the German, he was visible just for a moment. Jason fired two quick shots and then slid back down the bank. Again, he felt sick at his stomach.

"Do you think you got him? You only fired twice."

Jason was now really sick. "I got him on the first shot. I don't know why I fired twice."

"The Germans that are behind us are going to hear those shots and come our way. We got to move and move as quickly as we can slide on our stomachs."

"What about the young girl? We can't move her that quickly," the sergeant said.

"Leave her here. Maybe the Germans will take care of her. We will sacrifice one to save many," the lieutenant said as he looked at the priest.

The priest stared back at Lieutenant Forbes. "I am going to stay with her. Get the group moving."

"You can't stay. I need you to communicate with your people. Do as I say. We need to get moving."

Jason didn't know why he spoke up. "I am going to stay with her. The Germans will not know how many of us are in this ditch. I have four clips left. I will hold them off until you get out and bring back relief."

The lieutenant agreed. "Give me your M1, and you take my Thompson. I can leave you five clips. You will have one hundred and fifty rounds. Go slow with it, and you might buy yourself enough time for us to bring help. Let's get moving."

For a second time Jason smiled to himself. *I don't like the sound of you might in that sentence.*

The sergeant spoke up. "Wait just a minute. If you have to move her, she is going to start bleeding again. Here is a little more powder and some bandages. If the one she has gets blood soaked, and you have time, try to change it. Stick these into your supply belt. Good luck boy."

Soon Jason and the young girl were all alone. It was not long until he heard German voices. For the moment he no longer felt sick. In fact, he only felt one thing. He was going to die, and the fact that he felt that way lessened his fear. He looked at the girl. She was still passed out. "If we stay here it is just a matter of time until they are close and toss a grenade, and that will be the end." Looking up the dried creek bed, he could no longer see the group of Jews. At first, he thought he should try to move the girl up the dry creek to safety. Again, he heard German voices. They were getting close to his cover, and they sounded like they were now ahead of him. Looking out toward where he shot the sniper, he saw an area of very tall grass. "You go ahead and sleep. I am going to try to get us to higher ground." He pushed the girl up the bank and began to pull her along by holding on to the belt that held her arm in place. *You might not live through this, but at least I am giving us a fighting chance.* It seemed like forever until they reached the trees. He then swung the Tommy over his shoulder and carried her up the side of the small mountain. Fifty yards up he found a path leading away from his lines, but he knew the Germans were now between him and safety. He put the young girl down and leaned her against a tree.

"I got to rest," he whispered.

About fifteen minutes later he again picked her up and started along the trail looking for a place to hide. Again, he heard German voices. He quickly moved into the brush. "Now is not the time for you to wake up, he told her. His words fell on deaf ears. Leaving her in the brush, he moved down the trail until he found the source of the voices. Ahead of him he could see two Germans in a machine gun nest. Their position overlooked the valley, and they would have a perfect angle to ambush the Americans if they tried to move forward. He decided he would just wait. He went back to check on the young girl. As he sat in the bushes, he could make out the church down in the valley. As he was looking, it exploded and was completely leveled by three successive artillery blasts. *The Germans must have already zoomed in on the church. They have a plan. They were going to trap the Americans.* There was nothing left of the church. There was no way it could be used for observation. He was not sure where the shells that destroyed the church came from.

By the time Jason had gotten the girl hidden in the brush, the lieutenant had led the people of the church to safety and was telling the major about the situation.

The major didn't seem to listen to anything the lieutenant had to say. "You mean you don't know the enemy strength? I send you out there on a scouting mission, and you come back without any usable information."

"I did come back with information. We know the Germans are out there, and we observed German movement just three hundred yards from our lines. My guess is that they will destroy the church and keep us blind and trap us in the valley. I don't know their strength, but I would estimate that they have at least a company of men. If those men are dug in and have firepower on either side of the valley, we could lose a lot of men."

Suddenly there was a loud boom, followed by a second and then a third. A young soldier came into the tent. "The Germans have destroyed the church."

The major seemed to be unfazed. "You say you don't know the enemy strength. I do. I have photos of the area taken from our planes. These photos of the area were taken just yesterday. The entire German division has moved up the valley and left only a handful of men, and by now they are leaving. We are moving right behind them, and maybe we can stop them before they get to the high ground. To be safe, I am sending you and your company and Bravo company in right now. The church is gone. Fan out and move up the valley. There is high grass on the other side of the church. It will give you some concealment. I am sure if you meet resistance it will be light. Move quickly. Time is on our side."

"You seem to forget that the Germans have a big gun somewhere up the valley, or hidden in the hills."

The major scoffed, "They just blew up the church to keep us from getting a view of the valley. I would guess they are now moving the gun further up the valley."

Lieutenant Forbes was an experienced soldier. He knew if the Germans only blew up the church, and didn't attack their position with their artillery, they were inviting them to move into the valley. "Major, I need for you to listen to me. There is high ground on both sides of the valley. If the Germans have troops in those area, they won't need many men to…"

"Lieutenant, you have your orders. Move your men forward."

When he left the tent, Sergeant Harris was waiting outside. "What did you learn?"

Lieutenant Forbes scoffed, "I learned that the major is a damn fool. Let's hope we don't get destroyed by those German big guns. Get the men ready. Our first objective is to try to find Jet."

Thirty minutes later the two companies were spread out and were crossing the rock wall and moving past the church. They could not find Jason and the young girl.

Jason could see the troop movement and knew the Americans were in trouble. "I will be back," he told the girl, even though she could not hear him. Before he left, he checked her wound. It had started bleeding again. *She is never going to wake up if we don't get her some medical attention*, he thought to himself. He moved above the machine gun emplacement, and as he surveyed the area, he could see what looked to be a German 88 mm gun about seventy yards up the trail. *Oh shit. That must be the gun that destroyed the church.* Quickly, he moved to where he could toss his one grenade into the gun emplacement. One was enough, and five Germans and one 88 mm gun were no longer able to do any harm. Next, he took his Tommy gun and cocked it and without thinking ran up the trail as hard as he could go. He approached the machine gun nest, and before the two Germans could react and turn the gun toward him, he had killed two more Germans. As he approached the disabled machine gun nest, he looked up the trail and saw another German carrying ammo for the machine gun. The German dropped his load and was trying to get his gun ready to fire. Jason already had his gun cocked, and with a short burst of five shots the young German fell to the ground. Jason went to the German soldier and quickly kicked his gun away. He was badly wounded, but alive. He propped him up against a tree.

"The war is over for you, my German friend. I hope you live."

Moving back to the machine gun emplacement, he could clearly see down into the valley. He could see about thirty to forty Germans behind a bank waiting to ambush the Americans that were just passing the destroyed church. As he watched, the Germans fired five flares just over the American troops as they advance. *Why are they shooting flares during daylight? Are they marking our troops for their artillery?* The Americans quickly fell and hid in the grass. *What were the Germans doing?* Then he saw. The flares set the grass on fire behind the American troops. They were now trapped between the burning grass and the Germans. He had to do something, so he got into the German machine gun emplacement and opened fire on the Germans below. They were in range, and German after German fell to his constant blast of machine gun fire. Across the valley he could see another machine gun emplacement, so he turned his machine gun on it. It was barely in range, but it too was silenced.

As he was about to leave the gun emplacement, several shots were fired at him. Looking to his right he saw about seven Germans coming up the trail firing their guns at him. He ducked down behind the sand bags, and as he did, he saw three German grenades lying on the ground. Picking them up he quickly tossed the first, then the second, and then the third. Once he heard the third explosion' he grabbed his gun and started running up the trail to where he had left the girl. He then heard something behind him, and he cock his Tommy and turned to face whatever was behind him. A lone German fired his gun, and the bullet went into Jason's left leg. He fell to one knee as the German cocked his gun, but he fired a blast of about ten shots, taking the German down. He could hear other Germans shouting further away. The leg was bad, and he almost passed out from the pain. Dragging his leg, it was not long until he reached the brush where he had hidden the girl.

"We have got to get away from this trail." He swung his gun to his back and picked up the girl in his arms and carried her up the hill. He was in so much pain dragging his wounded leg. Luck was with him because about thirty yards up the hill, he found a small cave. Once he was inside, he spotted a large rock and dragged the girl behind it. *This will give us some protection.* He started getting weak. He was bleeding and bleeding a lot. He pressed his hand against the wound. He then looked at the wounded young girl. *Maybe one of us can get out of this mess.* He took the blood-soaked bandage from her wound and tossed it aside. He sprinkled the wound with what powder he had left and dressed it as best as he could. Then he passed out.

As Jason lay there passed out, he started to dream. He could see the woman who was killed by the Germans. He again saw the bullet pass through her head. He could see Germans lying on the ground, and they were bleeding. In his dream, he tried to turn away. Then all the visions went away. All he could see was a beautiful church. It was so peaceful.

In his semi-unconscious state, he could hear gunshots. He could hear voices. Sometimes they were German and sometimes they were English. Then he heard someone at the cave opening. He forced himself to wake up. He reached for his gun but again passed out.

An American soldier made his way over to him. "Jet, is that you? Damn, you killed half of the German army left here in Italy. Good thing you left a trail of blood, or we might have never found you."

The Lost Dream

When Jason woke up and opened his eyes, he could see Gabi. Her yellow sun dress was soaked with the rain and clinging to her body. "How long have I been here," he asked.

"I am not sure, maybe thirty minutes, or it could be an hour. Are you okay?"

"Depends on what you mean by okay. We have got to get out of here. We have to get back to the jeep and hope it is not under water."

The rain seemed to be coming down in waves as they worked their way back down the rock fence and to the river. They were lucky. The river was rising but was only about a foot over the sand bar. They waded into the water and got inside the jeep. In a few minutes they are making their way back up the hill. They did not talk until they were back at Jason's villa.

Once they were inside, Jason turned to Gabi and said, "Go to the bathroom next to Ana's room. You will find clean towels and a white terry cloth robe there. I will dry off down here."

When Gabi came back down the stairs, she was wearing the white robe and had a towel wrapped around her head. Jason had put on a black t-shirt and a pair of tan slacks. He had also lit a fire.

"I noticed the temperature had dropped just a little, and I figured that we needed to warm up. Are you okay?"

She heard the seriousness in his voice. "The question is, are you okay?" She took a seat on the floor and leaned back against the couch, which was in front of the fire.

"Do I have a memory of being here during the war? I guess the answer would be yes. I guess that is what you wanted, or you would not have taken me to see the ruins of the church." He took a seat on the floor and leaned back against the couch next to her. "Gabi, I know you are trying to help me, but I now know why my mind forced me to forget what happened. I saw and did terrible things. I did not want to know these things, but now I do."

"Gabi lightly touched the back of Jason's head. "The things you did during the war may be terrible, but if you didn't remember them, they were going to kill you. I know you and I both know that you would only do what you had to do. I think it may help you if we talk about what you remembered. Tell me why you think what you did was so terrible. War itself is terrible."

"I am not proud of anything I did. I didn't want any medals or recognition for fighting in the war. I saw an old woman killed. If I had not been so scared, I might have saved her. I am not proud of that. I killed, I don't know how many Germans. I am not proud of that. I did save a young girl. I am proud of that."

"Do you remember anybody that day?"

"I remember one face. That's it, just one face. I remember the old woman. Maybe she was not an old woman. I was just a young boy, and she seemed old to me. She was scared, but brave. There were several Jewish men and women in the church. There may have been as many as twenty or more. I remember no faces. There was a priest. I don't remember his face either. I just remember that I killed a lot of people that day."

Gabi continued to press Jason to talk about his experiences. "You mentioned a young girl. Do you remember her?"

"Not very well. I remember she was young maybe about fifteen years old. I remember her standing up and saying something in Italian and getting shot. I was really scared, and I seemed to want to save her. I think a lot of my actions were just trying to save her. I remember that I talked to her a lot. She does not know this, but our conversations kept me going. The last memory I have was trying to stop her from bleeding to death. At the time I felt her life was more important than mine, because I knew I was going to die. After all, I chose to join the army. She was just a poor victim. I wonder what happened to her. I would really like to know. Maybe not meet her, but know that she made it through the war and did okay."

Gabi leaned over and kissed Jason on the cheek. "I would say that she has thought of you often."

Without thinking, Jason leaned his head over on Gabi's knees. "I don't think so. From the point she got shot, she was unconscious the entire time."

Gabi again ran her fingers through Jason's hair. "There had to be many witnesses to the events of that day, and she would have been told about how she was saved by one brave soldier. She would think about you often."

She lay down on the rug in front of the fireplace. Jason moved down and moved up against her and put his arm around her waist. She did not move his arm. She instead turned and faced him and kissed him tenderly and slowly on the lips.

"I don't know what is going to happen tomorrow or the weeks ahead. I know you are going back home. I am staying here. Right now, I want you to just hold me."

He took his free hand and opened her robe and first kissed her neck, and then moved down to her breast. It was almost like a dream as they came together. They made love tenderly and said nothing to each other. After they made love they went to sleep in each other's arms, and an hour later they woke up and made love a second time. The next morning, they awoke in each other's, arms and made love a third time. They held each other for several minutes. Gabi was quiet and didn't say anything, but he could tell she had something on her mind. He pulled himself from the floor and put on his pants and shirt. She sat up and put the robe back on. "I would think my underclothes and dress would be dry by now. I am going to take a shower and get dressed."

When Gabi came down the steps, she had put on her sun dress and shoes on. Jason had made coffee. "Do you want some coffee and for me to make us some breakfast?"

"No, I am going to leave. I am going to go the Mass. I need to think." She walked toward the front door. Jason noticed how quiet she was. When they were standing next to her car, he said, "What are we going to do?"

She put her arms around him and laid her head on his chest. "I don't know. I really don't know. All I know is that you are leaving, and I have been unfaithful to the man I am going to marry. I don't think I could have made a bigger mess even if I were trying."

He reached down and lifted her chin and looked into her eyes. Her eyes were filled with tears. "You are right. I am leaving, but you can come with me. We can make a home in America. You would love Richmond, and they need doctors there too. Come with me."

She again looked down. "Tobia has done nothing. He has been so good to me, and I think I need to spend my life making up for what I have done. As I told you, I am going to Mass, and then I am going to meet with the priest. I am not a Catholic, but I do need to go to confession. Father Borrelli is more than my priest. He is my friend. I have got to go."

As Gabi drove away, Jason was confused. She had given herself to him freely and completely. *Does she not love me like I love her?*" he thought.

Later that morning Gabi, sat waiting for Mass to end. She stayed inside the church when the service ended, and while Father Borrelli was outside greeting members of the church she waited for him to come back inside. A few minutes later he came in and took a seat next to her. She turned in the seat to face him. "How is it that you Catholic say it? Forgive me Father, for I have sinned."

He reached out and took her hand. "I know what you are going to say. You have fallen in love with a man, and in about a month you are going to marry another man. I don't think that qualifies as a sin, Gabi. You just have to make some hard decisions. Did you tell Mr. Terry that you were the girl in the cave? Has he gotten back any of his memory?"

"He has gotten back his memory. What happened was a long time ago, and while he does remember the events of that day, he does not remember us. He knows there was a priest there, but he doesn't remember that it was you. He knows he saved a young girl but does not remember that that girl was me. What am I going to do?"

"Gabi, what are your choices? Maybe you really don't have any. If Mr. Terry asked you to go to America with him, would you go?"

"He has asked me, and I don't know. Everything I know is here. If you asked me yesterday if I love Tobia, I would have said yes. I think I still love him, and what I feel for Jason may be something else. I owe him my life. I have thought about going to America. He is not even going to be there. He has taken a job in South America. He is going to be there for two years."

Father Borrelli released Gabi's hand and put his arm around her shoulders. "You are right. You owe Jason Terry your life. I owe him my life too. There are maybe a hundred people that owe him their life. Do you think he expects anything in return? I can answer that. He does not. He does not expect anything from you at all. If he has fallen in love with you, it is because he loves you for who you are. Not because he carried you to safety during the war. You have a big question to answer. Do you love him for who he is, or do you feel you owe a debt that needs to be paid?"

"You make it sound so simple. How can I separate these feelings? Everything I know about him is who he is. He is a kind, loving man. It was this kind, loving man that saved me, you, twenty-three Jews, and many soldiers. I cannot separate those events from who he is now."

"Have you thought about just telling him who you are? I am sure this is something he would want to know. Using your own words, you cannot separate those events from who you are now either. Maybe telling him will release both of you."

"I have thought about this all morning. I think telling him will just complicate things more. He has asked me to go to America with him. I have said no. If he knows that I am the girl that was in the cave, he is going to … I don't know what he is going to do. All I know is what I am going to do. I am going to marry Tobia. If for some reason he comes looking for me, you must promise that you will not tell him that I was the girl in the cave. The girl in the cave might want to see him, but the woman that is going to marry Tobia does not. Promise me."

"As I feared, there are only three options here. You can go with him back to America. You can try to convince him to stay in Italy with you, or you can pick up your life before he came here and marry Tobia. I see you have made your choice. I promise that I will never tell Jason who or where you are. Would you pray with me?"

Going Home

On the following Monday, Jason returned to the construction site. The project had moved far enough along that he was not needed anymore. Going to the trailer, he poured himself a cup of coffee and waited for Michael.

It was only about ten minutes until he came through the door. "Are things in order? Are you ready to get back to America?"

"I am. I am leaving at the end of the week. I will need you to get me to the airport. In a way I am sad to leave." He was thinking of Gabi.

"We are sad to see you go. You have got things in good shape here. I want you to walk with me through the power station before you leave. The crew we hired out of Germany is doing a good job. Tomorrow we are going to do away with the cofferdams, and by the end of the week we should block off the diversion tunnels. By the time you see this baby again it should be full of water. We should be able to put the finishing touches to the dam in about a couple of months. It is my understanding that there is going to be a ceremony at the completion. Will you be back for that?"

"No. That won't be for at least two months, I hope to be at a new project in South America by then. You will have to handle it. After all, this is more your project than mine."

Michael scoffed. "There wouldn't even be a project if it were not for you. Speaking of projects, I am going to a new project when this one is complete. They are building a road in the north. My crew is going to build a bridge across a river. Looks like it may take about two to three years to complete. Oh, by the way, I need to make you aware of something. If things continue to proceed like I hope they will, you may need a new housekeeper."

Jason laughed, "I thought that might be the case. I guess I could live with that. I will have the boys to watch after things if good things come to pass. My flight is this coming Sunday. I think I will have a little get together this Saturday. Hope you can come. I am not going to have a lot of people. Just you, Bonita, Luke and Ana. It will not be at the villa. It is going to be at Angelo's. We plan to eat at seven."

That night he drove into town and stopped at the hospital. He went to Gabi's secretary and asked if she were in. Marie told him that she had left early that day. "Would you give her this note? I will not be back in town until the weekend."

The next day Gabi came into her office and saw the note in the middle of her desk. She opened it and read:

This is my last week in Caseno. I hope you have reconsidered my request. If you have, come by the house. If you have not, I am having a dinner at Angelo's this Saturday at seven. Please come by. I would not want to leave without seeing you.

Each night Jason waited to see if Gabi would come by. She did not. He retrieved his art supplies and pulled out the two drawings he had made of Gabi. He looked at the large canvas and said to himself, *let us see if we can get an image that captures this beautiful woman.* As he started to paint, he found that he relied on his memory and vision of Gabi more than the two pencil sketches. Each night he worked long hours into the night and by Friday it was finished. Looking at the finished painting he wondered if this would be his last vision of her. He sat the painting up on the mantel of the fireplace and lay back on the couch. He closed his eyes and thought of Molly. *What if she had waited? Would I even be here?* His thoughts turned to Maggie. Maybe he should have gone to Boston and tried to get her back. No. If I had done that, I would never have had Gabi in my life. She had not come to him. Maybe he should go to her. No, the ball is in her court. He had told her how he felt. All he could do was wait.

On Friday, Gabi asked Marie to have lunch with her. She decided not to go to Angelo's because she was afraid that Jason might come by. Once they had ordered, she said, "I need to apologize to you."

Marie was caught off guard. "Why would you need to apologize to me? You have always treated me like a friend and not like a secretary."

"I got mad when you called Jason Terry my other boyfriend. The truth is you were right. We have become rather close. He has asked me to go to America with him."

"My gosh. What did you tell him?"

"I have told him that I would not go. The truth is, I want to go. I think I am in love with him."

Marie leaned forward in her chair. "Gabi, you can't think you love someone. You either do or you don't."

"There is more that you don't know. In a way I feel I owe him something. I prefer not to tell you a lot, but believe me, there is a lot more to the story. I need to know what to do."

"I can't tell you what to do. You need to just take a close look at your options. Tobia is here. He travels a lot, but he will be with you most of the time in Rome. If you live in Rome, you can still be a doctor. Jason Terry has asked you to join him in America, but is he even going to be there? He travels with his work. Look how long he has been here. Do you even know where his next project will be?"

"He said when he gets back to New York, he is going to get a month's leave, and then he is going to a project in South America."

"Good grief Gabi, is that the life you want? It might be better to want something you don't have than to have something you don't want. Do you not love Tobia anymore?"

"Tobia will take care of me. He loves me very much. I am sure we will be happy together."

"That is not what I asked you."

Gabi was silent. She was thinking of the conversation that she and Jason had had back at his villa. He had asked the same question and had told her that she wanted security more than love. Maybe he was right. She did want security, and he was offering her none. She thought back to his conversation. He asked her to come to America. He did not ask her to marry him. Tobia had asked her to marry him. He was going to provide them a home in Rome. She could continue to be a doctor.

"Marie, thank you for coming with me to lunch and talking to me. Let's talk about something else. Things are going to work out."

That night Gabi stayed at the hospital to be near the square. She had decided she was going to go to Jason's farewell dinner and say her goodbyes. She owed him that. About seven o'clock she started to make her way to Angelo's but was stopped by a nurse that told her she needed to see one of her patients. This cost her about thirty minutes, and when she was just outside Angelo's she could see Jason and his party. She watched for a minute. She knew she loved him. She also knew she loved him enough to let him go. Tears begin to roll down her cheeks. *I can't do this,* she said to herself. She turned and walked away.

The party lasted until about nine o'clock, and by ten, Jason was doing the last of his packing. He spent a restless night. He had really expected Gabi to come to his dinner. The next morning Michael came by and helped him load his luggage. He had one package wrapped in brown paper that he left sitting just inside the front door. It had a note taped to it. His plan was to drop the painting off at Gabi's office on the way to the airport, but he had changed his mind. Seeing Gabi again would serve no purpose. It would only cause pain for both.

Three hours later, he was sitting in an airplane ordering bourbon. When it came, he quickly swallowed it down and ordered another. Two bourbons later, he was in a deep sleep and dreaming. In his dream he was in the cave. He was not scared. He changed the bandage on the young girl and felt at ease. He felt that if he died because of his leg wound, she would live and do something good.

While Jason was flying back home, Ana had found the package he left by the front door. He had written a note for her. "Please take this to the hospital and give it to Gabi."

The next morning, Ana asked Bonita to take her to the hospital. Gabi was not there, so she left the package with her secretary, Marie.

When Gabi arrived, Marie said, "You have a package. It is large. I put it in your office."

"Do you know who sent it?'

"Yes, it was left by Ana Marino. She said that she worked for Jason Terry."

Gabi went to her office and began to open the package. The brown paper had been secured with twine. Taking a pair of scissors, she cut the twine and unwrapped it. What she saw was amazing. Removing the last of the paper released a white envelope. As she gazed in amazement at the painting, she reached down and picked up the envelope. The painting was about forty inches by thirty-two inches. It was of her, sitting on a large rock in the middle of the river. The water was cascading around the rock, and she was sitting there in her yellow sun dress. He had captured the light coming from behind her and highlighting her hair. One strap of the sun dress had fallen off her shoulder, and even she thought she was beautiful. *Is this how he sees me,* she thought. Looking closely at the painting she could see that he had painted her with the scar on her shoulder. *I wonder why he has not put me and the girl in the cave together.* Turning away from the painting, she opened the letter.

Dear Gabi;

You are now looking at the painting of the last day we spent together. You are asking yourself two questions. One question is, when did he find time to complete the painting? The other question is, am I really that beautiful? I will only answer the second question. You are that beautiful. I cannot thank you enough for helping me. I am at peace with the war. I think I can live with the fact that I killed so many that day, and I became that so-called hero. I am including my address at the bottom of this letter. I am going to ask you a favor. The young girl who was with me in the cave must have gone to the Church of Three Bells, and you told me that you gave the wooden relief to the church. I think your friend; the priest will know who she is. Please try to find out what happened to her. I don't want to meet her, but I would like to know what happened to her.

You will always be a part of my life, and I hope you and Toad Frog (Tobia) find all the happiness that I hope for you.

Jason Edward Terry
403 Main Street
Richmond, Kentucky

When Gabi started to fold up the letter, she noticed several large tear stains on the letter that were causing some of the ink to smear. *That's good,* she thought. *Both the ink and my life are really starting to smear.*

When Jason got back to New York City, he was delighted to see the office staff. When he met with Jerry Merrick, he got the news that the project had gone so well that he was to receive a bonus. It was large, and Jason felt he was just doing his job, but the company insisted that he was worth it, because the project was about to be abandoned until he took it over. Later that night, he had dinner with Mary and JoAnn.

They were having so much fun laughing and enjoying each other's company that they were afraid they were going to be asked to quiet down. Later in the evening, JoAnn left, and Mary and Jason were left alone. Mary took his hand and said, "You wrote to me about a Dr. Acosta. What became of her?"

"We got to be good friends. During our friendship she forced me to relive the war. It has helped. I have not had the church dream since."

"Jason, you have never talked to me much about the war. JoAnn and I were with you that day you were presented the Congressional Medal of Honor. There must be a story there that needs to be told. What happened to you during the war that has caused you so much pain?"

"I have not told you much because until recently I haven't remembered much. The only part I did remember was that I was found in a cave with a young girl. I was not sure if this is something I remembered or something I was told. We both had been shot. She was shot in the shoulder and me in the leg."

Mary didn't say anything for a minute. "What became of her?"

"I don't know. When my company found me, I was passed out. When I did wake up, I was on a hospital ship and was taken to England."

Mary continued to asked questions. "Do you remember now how you got into that cave?"

"I do. She and several other Jews where hiding in the church. I help to rescue them. As we left, the young girl was shot by a German sniper. She was left behind, and I stayed with her. Later I had to move her, because we were about to be discovered by the Germans. We took shelter in the cave."

Mary was becoming even more engrossed in the story. "Don't you ever wonder what ever happened to her. Did you try to find her while you were in Italy?"

Jason took a drink of wine. "Not really. Until Gabi forced me to remember, I had no desire to remember the war. I did want to know about the young girl, but I didn't try to find her. Before I left, I asked Gabi to try to find some information."

"You must have done much more to receive the Congressional Medal of Honor. You have not told me everything, have you?"

Pushing his chair back a little from the table he said, "No, and I am not going to talk about that day. I was forced to remember it, but I don't want to talk about it. When I got back to the United States, I was to receive the medal in a ceremony at the capital. It was to take place on August the 6th. That is the day we dropped the first atomic bomb on Japan. Things got pushed back, and I didn't stay. I went home."

"So, your friend Gabi helped you remember the missing parts of the war. When you say good friends, how good friends were you?"

"We were good enough that I asked her to come back to the States with me. She turned me down."

Mary thought for a moment. "Did you ask her to marry you or just come to America with you? You understand that those are two different questions."

"No. I didn't know. I would assume if you asked someone to come with you, they would know that includes a proposal of marriage."

"Jason, you are the smartest person I know, and sometimes you are so damn dumb. I know you see those two questions as the same. Most women would not. You said that you asked Doctor Gabi to help you find the girl who was in the cave. I just had a strange thought. What if Gabi was the girl in the cave?"

"That is strange that you would think of that. I did a painting of Gabi just before I left. When I did a preliminary drawing, I noticed that she had the scars of a bullet wound in her shoulder. Just for a moment I had the feeling that we had a connection. When I got my memory back, I thought she might be the girl in the cave. Then I dismissed it. It didn't fit. What I knew of her told me she could not be the girl in the cave. I also think that if she were the girl in the cave, she would have told me. She was trying to help me regain my memory. If she were the girl in the cave, I think she would have used that information."

"From what you have told me I think you are right. Why don't you forget building a dam in South America and go back and get her?"

Jason scoffed, "It is too late to do anything about it. *Alea iacta est.* I am leaving this weekend to go back to Richmond, and in about four weeks I will be on my way to some place in South America. I will be there for at least two years. I might not be able to get away to even make a home visit."

"Jason, do you even know where in South America you are going?"

Jason laughed. "Of course, I am going to Peru. It is going to be a tall dam which is going to create a very large lake. It is hoped that a large lake will create stability for the people who live in the area and create some growth. The dam will generate some much-needed power for the area. My problem is that the nearest town is about one hundred miles away from the dam. I am going to live in a tent city. The only good thing about this project is they are going to pay me a fortune."

"Jason, you don't need a fortune. I bet you could just about buy that company you work for. What you need is someone to share what you already have. Why don't you quit that darn job, go back to Italy and ask that doctor to marry you, and if she won't come to America, stay with her."

"I wish it were that simple. I have already committed to build the South American dam. By the time I get back to Italy, she might already be married. No, I don't think she would be married, but the wedding date would be getting close. I think she made it rather clear that I was not going to be a part of her life."

Mary and Jason continued their conversation while he walked her back to her apartment. When they were in the lobby there were several people there. "Shall we put on our show?" He took her in his arms and gave her a passionate kiss. She then gave him a hug. "You be careful in South America. There is a jungle down there. You are the best friend a person could have, and I don't want to lose you."

Margie

Jason had not told Billy he was coming home. He would just surprise him. When the taxi dropped him off in front of his house, he left his luggage sitting at the foot of the steps and walked to the door. Knocking on the door, he was surprised when a strange woman opened the door. "May I help you," she said in a kind voice.

"Yes, you can. Where is Billy?"

The strange lady leaned back into the doorway and called out, "Billy! Someone is here to see you." She did not invite him in. She stepped back from the doorway and waited for Billy.

In a few moments Billy opened the door, and a smile greeted Jason. "My it is so good to see you. Why didn't you let me know you were coming? I know Rachel would like to know that you are here. You know her room is decorated with the souvenirs you have sent her from Italy. She now plans to visit all those places you have told her about." The strange woman left the two men talking and went toward the kitchen.

"It is really good to see you and to be home, but I have to ask, who is the lady that opened the door?"

"Oh, that is Margie. I hired a cook."

Jason took a deep breath. "Billy, you are a cook, a good cook. Why do we need a cook? How much are we paying her?"

Billy smiled. "We are not paying her anything. I just let her live here. I got us a free cook."

"Where does she stay? Which room did you put her in?"

"Oh, she stays in my room," Billy leaned back inside the door. "Margie would you come here for a second?" In just a moment, Margie was back at the door. "Margie, I would like for you to meet our boss. This is Jason Terry. Jason, I would like for you to meet my wife, Margie Ballew."

Jason started to laugh, "Billy, you are an old rascal. Why didn't you let me know? I would have loved to come to the wedding."

"I know that. That is why I didn't let you know. I felt it would have been too much of a hardship to come from Italy. We had a small wedding." Billy started down the steps. "Please let me help you with your bags, and let's get you settled. How long are you going to be here?"

"I am going to be here for about four weeks. I need to sign some papers and get several things in order before I leave. I wrote you and told you that I was going to a project in South America. I hope I can get to see Rachel while I am here."

The next day Jason made an appointment with Elmer Hall. When he was seated in front of him, Jason said, "You have been sending me reports, and I just need to know if I need to make any changes or adjustments in my investments?" You know that I work with another investment firm in New York. I have copies of their reports with me. They had suggested that I sell my gold or at least half. I took their advice and sold half. They invested the profit from the gold into up and coming companies. You will be able to see that I have done very well."

"I don't think you need to make any changes in your investment here. Some of your New York friends have given you very sound advice, and that advice has made both of us a lot of money. Your net worth has almost doubled in the last five years. You are a very rich man. How long are you going to be here? Are you going back to New York?"

"I am going to be here about a month, and when I leave, I am going to Peru. I have taken on another dam project. I believe it will take about two years."

"Jason, you have enough money to never have to work again. You could spend thousands each month and never run out of money. Why are you working so hard?"

"I don't know. While I was in Italy, I thought about retiring and living there. I have told you about the villa I bought. I had planned to sell it once the project was completed, but now I think I will keep it as a vacation home. While I am here, I need to change my payments for Ana Marino. As you know she is my house keeper, and her brothers are running the farm and setting up wine production. They are up and running and on solid footing, so we need to set up payments out of that account. We need to stop payment on this end, and I will let them know that she is to be paid out of the farm account."

"I stopped payments to Rachel. I informed you of this in a letter. She is not living in your home and is now working and making a good salary. Is there anything else?"

"Yes, Billy has hired a cook, or sort of. I want to set her up to receive a salary."

"Do you really need a cook? How much are you ever here?"

"I don't need a cook, but Billy has gotten himself married and maybe this will help her feel a part of things, and I approve of her."

How much do you want to pay her?"

"Whatever is standard. You will know more about this than I do. I hope to see you again before I leave. Thank you for what you do for me."

"It is me that should be thanking you. The fees I get for managing your money, and the tips from the stock market are making me a real nice retirement nest egg. I will see you before you leave."

Jason found he really liked Margie, and he had to admit that she was a better cook than Billy. For the first few days, he just stayed around the house and did some outside work himself.

On the weekend Rachel came in, and he was really interested about how things were going for her. She was working in an office for a large factory in Lexington. She was now living in an apartment not far from the office complex that she worked in.

That Saturday, Rachel and Margie fixed up a meal of fried chicken, mash potatoes and gravy, made from scratch biscuits, green beans, corn pudding, and apple pie. When he had finished his meal Jason said, "That was pure heaven. That has to be the best meal I have ever eaten." He turned to Margie, "If I had met you before Billy and knew you could cook like that, I would have married you myself. That was good. Thank you and thank you Rachel for coming to visit and helping prepare this meal."

Rachel had a serious look on her face. "Jason, I have a question. I know you were joking about marrying Margie and was paying her a compliment, but if you really fell in love with a black woman, would you marry her?"

Billy spoke up, "Rachel why are you asking such a question?"

Rachel smiled, "I was hoping that Jason would marry me."

The table got extremely quiet. Rachel got serious. "You know that I am joking. I work with a young white boy about my age. I sense he likes me very much. Sometimes he even flirts with me. I think he even wants to ask me out. If he does, I am not sure how to respond."

Jason turned in his chair and faced Rachel. "I don't know how to answer your question. I don't think we have any control of the people we fall in love with. When I was in Italy, I fell in love with a woman who was engaged to be married to someone else. I don't think it would matter to me what her race was, if she would agree to marry me. I love you, and I love Billy and I hope to love Margie, but that does not answer your question. If you and this admirer of yours fall in love, it would be difficult. My only counsel is that you need to weigh all the problems that an interracial romance would involve and if you don't think you can handle it, don't let it start. I don't think you would have any legal problems in Kentucky, but you might if you moved to another state."

Rachel immediately changed the subject. "Tell us about the woman you fell in love with in Italy."

"I got hurt on the job, and she is a doctor. We started out not liking each other, but as we got to know each other, we fell in love. At first, she would call me Mr. triple A, and I would call her Doctor Bubbles."

Rachel had a smile on her face. "I don't think Mr. Triple A is a compliment."

"It is not. It means arrogant American, asshole."

Everyone was still laughing when Rachel said, "If you two fell in love, why is she not here sharing this meal with us?"

"I did not ask her or at least not directly, and I think my lifestyle scared her away. I have not told you this Rachel but in about three weeks, I am headed for Peru. It is a rough job. I will be at least a hundred miles from the nearest city. That is not much to offer someone."

Rachel was blunt. "Jason, everyone knows you are richer than sin. You don't have to work, you just do. It was you who did not commit to the relationship. Shame on you."

Billy responded in a soft voice. "Rachel, that will be enough."

Rachel answered Billy in an equally soft voice. "I am sorry Jason. I was cruel, and I was not trying to hurt you. If I have, I am so sorry. Please forgive me."

"You have nothing to be ashamed of. You should not be condemned for telling the truth or speaking your mind. You are right. My friend Mary in New York said the same thing, but in a different way."

Rachel was curious. "Tell us about Mary. I don't think you have ever mentioned her."

Jason became very serious. "Mary is gay. Her girlfriend, who lives with her, is JoAnn. They are two lovely people, but she faces the same problem that you might face. Many, many people do not accept homosexuals. They must keep their love a secret. So, Rachel, I don't think you are going to have any luck marrying me off. It looks like the only women that I fall in love with are either married, going to be married or just not available."

The following Monday afternoon Jason got a call from Elmer Hall. "Jason you need to come by the bank. I need to talk to you about your portfolio. I know you have money scattered in several banks and many bonds and stock investments, along with considerable property. I don't think you even know the extent of what you have. I want you to sit down with me and we need to update everything you have." They agreed to meet the next day. When they finished, a copy of the portfolio was made and given to him. "Jason, being a young person, I bet you have not even thought about having a will. I would advise you to get a will made before you leave for South America. If something were to happen, you have no family, and who knows what would happen to your estate. This is something you will want to have control of."

During the next couple of weeks, he just relaxed. He took in a couple of movies. Read a few books and did anything he could do to not think of Gabi.

Jason Needs a Will

Before he went to Peru he was called back to New York, and he and a local team worked on the preliminary plans for the dam. At the meeting he found out that one of his team members was Glenn Whitamore. Jerry Merrick made sure Jason recognized him, and told him he had nothing to worry about, because he had learned his lesson and he had checked the data and rechecked it.

After the meeting he turned to Jerry Merrick and asked, "Do you know a good law firm that could help me draft a will?"

"I do. I work with Mills and Mills. The firm is run by two brothers. If you were a millionaire, they would have a senior lawyer help you, but everyone else is assigned a junior member of the staff. All you must do is make an appointment, and they will have someone help you. All the lawyers in this firm are top of the line. They are in this building. They handle our legal affairs. I can call, and they will assign someone on the senior staff to see you. It takes a little longer to see a senior member. If you want this done before you go to Peru, you might not want to see one of the senior lawyers."

"No, that won't be necessary. My needs will be simple. I would assume that any lawyer could make my will. I will make the call and see when they can see me."

The next day, Jason was sitting in the waiting room of Mills and Mills. He did not have to wait long. A receptionist escorted him to a small conference room. "Someone will be here in just a moment. Would you like a cup of coffee?"

"Yes, that would be fine."

Before the coffee was brought back, the door opened, and Jason looked up. There stood Maggie Black. He said nothing but just stared at her.

It was Maggie who spoke first. "When you were assigned to me, my first thoughts were to ask someone else to handle this. But then I decided that I wanted to see you. I know that you have gone through several years of hating me. I sometimes hate myself. Do you want another lawyer?"

"No, I don't. It is good to see you Maggie. I have thought about you often. You are wrong about me hating you. I was hurt, disappointed, and many other things, but I don't hate you. I came to understand and accept our fate. I moved on, and I hope things have worked out for you."

"Let's do the preliminaries for the will, and then if it is okay with you, we can talk?"

"That will be fine. I don't have a lot of time to get a will prepared. My company is sending me to Peru to start a new dam project. The area is remote, and I will barely be able to communicate with the main office, let alone travel back and forth to see my family or friends. The will is not going to be complicated. I want to leave what I have to seven people. My assets will not be divided equally, and this is where I will need your expertise."

"Is there property involved, and how large is your portfolio?"

"Yes, I own two homes and two farms. Some of the property is in Italy. My farm in Italy has a villa on it and I need to put the villa on a separate deed. My portfolio is more than fifty million dollars."

There was a long silence. "Did you say fifty million dollars?"

"I did. I have a list of my holdings with me. Things are divided into four areas: cash, stocks, bonds, and property."

"Jason, Mills and Mills will not let a junior member of the staff handle this large of an estate. I will have to turn you over to a senior member of the staff." Before Jason could say anything, Maggie picked up her legal pad and left the room. In just a few moments, she and an older man returned. "Jason this is Alex Anderson. He will help you. Before you leave, please stop by my office."

Jason closed his folder and stood up. "Mrs. Black is helping me. I have already started with her. I want to continue with her. If that is not possible, I will find another firm."

"I assure you that you will not find another firm better than Mills and Mills. Mrs. Black has only been with the firm for less than a year. We want to give you the best service possible. You will not be disappointed."

Looking at Maggie, Jason extended his hand and said, "It was good to see you again. I am leaving the country again soon. I hope we can see each other again before I leave." Jason left the office and returned to his own office. He again started to review the South American dam project. In about thirty minutes a secretary was knocking on his door. "There is a Mr. Franklin Mills to see you. Are you able to see him?"

"Yes, send him in." Franklin Mills was not quite as old as Jason thought.

"I am so sorry that you were disappointed in the way you were received at our office. I hope you will accept my apologies, and let me do what is necessary for you to come back. Sometimes our policies get in the way of good personal service. The truth of the matter is that some of our upper end clients would be insulted if we let one of our junior members handle their affairs. I guess we must cater to some snob appeal. If you want Mrs. Black to handle your legal matters, then she shall. You and this company are very important to us. If you will return to our office Mrs. Black is waiting."

In less than ten minutes, Maggie and Jason where going over what he wanted for his will. "As I told you I want my holdings divided among seven people. Three are Americans, and the other four live in Italy and are of course Italian. There will not be an equal division."

Maggie was writing on her legal pad. "Tell me what you want. The fact that you are leaving part of your estate to foreigners creates some complications, but I will research it and make sure it is done right. The problem will come if you should die, but I will get it covered." She was beginning to relax around Jason, and she gave him a smile and said, "The best thing is not to die."

"My home in Richmond has a small farm behind it. I want both the house and farm left to Billy Ballew. My home in Italy I want to be left to Gabi Acosta. She is getting married, and I will get you her married name. It also sits on a farm, and the home needs to be on a separate deed. I want the farm in Italy to go to Ana Marino, Bonita Aparo, and Luke Aparo. I have some stock in Merrick Construction and some mineral rights. I would like those to go to Rachel Ballew."

"How much stock are we talking about?"

Jason turned his folder toward Maggie and pointed to some figures.

"Good Lord, Jason, does the Merrick company know how much of their stock you own?" Then she laughed. "You have got to be the most stupid man alive. Here you are going to someplace in South America, and you could just about buy the company that is sending you there."

Jason smiled. *It is good that she can talk to me so freely. It feels like old times.* "It seems like I am hearing this a lot. I think this may be my last project. To answer your question, the company does not know. I have a holding company. The stock is held by this holding company. The rest of the stock and cash can be divided equally among the six people I have mentioned, plus one more."

"Do you want to include Rachel Ballew in the distribution of the remaining stock and cash?"

"I do. And I want Mary Westfall included in this distribution. How long to you think it will take to get this ready?"

"Preparing the will won't take long. You need to give me a list of the names and addresses of the seven people that are listed in the will. When are you leaving?"

"I have them listed on the back of this folder. If there are no delays, a week or ten days."

Looking at the notes she had taken, she said, "The creation of the will is not going to be a problem. The administration of the will, if necessary, will be complicated, and fees will need to be built into the will to cover the cost. In an estate that is this large, the fee would be three percent. That would be roughly about one and a half million dollars depending on the size the portfolio at the time of your death. Gosh, I hate saying this like you are going to die. Let's hope you outlive everyone included in this will. You need to understand that the three percent covers the cost of transferring your stocks, bonds and cash to seven people. The cash would not be a problem, but working with the Italian government is not easy. I will get back to you on the creation of the new deeds you need, and that fee needs to be paid at the completion of the will. Who do you want listed as the wills administrator?"

"Please list Elmer Hall. I have his information also on the back. How much will I need to pay up front?"

We will need two hundred and fifty thousand. The money will be put in escrow. Should you want to change the will and not leave anything to people living outside the country, the fee will be adjusted. Should something happen to you, we will put the wheels in motion to carry out your wishes. I am just guessing but it might take a year or more to make this happen. Is there anything else?"

"Yes. Would you like to have lunch with me?"

"I can't. I must be in court in about an hour to assist on another case. I can meet you at five this afternoon, and we could have drinks and maybe eat an early dinner."

"I will meet you at our meeting place out front. See you at five."

As Jason left the office of Mills and Mills, he wondered if he had made the right decision to meet Maggie for dinner. Maybe he should call her and cancel. No, he wanted to see her. There were some things he wanted to know, and other things he needed to know to move on.

Maggie Roth

May Margaret Roth had lived a charmed life as a child growing up in Boston. While she was just a baby, her father started calling her Maggie and it stuck. She spent the first eight years of her education enrolled in a private school. While in grade school and junior high she mastered the piano and was the center of many of the school activities. At the end of her eight-grade year, she asked her parents to put her into a public school. She was quickly accepted and became a cheerleader and became active in the drama club. In her junior and senior year, she joined the mock trial team and developed a passion for the law.

After graduation she decided to attend Boston College, where her mother was a teacher and majored in pre-law. Her senior year she became an apprentice at a small local law firm, and when she graduated, she was hired as a legal aide. She fully intended to go on to law school, but at the time she was living an active social life. She was dating regularly but had no steady boyfriend.

One afternoon, Carol the receptionist asked her if she would mind taking care of the desk while she took a break. She was not feeling good, so Maggie told her to take the rest of the day off and go home. It was only an hour until the end of the day, and she was left in the office all alone. The day was just about to come to an end when in walked a tall, very distinguished, gentleman. She guessed his age to be in the forties. "May I help you?"

"Yes, I am her to see Mr. Jones. We have a four thirty appointment."

"Mr. Jones is not here, and this is not my work station." She shuffled through the material that was scattered on Carol's desk and found the appointment book. He was right. He had an appointment with Mr. Jones. She also found a note attached to the page. The note read: "Mr. Jones was called out of the office. Reschedule Mr. Black." Written in pencil below the note was another message. "Cannot reach Mr. Black." She showed the note to Mr. Black.

"Well, what I need is simple. Just about any lawyer will do. Who else is here?"

Maggie again looked at the appointment book. "Just me, and I can't help you. We have three lawyers in our firm, and they are all out of the office at this time."

Looking down at her name tag, he said, "Well, Miss Maggie, what time do you get off? Your firm can buy me a drink for wasting my time."

For some reason, there was something about him she liked. "How do you know I am a miss or that I don't have someone waiting for me when I get off?"

"I know, because you have not said no yet."

Maggie looked at her watch. "I am the only one here, and I need to lock up. There is a bar across the street named Big Jim's. I will be there in about twenty minutes."

A few minutes later she was being seated in a booth where Cam Black was waiting. "I am glad you came," he said as the waiter placed a glass of water in front of her. "What would you like?"

"Oh, I feel like something refreshing. Bring me a strawberry daiquiri." She looked at him, and she felt very much at ease. She was not bothered by the fact that he was much older than herself. She was just in her twenties, but for some reason it did not make any difference. She liked him, and they spent the next hour talking. About six o'clock he told her he had to leave but asked if she would have dinner with him on the weekend. It was the first of many dates to follow, and they were married six months later. She was somewhat disappointed that he didn't want her to work, and she couldn't seem to connect with his three children from his previous marriage.

One month into the marriage, she noticed that he seemed to change. He was moody and didn't seem to want to do anything. Over the next few months, he started disappearing from work, and she could not account for his missing time. She called his work, and he would be gone. When she confronted him about it, he would simply say he needed to get out of the office for a while. She concluded she was nothing more than a trophy wife, and he was having an affair. It was then that she decided to leave and go to New York.

When Maggie left from her office she was running late. She grabbed her purse and headed for the elevator. She looked at her watch. She was going to be twenty minutes late to meet Jason. She wondered if he would still be there. Exiting the front door, she spotted him and gave a deep sigh of relief. "I am so sorry," she said as she approached him. The meeting took longer than expected. I guess I should have called your office. I am so sorry."

He laughed and said, "That's okay. I once had a date with a girl, and she never showed up at all." The smile left his face. "I am sorry. That was cruel. Please forgive me."

"No, the cruel thing was the girl not showing up. She did not have the courage to face you. She acted like a child and sent her father. It is you that I hope someday can forgive me. You said you were going to take me to dinner. Where would you like to go?"

"Some place quiet and maybe not so crowded. How about Anthony's?"

"I am not really dressed for Anthony's, but if it is okay with you, I can go home and change and meet you there at six."

They both went to their apartments and cleaned up, and at six o'clock he was taking her by the hand and helping her out of a taxi. She had changed into a silver dress that really accented her figure. He decided he would not say anything about how striking she looked. The maître d took them to a table, and like always the restaurant was not crowded. Jason felt this was by design, because the prices were extremely high, but the food was magnificent.

Soon a waiter was pouring water into their glasses and saying, "Can I get you anything from the bar?"

Turning to Maggie, Jason said, "Would you like some wine?" She simply nodded yes.

"Bring us a bottle of Dubonnet," Jason said as he turned back to Maggie.

As the waiter left the table, Maggie shifted in her seat. "You have changed. When we were dating, I don't think you would have known a good bottle of wine from a beer. When did you become such an expert?"

"When I said I owned a farm in Italy. I didn't tell you that among other things it is a winery. Wine in Italy is more plentiful than water. I wish I had one of our labels to share with you."

The waiter returned and poured the wine. "Are you ready to order?"

Orders were placed, and Jason asked, "What happened after you left New York and went back to your husband? Your father told me he was extremely ill."

"Going back to Boston was the second hardest thing I ever had to do. If I had stayed, I would have had to explain to you that I was a married woman, and our love would have become nothing but an affair. You were not having an affair, but I was. That would have been very difficult to explain. I had to go back to Boston and explain you to my husband. The strange thing is he forgave me. I didn't leave anything out, and he forgave me, but his children did not. He fought a good battle against cancer, but he lost. I have been a widow for several years now. He left all his property to his three children. I got one fourth of his other assets and a very large insurance policy. I took the money, studied for the LSAT, passed it and went to law school. The rest you know. I was hired by Mills and Mills. Dad sold me the apartment. So here I am, sitting with a man that I have no idea of how he could not hate me, and yet he is taking me to dinner. Can you explain that?"

He smiled and said, "I thought you were paying. I told you back at the office. I don't hate you. I have moved on. Have you moved on?"

"I am seeing someone. Like me, he has been married before. He is close to my age. Unlike me, he is divorced. We were going to have a date tonight, but when I got back to the apartment, I called him and told him a friend was in town and would only be here a short time."

"Maggie, you should have been more complete in your explanation of me. I was more than just an old friend."

"I know. I have done it again. I have not told him the complete story. It would be very hard to say, I am going to dinner with an old friend who was going to ask me to marry him."

"How did you know I was going to ask you to marry me that night?"

"Dad saw the ring. I know you left the ring in the apartment to show Dad that you were more that a man just having a fling with a runaway wife."

"I had no intention of your father telling you about the ring. Why would your dad tell you that? Was he trying to make your life more difficult?"

"My father is like my mother. He is a teacher, not by trade, but he is a teacher. He wanted me to know the damage that I had done. Let's talk about something else. You said you had moved on. Please tell me how you have moved on besides becoming the richest man I have ever known. You said that we both had moved on. Are you seeing someone?"

"No, no I am not. While I was in Italy, I met a woman. We became more than friends, and I asked her to come back to the U.S. with me. The problem was she was engaged to be married. It was complicated to say the least. I got hurt on the job, and she was my doctor. That is how we met. Her boyfriend was a wine broker and was out of town a lot. As friends we started seeing each other. We started meeting for lunch and one thing led to another and… Well let's just say it didn't work out. I guess we have one thing in common. We have not been lucky in love. What is the name of your new man?"

"Eric Sims. He is also a lawyer. We don't work at the same firm, and we have talked about going to Boston to start our own practice. I guess we are all dreamers."

About that time the waiter came to the table and said, "Will you be requiring anything else?"

"Just the check please." Jason then turned to Maggie, "I guess that was our cue to leave. I am glad we had this dinner together. I hope we can always remain friends." After paying the bill, they went outside and hailed a taxi.

Just before Maggie got into the taxi, she put her arms around Jason and said, "Thank you. I will call you when the will is complete. I may just come to your office. After all, you are just four floors down. How much longer are you going to be here?"

Maggie released her hug and stepped back. Jason looked into her eyes, and just for a moment he wanted to go back to the day she left to go to Boston and ask her to stay with him. She had tears in her eyes, and he knew she felt the same way. He pulled her close again. "I am not sure." He then kissed her on the forehead, and then she got into the taxi and he watched as it drove away.

The next morning, Jason was in his office when he heard a light knock on the door. He looked up and saw Jerry Merrick standing in the doorway. "I got news, and I am not sure if you will see it as good news or bad news."

"What is going on? I am packed and ready to go."

"That is just it. I am not sure you need to go yet. I have just been informed that the paperwork has not been cleared yet. This is always a problem when you deal with foreign governments. The government has promised they will build a road to the dam site. If we don't get a road to the site, we are going to be dead in the water."

"That is not something that I wanted to hear. I wanted to get started on this project. I don't want to be an old man when I return from Peru. How long are we talking about?"

"A few days, a few weeks or maybe a month. I am not sure. If you want, you can fly down and set up the site. But you are going to be living in a tent for a while, and I believe you need to stay here until the camp is ready. You just need to enjoy New York for a while. Just check in to the office each day and hopefully we will get going soon. One thing I am going to need is a painting of what the completed project is going to look like."

"I have already completed one. I thought I had already sent it to you. I guess I have had too much on my mind. I have one right here."

That afternoon, he walked up to Central Park. He had never taken the time to explore all the city. Except for showing Billy and Rachel the tourist sites, he had never really toured the cultural part of the city.

In the next couple of days, he took in all the attractions and really developed an appreciation for the city's history and culture.

A couple of days later, he decided he needed to stop by the office and check on the progress of the project and check his messages. Finding he was still on hold, he decided to have lunch at the hotdog stand. He was standing in line when he glanced over to the small wall that he used to sit on, and there sat Maggie. He got his hotdog and coke and walked toward her. She had not seen him, and for a moment his feelings for her came back. She was a gorgeous woman. He walked closer. "How about some company?"

She looked up and when she saw who he was, she smiled. Saying nothing, she moved her purse to the side and patted the area next to her.

He took a seat. "I was going to call you to check on the progress of the will, but I have found that my trip to Peru is on hold, and we have plenty of time."

It will be finished today. Just call in the morning, and we can arrange a time. What are you up to today?"

"Well, I am not doing any work here. I am just waiting. Did you tell Eric about me?"

"I did, and it did not go well. He told me that I could not see you anymore. I told him that I was your lawyer, and he was not going to tell me who I could see or not see. He got mad and walked out. Later he called me and said he was sorry, and I told him to go to hell."

"Surely you two didn't break up."

"No. He has sent me a bouquet of flowers with a nice note saying he is sorry. I will keep him on hold for a few days. I have let my father and my husband control my life. Eric will not. I care for him, but he will have to understand, I am going to be an independent woman."

"How about a non-date?"

"What do you mean a non-date?"

"I was going to take my friend Mary to a play tonight. I purchased three tickets because JoAnn was going to go with us, but for some reason she can't go. Why don't you join us? We are going to see the King and I."

"Sounds like fun. Non-date. Friends going out and having fun. What time do I need to be ready?"

"The play starts at eight. How about I pick you up at six-forty-five?"

When the taxi arrived at Maggie's apartment, Mary and Jason were already in it, and Maggie was sitting out front waiting. They went straight to the theater. When it was over, they walked down the street to a bar and had drinks and talked about the play. When they got into the taxi, Mary insisted that she be dropped off first, and it was almost like she wanted Maggie and Jason to spend time together. From what Jason had told her, there was no chance for Jason with Gabi, and he might never see Gabi again. She liked Maggie, and she thought they were a perfect match for each other. After Mary was dropped off at her apartment, Jason and Maggie were in the taxi alone. Jason felt somewhat guilty. He was alone with a woman that was seeing another man. Should he even care? His thoughts turned to Gabi, but as he looked at Maggie, he pushed the thoughts from his mind.

When the taxi stopped to drop off Maggie, she leaned over and kissed Jason. It was not a passionate kiss, but it was on the lips. It was a brief kiss and after she left the taxi and had entered her apartment, he found himself wanting more.

On Thursday morning, Jason stopped by his office to find out that the paperwork had all been approved and that he was ready to leave on Saturday. He decided to stay in his office and go over the last details, knowing he would have limited contact with the home office while in Peru. About ten o'clock a secretary handed him a note from Maggie telling him his will was finished and for him to stop by and sign. He decided he would just go ahead to her office and get it finished. When he got there, she was not busy, and he was soon sitting across from her desk.

"I have completed the changes that you requested. We have named Elmer Hall as the executor of your will. You have requested this company to assist Mr. Hall in carrying out your wishes. Mr. Hall will receive three percent for his role in being the executor and this company will receive three percent compensation. I will need for you to sign this. I have asked Mrs. Lewis to witness the signing."

Jason was given a copy of the will, and the law firm filed the other.

Jason picked up his copy of the will and stood up. "My time is up. I am leaving this Saturday for Peru. I am not sure when I will be back. It may be a real long time. I was wondering if you might have dinner with me tomorrow night. I really could use the company."

"I really and truly wish I could, but I can't. Eric's parents are in town and we are having dinner with them. I guess we might not see each other again for a while." She came around the table and gave him a hug. They lingered for just a moment before they parted. When they stepped apart, she said, "Thanks for coming to see me and insisting that I handle the making of this will. It means a lot."

He returned to his office and went around and told the staff goodbye and went to his apartment. What a waste he thought. *I am paying a fortune for this place and I am very seldom here.* He picked up the phone and called Mary.

"Mary, I need a favor. When I get back from Peru, I am going home, and I will not need this apartment. When I hang up this phone, I am going to call the building manager and inform them that I no longer want this suite. I need for you to clean this place out and send my belongings to my home in Richmond. It will just be my personal items. Everything else stays with the apartment. I am leaving on Saturday. I am going to pack up tomorrow, spend my last night here and look forward to seeing you when I get back."

By Friday night he had his bags packed and waiting at the door. He took a shower, put on a pair of sweat pants and a tea shirt and poured himself a glass of wine. He had started reading, *The Fountainhead, by* Ann Rand. He had started reading it on the trip back from Rome but had not had time to finish it while back in New York. He became engrossed in the story and time slipped away. It was about midnight when he heard a gentle knock on his door. He looked through the peep hole to see Maggie standing there. He opened the door and she said, "I couldn't let you leave without seeing you one more time."

Neither moved as he asked, "Where is Eric?"

"It doesn't matter. He took his parents back to their hotel."

Jason reached for her hand and gently pulled her inside the apartment and closed the door. He took her in his arms and kissed her first on the lips and then down her neck. Neither said anything as he guided her into his bedroom.

It was almost three o'clock. Jason was awake staring at the ceiling. Maggie was asleep and had turned away from him. He turned toward her, and the light from the street gave enough light for him to see her in the dim light. He reached out and took his finger and traced a question mark out on her back. She awoke and turned toward him. "You can't sleep?"

"No. I was just thinking. My life is a mess. What if I asked you to wait for me? I could finish this project or maybe get someone to take it over once I get it started."

"What if I asked you not to go? If you asked me to wait, that would be unfair to me, and if I asked you to stay, that would be unfair to you. I am not going to wait, and you are not going to stay. It is what it is. If we could go back in time, could we fix all of this? We can't. When you came back from Rome, you told me that you had moved on. Have you moved on? What was her name? It was Gabi, wasn't it?" She moved closer and pressed against him. I am never going to tell Eric about this night, and if by some miracle you can be with Gabi or even someone else, you will never tell them either. This night belongs to you and me."

South America and Beyond

On the trip to Peru, Jason found that he regretted his decision to take on this project. He had to change planes three times on the trip. When his plane finally landed in Lima, and he debarked from the plane, he saw a large man holding a sign with his name on it. He approached the man and said, "I am Jason Terry. I am so glad you have come to meet me. I need some help finding my way around."

"No hablo inglés. ¿Hablas español?"

Jason reached up and scratched his head. "Oh shit. I am really in trouble now."

The big man grinned. "Shit is not a Spanish word. I was joking with you. I don't know much more Spanish than I just spoke. Well, maybe a little more. Let's get your luggage and get you to the hotel."

The man's name was Lewis Grant. On the way to the hotel, Jason was able to find out the site for the dam was set up and waiting for him. The road to the site was not much more than a cow path, and it would take at least four hours to get there. He was to spend the night in the hotel, and if he needed to make any phone calls, that would be his last chance for a while. Communication from the site was by short wave and limited at best.

Lewis was right. It was a rough ride to the site. When they had traveled for about two hours, Jason, who had talked very little said, "I thought that the government was going to build a road to the site."

Lewis, with a grin on his face said, "They did, and this is it."

"You got to be kidding."

"I am. They have promised by the time we need major materials from Lima the road will be completed. Don't expect much, but anything is better than this."

They had to cross the mountains. The road was narrow and winding, and a couple of times they had to stop to let Jason throw up. It seemed to take forever. When they came to the site, he found they had set up a large tent for him to live in, and there was a construction trailer to work from and to hold meetings in.

"How in the hell did you get that trailer here?" he asked.

"Don't ask, but we did. It took several days."

Construction was slow and nasty. The government of Peru improved the road and put down gravel, and that speeded up the delivery of the needed materials for the dam. If it wasn't hot and dust blowing in your face, it was raining, and they were wading in mud. Living in a tent produced its own set of challenges. Twice during the first year there, his tent was destroyed by high wind and heavy rain. The rain and wind also destroyed parts of the road, and that delayed the project. It took about a year for the dam to start to take shape. During the first year he went back to Lima only a couple of times. His only contact with the New York office was by short wave radio to Lima, and he had to communicate through a third party. The road with all the heavy traffic was getting better, and the four-hour trip to Lima could be made in two. At the end of two years, the dam was behind schedule. The project was more demanding than anyone had anticipated. Jason was now spending more time in Lima. He could call his office and keep track of his businesses and friends. He called Billy once a month and the Aparos about every two months. Each time he called Italy he was tempted to ask about Gabi, but he did not. That part of his life was now behind him.

Heavy rains had delayed the project several times, and his stay in Peru was going to be a year longer than expected. As often as he tried not to, he often thought of Gabi. She would be married, and maybe she was a doctor in Rome. He wondered if she had children. During the third year of construction he found himself spending more time in Lima. He had found a bar which had a restaurant in it. It was called El Gato Rojo. He was beginning to really enjoy food with a Latin flavor.

Each time he came to Lima, he would spend his nights there. He would eat, then go to the bar and order drinks and listen to the singers. He even found he was picking up the language.

After a long three years, the project came to an end, and he was flying back to the States. When he got back to New York he again received a large bonus. He also had not been anywhere he could spend his money. *A nice problem to have,* he thought. *I have three years of income to figure out what to do with.*

Before he left New York, he spent time with Mary and JoAnn. Billy had forwarded his mail to him in Peru, and he had not received any correspondence from Gabi. Perhaps she had not found out who the girl in the cave was, or she did not want to have any contact with him. He also found out that Maggie had married Eric Sims, and she was expecting her second child. *Water under the bridge,* he thought.

As the plane left the runway, Jason could see the city getting smaller as the plane gained altitude. A chapter in his life had come to an end. He was not coming back to the construction firm. He had a deep feeling of sadness. He had accomplished so much. He was rich, but he had no one to share it with. He couldn't see spending the rest of his life in a big house with just himself and Billy and Margie. He then thought of Rachel. She was very much a part of what he wanted to do. He wanted her to be a part of his new business adventure.

He had been back in Richmond about two weeks when he carried out the decision he had made before he left New York. He would leave the New York office. He sent a letter of resignation that very afternoon and called Rachel. On the phone he said, "Rachel, this is Jason. Can you have dinner with me tonight?"

She agreed, and he called the Land's End Restaurant and made a reservation. It was a very liberal establishment and allowed African-Americans. But because their prices were so high, few people of color could afford to come. At 8:00 they were seated at a very private table. "Jason this is so nice, but why have you asked me here? I have not seen you for three years, and during that time you have only written to me about six times."

"I need to ask you some questions."

"You did not need to bring me here to ask me questions."

"You are right, I didn't. I wanted to see you, and I hope we can turn this into sort of a celebration. The first question. You have been working for the same company for more than four years. Have you received a raise or promotion during that time?"

"No, I have not, but I am paid more than any person of color that I know. The pay is good, and I am happy."

"Would you leave if a company offered you more money?"

"No, I am content, and I like the security. I like living in Lexington. There are many things to do, and I am close to Billy and Margie. Money is not that important."

"Would you leave if you were offered more responsibility?"

Before she could answer, a waiter came to the table. "Would you like to place a drink order while you look at the menu?"

Jason looked at the wine list, and then looked up at Rachel. "Would you like some champagne?"

Rachel did not let on that she had never had champagne. "Yes, I would like some champagne."

Jason turned back to the waiter and said, "Bring us a bottle of your best champagne please."

The waiter did not move. He leaned over and quietly said, "Sir, are you aware that would cost a hundred dollars a bottle?"

Jason almost whispered back, "If that is all it costs then bring two bottles. If we don't drink the second bottle, we will take it with us. If we drink them both, we will get a third."

The waiter quickly left the table and Jason said, "Where were we? Oh yes, I had just asked you if you would leave your job if you were offered a job that had more responsibility."

Rachel did not answer the question but said, "What are you getting at? Where are all these questions leading?"

Jason picked up his menu and said, "Let's decide what we are going to eat, and I will let you know."

It wasn't long until the champagne came, and they had placed their orders. Rachel could not even pronounce what she had ordered. Jason had to explain it to her. She fell in love with the taste of champagne, and she was on her second glass before the food arrived at the table. "Go easy on the grapes, Rachel. You need to have all your senses about you to answer my next question."

The champagne had already done its thing. Rachel giggled, "Okay."

Once they had finished eating, Jason said, "I am leaving the New York firm. I am going to start my own firm here in Lexington. You do not need to let me know right away, but I would like for you to come and work for me. I will start you out at twenty-five percent more than you are making now, and you will have your own office. If things go well, we will discuss a partnership."

"You don't even know how much I make. How can you make me such a deal?"

"I have done my research. I know what I must do to create a company that can produce a great product and make money. I know there is a need here. In the future this area is going to need roads, taller buildings and schools. This is what we can design and create. I know how much you make, and all I am doing is offering you what you should be making anyway."

"Mm let me think about it. Okay, I thought about it. The answer is yes, yes, yes."

"No, I want you to really think about it. You don't have a clear head. We will discuss it over coffee in a day or two. You can have more champagne now."

The next day, Jason went to the basement and opened a room that he kept locked. There was a cedar chest, and it too was locked. He opened the chest and took out a box that contained his medals. He opened the case that held the Congressional Medal of Honor. Inside there was an envelope. It contained the events of the day when he became a hero. He had never read it. It had a list of witnesses, and as he scanned down the list one name stood out. It was a priest, Father Danti Borelli. The next day, he booked a flight back to Rome.

On the flight to Rome, he could not stop thinking of Gabi, but she was not the purpose of his trip. He really did not want to see her. He didn't want to have to go through all the pleasantries of saying, "How is Tobia, do you have children, are you still practicing medicine?"

Bullshit on that. It would be just too difficult. He had to move on. She had moved on. He thought of Father Borelli. Gabi must have told him about the person who carved the relief of the church. Why didn't he seek him out? There were many questions that were not answered. He made up his mind that he would not leave Italy until he had all the answers.

When he disembarked from the plane Jason decided he would be in no hurry. He would tour the city. His first full day in Rome, he took a tour, and on the second day went to Pisa. He had rented a car, and on the third day he was on his way to Caseno. He knew that Gabi would no longer be there. When he got to the city, he drove straight through and made his way to his villa.

He stopped his rental in front of the villa and made his way up the steps to the front door. *I have got to get rid of these iron monsters that serve as door knockers. They are no way to greet guests.* He brought down the monster's head three times, and waited until he heard the latch of the door turn on the inside. When the door opened, there stood Ana. She called out his name and gave him a big hug. "When did you get back in Italy?" She did not wait for him to answer. "Please come in?"

After a few minutes, she was pouring him coffee, and he started inquiring about her brothers. She informed him that they were out on the farm working, and if he wanted to see them right away, she would walk with him. "No, that can wait. I want to sit here and enjoy the coffee. You Italians drink your coffee much stronger than we do in America, and I have missed this strong flavor."

Ana poured herself a cup of coffee and took her seat at the table. "How was Peru?'

"Like dying and going to hell. I thought that I would never see the completion of that dam."

"Where are you going next?"

A big smile covered his face. "I am going back to my home town. I have left the New York firm and I am thinking about starting my own construction business."

Ana took a sip of her coffee. "Good for you. I keep telling Michael he needs to slow down. He seems like he is gone so much."

"Where is he now?'

"He is in Caseno. He is between jobs. He will really be excited to see you. He should return in about an hour."

Jason stumbled for the right words and then said, "Did you attend Gabi's wedding? You two seem to have become friends."

"I have something that I need to tell you. I did not attend the wedding. Shortly after you left, Michael and I got married. He took a short leave from his company, and he took me to Paris. We spent several weeks seeing the sites of Paris and the French countryside. We have an apartment in Caseno. When he is on a job, I stay here. When we got back from our honeymoon, Gabi was gone."

"That is wonderful. I mean about your marriage. I wish you would have let me know. I would have love to attend." *This damn job in Peru has caused me to miss the wedding of two of my best friends and maybe any chance I had with Gabi.*

"We talked about it. But we really didn't know where you were. You were either in America or getting ready to travel to Peru. It would have been so unfair for you to have to fly back to Italy and then make that long journey to Peru. Now to answer your question. When we returned, Gabi was gone from Caseno. I thought she might drop me a letter, but I have heard nothing. You have not heard anything either?"

Jason stood up. "No, I have not. I am going to my room. I need to clean up and rest a while. When the boys get here and Michael returns, do you want to go to Angelo's for dinner?"

"No, we are not going to do that. I am going to fix us a meal here, and we can enjoy each other's company and get caught up."

After he took a shower, he felt much better but tired. He stretched out on the bed and soon was asleep. He dreamed of the day he and Gabi had picnicked along the creek. In his dream he was so happy. When he awoke from the dream, he said to himself, *I wonder where she is?* He dressed and went downstairs to find Michael reading a newspaper in the great room. When Michael saw him, he rose to his feet and gave him a hug.

"You were right. You told me just before you left that you were going to steal my housekeeper away, and you did. Congratulations."

"Well, I didn't steal her completely. She still takes care of your house. She does come to my job sites some, but the brothers take care of the house when she is away."

That night Ana had fixed a very traditional Italian meal. Bread baked Italian chicken, salad, and wine. While they were eating Luke spoke up. "Jason what do you think of the wine?"

Jason picked up his glass and took another sip. "It is very good. I really like it."

Bonita smiled. He handed the bottle to Jason. "Take a look at the label."

Jason looked at the label and read it. It said Ana Marino's Villa Red. "I have not checked, are we in full production?"

Luke picked up the bottle. "We are, and this is one of four labels. Sales are going well. We have been working with a company that represents us. Our wines are now in sixty-two wine outlets in Italy and thirty-six restaurants in Rome and Naples. We even have one on the Isle of Capri. We are making money. Our vegetable business is now only a small percent of our total bottom line. We need to sit down with you, because we may need to hire someone else for our vegetable sales."

After the meal, and when all the dishes were put up, Jason sat down on the couch in the great room. Bonita and Luke went to their trailer, and Michael and Ana came in and joined Jason. Michael looked at his watch. "I think we are heading back to town now. Will we see you sometime tomorrow?"

"Michael, you don't have to keep an apartment in town. This is now nothing more to me than a vacation home. You and Ana can live here. When I come back to visit, I could be your guest."

"That is so kind of you. Ana and I will talk it over. Do you want to visit the dam site while you are here? You know they put a brass plate on the base of the dam. It lists you as the architect. I understand that was your first job."

"It was, and I would like to see the dam. Why don't we drive out there in the morning?"

That night, as Jason went to sleep, in his dreams he found himself back in the cave. It was not a nightmare, but in the dream, he was a hero. When he woke up he thought about the dream. Maybe he would soon know what happened to the young girl. It would bring closure to the events that occurred so long ago.

The next day he was standing at the base of the dam looking at the brass plaque. "I didn't bring a camera, but someday in the future could you take a photo and send me a copy. I would like to put it in my scrapbook. I can't get over how much the vegetation and bushes have grown in three years."

Michael started walking up the hill toward the top of the dam. "The government has stocked the lake with fish, and about a mile up the lake they have built a beach. Recreation in this area is really picking up. It is my understanding that they are going to make some road improvements. That will help even more."

By noon Jason was standing in front of a church. He opened the door and walked in. The first thing he saw was the wooden relief that he had given Gabi. It was displayed on the wall just inside the front door. There were just a few people inside. Most were old, and most were women. He took a seat four rows from the front. He sat and waited until he saw a priest come from the right. The priest spotted him and came over and took a seat next to him. "Are you in trouble my son? I have not seen you here before."

Jason spoke in a very low voice, "I am in trouble, and I think you can ease my mind. You said you have never seen me before, but I don't think that is true."

"No, I don't remember seeing you before." Father Borrelli was becoming just a little uncomfortable. "You don't go to church here. How is it that you think you know me?"

"You and I have a common friend. Her name is Gabi Acosta. I did the relief of the Church of the Three Bells. I found out just about a week ago that you were the priest of the church before it was destroyed."

All this time the priest had been facing the front of the church, but now he shifted and faced Jason. "You are Jason Edward Terry. I along with many other people, owe you my life. I know from what Gabi has told me that you did not come here expecting any gratitude. You have been gone for three years. Are you doing okay?"

"I am, and you are right. I came to find out one thing, but since I got here, I need to know two. I want to know the name of the young girl who was shot and found with me in the cave. I don't want to find her, I just want to know what ever happened to her."

"You said you wanted to know something else. What would that be?"

"I would like to know where Gabi is. I would like to know if she is okay. I really don't want to see her or the young girl that was in the cave. That is not the purpose of this visit. I just need some closure to the events of the war."

Father Borrelli turned back and again faced the front of the church. Not looking at Jason he said, "You are not going to like either answer, because they are the same. Gabi left Caseno after you did. She told me if you ever came looking for her not to disclose where she is. The young girl gave me the same request. She did not want anybody to know who she is. It is not that she is not grateful for what you did for her. She is. I think this may be a part of her life she wants to leave behind her. You said that you are not looking for her, but you just want to know if she is okay. I assure you she is. I gave my word, and I will not tell you who she is or where she lives." Father Borrelli did want Jason to know the entire truth, but he had given his word he would not disclose where Gabi was.

"Father Borrelli, I understand you keeping your word, and I respect that. But this makes no sense. The young girl would not know who I am. After all this time why would she think that I would come looking for her? If I did want to meet her, why would she not want to meet me? You said that she does not want to relive this part of her life. Wouldn't she want some type of closure? I have come a very long way for this information. I know that Gabi told me that she would be moving to Rome after the wedding. I am not going to Rome looking for her. I understand why she does not want to see me. I fell in love with her. I asked her to come back to the United States with me. She said no, even though I think she might have loved me too. It looks like I have made a long trip for nothing. Thank you for your time."

"The girl with you in the cave knows who you are. She has seen the relief. I think I know why she doesn't want to meet you. She lost a lot during the war. Like you, I don't think she wants to face it again." Father Borrelli stood up. "Do you have time to make a short trip with me? I think it may help you." *I gave my word that I would not tell Jason anything. I said nothing about showing him things.*

Jason agreed, and in a few minutes, they were in Jason's car going up a long hill. Jason could see grave markers on both sides of the narrow road. About half way up the hill, Father Borrelli said, "Turn to the right, here. Go until you see a large grave stone that has fallen. It will be on the right. When you see it, stop."

Jason did as he was told, and the two men got out of the car. "Follow me," Father Borrelli said as he started walking up the hill. Then he stopped.

Jason being somewhat confused said, "What is it that you want to show me?'

Father Borrelli stopped and pointed at a grave. "I wanted to show you the grave of the woman you did not save that awful day." He pointed at the grave marker.

Jason fell to his knees and said, "I am so sorry about that day. If anyone deserves a medal that day it was you." He read the name, Gabrielle DeSantis, Loving Wife, Mother and Grandmother. Jason did not get up. His eyes turned to a smaller marker on the same lot. He read the name, Sofia DeSantis Acosta. He read the name a second time. Sofia DeSantis Acosta. It was like he was kicked in the stomach. *How could I have been so blind?* Tears began to roll down his cheeks. When he got himself under control he turned to the priest. "Why did she not tell me that the lady in the church was her grandmother and she was the girl in the cave?"

Father Borrelli walked over and placed his hand on Jason's shoulder. "There is a lot more to the story, but only Gabi can tell you. Listen to what I am going to say. I have a brother in Rome. His name is Doctor Alonso Borrelli. If you ever see him, give him my regards. Jason, would you pray with me?"

Jason drove Father Borrelli back to his church. As he got out of the car he said, "Jason, I don't know what you are going to do, but I am going to ask you to forgive me and remember this. Sometimes you do the wrong things for the right reasons. There is more to your story than you know. If you want to know the rest of the story, you will have to find Gabi. Whatever you do, or you don't, it is up to you. When I found out that you were in Caseno, I did not seek you out. I should have, and I thank you for what you did for Gabi. I thank you for what you did for me and many of the people of this city. If you stay in Caseno for a while, please come to Mass. I know that you are not Catholic, but it would mean a lot to me."

As Jason drove away from the church, he wondered what Father Borrelli meant when he said that there was more to his story. He thought he knew everything he needed to know. He had met Father Borrelli. He knew who the girl in the cave was and knew where his dreams came from. What else was there? What did Father Borrelli mean when he asked him to forgive him, and said that sometimes we do the wrong things for the right reasons? He glanced down at his watch, and it was 1:30. He wanted to get something to eat, so he decided to stop by and see Angelo.

Angelo was delighted to see him. He showed him to a table. He left and came back with a bottle of wine and two glasses. "You will like this wine. It comes from your winery. Tell me where you have been. How long has it been, over three years I think?"

"I have been living in Peru, and it was not the best experience of my life."

Angelo raised his hand, and a waitress came to the table. "Do you want the special? It will be my treat."

Jason nodded, "That will be fine. What ever happened to Gabi? Did you go to her wedding?"

"That is the strangest thing. She was going to be married here at the Catholic church. Father Borrelli was going to do the ceremony even though she never considered herself a Catholic. About two weeks before the wedding, she comes to me and says that she has decided to get married in Rome. Can you believe it? She decided to get married in Rome? She tells me that she has decided she wants a private wedding, and the only guests are going to be her family. I thought I was her family. She left her job at the hospital, moved to Rome, and I have not seen her since."

At first Jason did not say anything. He was thinking about what Father Borrelli had said about him not knowing the rest of the story. Was this what he was referring to?

"That is strange. Before I left Caseno to go to Peru, I gave Gabi my address and asked her to write to me. She did not. Before I came back to Italy, I had made up my mind not to try to find her, but now I might. I am just not sure. I am going to stay around here for a few days, and then I am going back to America. I am going to start my own business."

Angelo got up from the table. "If you find Gabi, tell her that I love her, and I wish she would come and see me?"

When he finished eating, he went back to the villa. Ana was working in the kitchen and Michael was sitting at the table. He greeted them and walked over and got a coffee cup from the sideboard. "Is this coffee hot? I could use some."

They talked about the dam project and Michael's new project and then Michael said, "Jason, I am going to ask you something and if you say no, we understand. You will not hurt our feelings."

Jason blew on his coffee to cool it down. "Say what's on your mind."

"Some of your property in the front borders the main road. There is a corner section that would make a great place to build a house. A short driveway would give that lot easy access to the road. Ana and I would like to buy an acre lot from you to build a house. We want to live here."

Jason did not smile, "No, I am not going to sell you an acre." He paused and then broke into a big smile. "I am not selling you a lot. I am giving you a lot for a wedding present."

Ana rushed to him and gave him a big hug. "You don't have to give it to us, we will gladly buy it."

"No, I am going to give it to you. I will call my lawyer, who arranged for me to buy this villa, and make all the arrangements. I also need to separate the villa from the rest of the property. We can get these both done at the same time."

Ana looked somewhat confused. "Jason, are you going to sell the villa? After you left to go to Peru, a couple of men came by and surveyed the property. Michael asked them what they were doing, and they said they were going to put the house on a separate deed."

"No, I don't have any plans to sell it. I just needed to expand my options."

The next morning Jason and Michael went to see the lawyer and started the process. They were told that once a survey of the property was done, he would have the papers ready to sign. Jason told him he planned to go back to America in a few days and if the papers were not ready, send them to his home in Richmond.

The next day Jason was on his way to Rome. Once he was in Rome, he went to the first hospital he could find. The hospital did not have a Doctor Alonso Borrelli, but he was listed in their directory. He was able to find out which hospital he worked in, and looking over the receptionist's shoulder, he saw his home address. Asking directions several times he finally found the home. For a few minutes he sat in his car and rehearsed what he was going to say. *My name is Jason Terry. I am a friend of Doctor Gabi Acosta. I have been out of the country for the last three years and have lost track of her. Could you tell her that I came by and would like to see her? If she is not here in Rome, just tell her I will be at the villa for the next ten days and to give me a call.*

Walking up to the door he almost changed his mind. He knocked on the door three times and almost wished that no one would come to the door. In a few moments, the door was opened and there stood a woman in her sixties, streaks of grey in her hair, an elegant woman. Next to her was a little girl about two years old. Her hair was jet black, and she had large oval eyes, and before he could speak the little girl wrapped her arms around the lady's legs.

"Don't be scared. The nice man is not going to hurt you. I am sorry, she is a bit shy. Once she warms up to you, you can't stop her from talking. Can I help you?"

"I am here to see Doctor Borrelli. Is he in?"

"Please come in. Doctor Borrelli is at the hospital. If you will wait here, I will get you one of his cards that will have his office phone number and address." She walked away and went to a desk that was in the foyer. The little girl was about to walk away when Jason said, "What is your name?'

"Sophie."

"That is a nice name. Are you Sophie Martin?"

"No silly. My name is Sophie Terry."

At that time Mrs. Borrelli came back with the card. "If you give my husband a call, I am sure he can make you an appointment."

Jason was in shock. Why did the little girl refer to herself as Sophie Terry? As Jason took the card, he could see into the living room and on the wall was the painting of Gabi at the creek. "I can see you have a painting on the wall. Is that your daughter?"

"We think of Gabi as our daughter. Would you like to take a closer look at the painting? We are so proud of it. It is a source of great pleasure, and it is also a source of some pain."

As they stood in front of the painting, Jason said, "I see the artist signed his name as Jason Terry, and the little girl just told me her name was Sophie Terry. Is there a connection?"

"Yes. There is. The painting was done by Gabi's husband. Right after their wedding, he said he had to go back to America, and he never came back. He does not even know he has a daughter. I don't know why I am telling you all this. I am sure you will have no trouble making an appointment once you get to the hospital, or you could just make a phone call. Do you want to call from here?"

"That won't be necessary. I will go to the hospital. Thank you so much for the information." He then looked at the little girl. *What in the hell is going on?*

A confused Jason made his way back to his car. Taking a seat behind the wheel, he said out loud to himself, "What is going on? I have a daughter and I am married to Gabi? Am I living in some type of alternate universe?" He sat in the car for about ten minutes, and then reached for the ignition key, turned it to the right and started the car. Before he pulled away from the Borrelli's he looked at the card that Mrs. Borrelli had given him. *I will go to the hospital and see Doctor Borrelli.* Then he thought for a moment. He was confused. Was Sophie his daughter? He thought about the night that he and Gabi had spent together. Maybe she was. He wanted to go back and see Sophie again. *No, that is not a good idea.*

After driving for some thirty minutes and stopping to ask questions four times, he pulled into the hospital parking lot. Wasting no time, he was soon in the reception area looking at the directory posted on the wall. The first name listed under Doctors was Doctor Alonso Borrelli. Then another name caught his eye. He saw the name, Doctor Gabi Acosta Terry. He left the directory and walked to the reception desk. He was greeted by a young lady who smiled and said. "May I help you?"

His voice barely came out, and he choked a little. "I would like to see Doctor Terry."

The young lady continued to smile and said, "I am sorry. Doctor Terry is on the hospital staff, but she does not make appointments. She takes care of patients who have been admitted to the hospital. Do you wish to make an appointment with another doctor?"

Thinking fast, he answered her with a lie. "I am a patient. I think I might be having a heart attack, or maybe it is another panic attack. I just don't know. Doctor Terry told me to rush back if I didn't know what to do. I need to see her now."

The young receptionist stood up and called for an orderly. "Bring a wheelchair quickly," she shouted, and soon Jason was being wheeled down a hallway to an emergency room. It wasn't long until a nurse was taking his temperature and taking his blood pressure. "You must have had a panic attack. Everything seems normal now. We will have Doctor Terry look just to be safe. While we are waiting, I need some information for your chart. What is your name?"

"My name, my name is Jason Edwards."

"Mr. Edwards, if you will lie back on the examination table, I will see what is keeping Doctor Terry."

It was not long until Gabi came through the door. She didn't even look at Jason but picked up his chart and started looking at it. She didn't even look up. "I don't remember treating you for panic attacks before. Mr. Edwards, how long have you been having these panic attacks?"

Jason sat up and positioned himself on the side of the table. "Ever since I met you. I have been in a constant state of panic."

Gabi turned and faced him. She said nothing. She just stood there. About that time the nurse came back into the examination room. "It's okay. Leave us alone. Mr. Edwards is not sick. I will see that he checks out."

Jason got up and walked over and stood in front of Gabi. "When do you get off work? You have a lot of explaining to do."

"I do, but I cannot do it now. It is good to see you, Jason. I can see you are back from Peru. Meet me out front in about an hour."

One hour later Gabi was walking through the hospital parking lot. Jason got out of the car and walked around and opened the door for her. Once he was back in the driver's seat, he shifted around toward her and said, "I feel very uncomfortable. A part if me wants to take you in my arms and hold you forever. There is another part of me that wants to smack the hell out of you. Gabi, I need answers. Where can we go to be alone?"

She told him of a tavern that was about a half mile away. She did not speak again until they were seated in a small booth in the back. They seemed to be completely alone. Then she spoke. "Jason, I need the part of you that wants to give me a hug to hold me just for a moment."

He got out of his booth and came over and sat down beside her. As he put his arm around her, she laid her head on his shoulder and started to cry. He did not say anything but started thinking about his conversation with Father Borrelli. *Is this what he meant when he said, I didn't know all my story and only Gabi could tell me? What did he mean when he said, sometimes you have to do something wrong for the right reason?*

When she stopped crying, he said, "You know we have been in much worse situations."

"I can't think of any," her voice barely came out.

"Several years ago, we were lying in a cave bleeding to death. I don't think either of us is going to die today. Today I find out that I am married, and I didn't enjoy the wedding. I have met Sophie by the way. She is amazing. She is my daughter?"

Jason got up and took his seat opposite Gabi, so he could see her as they talked. He motioned for the waitress and ordered two glasses of bourbon.

When the waitress returned, she set the bourbon on the table. "I think you will like this. It comes from Kentucky in the United States."

He gave her a smile. "I am from Kentucky. This bourbon is made about sixty miles from where I live."

The waitress left, and Jason looked at Gabi whose eyes were red from crying. "I don't like bourbon, but I think we both need something strong."

"After you left, I found out I was pregnant. I knew you were the father, because until you and I spent the night together, I had never been with a man. I did not know what to do. You were who knows where. You had given me your address, and I couldn't figure out if I should write you or not. It is not good for an unmarried woman to have a child. Sophie would have become an outcast. I knew that if I told Tobia, he might marry me anyway, but I didn't want to do him that way. I went to see Father Borrelli. We came up with a plan. It may have been a stupid plan, but I left the hospital in Caseno and went to Enna. The Borrellis have a cousin there. I stayed with her until the baby was born. While I was there, Father Borrelli was telling everyone that I had left Italy and gone to the United States. People were told that while I was in the United States, I got married. When I returned with the child to Rome, we told everyone that you took a job in Peru and left me. I have made you a villain in Rome. I have not been back to see anybody in Caseno, because there was a chance you would come back there. I thought you would be gone for two years, but looks like it was three. I have been staying with Doctor Borrelli and his wife. As far as they know, you abandoned me with a child, but they feel like proud grandparents. I named Sophie after my mother."

All Jason could say was, "Wow." *Sometimes you must do something wrong for the right reason.*

"Wow is right. What are we going to do?"

"Do you think that we could get by with the truth?"

Gabi reached up and wiped a single tear that had made its way onto her cheek, "I think we are beyond the truth. I know that some part of you must hate me. I should have written to you and told you the truth. I can't correct that. I think we should leave things as they are. You should go back to the United states and let everyone think I am an abandoned wife."

"Gabi, you are not thinking. Do you not know me at all? There is no way I am going to leave my daughter in Italy growing up without a father. We must come up with something else. When we were getting to know each other back in Caseno, you called me Mr. Triple A. I never told you a lot about me. You assumed I was rich, but I have not always been so. You were right. I am not just rich. I am really rich. The villa doesn't even represent a fiftieth of the wealth that I have. It seems to me, I should have enough money to fix our problem."

"This doesn't seem to be a problem that money can fix."

"Hear me out. The first thing we need to do is fix our wedding. It must go from a fake wedding to a real one. Father Borrelli is already complicit in this. I think he may take a bribe and marry us for real. He needs to be convinced to back date the marriage to when you and he faked the marriage. We will need witnesses to the wedding. Ana and Michael will help us. The last thing will be the toughest." He gave her a big smile. "You will have to forgive me for abandoning you."

Gabi was not smiling. She was overwhelmed by the events of the day. "You are still willing to marry me?"

"Don't ask silly questions."

"This question is not silly. Father Borrelli might go along with doing this, but do you think the government officials will record a back dated marriage?"

Jason laughed. "From what I know of Italian officials, they will do anything if the price is right. If they can't be bought, we shall fly to the United States and get married there. Can you get some time off to come to the villa? We need a few days alone for you to forgive your cruel husband and to get things rolling. While we are there, I will paint a picture of Sophie to soften the Borrellis, and maybe they will start to forgive me."

Tears started rolling down Gabi's cheeks again. She didn't say anything, she just sat there.

Jason got serious. "I am sorry, Gabi. This may not be what you want. But it is what I want. I need and want you, and I want to be near my daughter."

"Are you going to be near her? Your last job took you out of the country for three years. That is one of the reasons I didn't leave with you when you asked me. I was in love, but love was not enough. You were asking me to come to America and live alone for two years that ended up being three. Do you know where you are going next?"

After taking a drink of his bourbon, he said, "I hope to be going home. I want my family to meet my wife and daughter. I have quit my job in New York. Rachel and I are going to start our own business, and we will only be bidding on local jobs. If you can't agree to that, would you try to get your job back in Caseno. We could live in the villa."

"You need to take me home. I know you want to meet your daughter, but I think it best that we both get to know you again. You need to go back to the villa and wait for me. Tonight, I am going to tell Alonso and Vanna that my husband has come back. I will tell them that you want to come back into my life, and I am willing to try for the sake of Sophie. They know that you own a villa just outside of Caseno, so I am going to tell them that I am going to take Sophie there to meet you."

Jason drove Gabi back to the hospital. And when he pulled the car to a stop, he leaned over and kissed her. It was a gentle kiss, and it made her feel that everything was going to work out.

"I am looking forward for you and Sophie to come to the villa. I know you must make arrangements and it might take several days. Meanwhile, I will start my painting of Sophie."

A surprised look came on Gabi's face. "You have been to the house, and you have seen Sophie. Did Vanna know who you were?"

"No, I did not introduce myself. I told Mrs. Borrelli I was looking for Doctor Borrelli. I didn't know anything about Sophie until I asked her name. She said, I am Sophie Terry. She looks like her mother. At first I thought she was Tobia's child."

After Jason dropped off Gabi, he made the drive back to Caseno and to the villa. He sat down with Ana and Michael and told them his incredible story. Michael came to Jason and gave him a hug. "You come back to Italy after three years and find you are married and have a child. You and Gabi are going to have to make some very hard decisions."

"The first thing we are going to do is make our marriage legal."

Michael looked down at his empty wine glass. "How are you going to do that without exposing Gabi, and your child? We have a lot of hypocrites that will judge her."

"I have a plan. Gabi has presented herself as being married three years ago. We are going to make that fantasy a reality. Gabi and I are going to get married again. You and Ana will be our witnesses and I am going to slip an official some money to back date the certificate. That is the plan."

Ana went to the kitchen and got another bottle of wine. As she was refilling Michael's glass she said, "Do you think that you can convince Gabi to leave Italy?"

"It does not matter. If she won't come to America, I will live here."

"Damn, this is good wine." Michael took another drink and then set his glass down. "What do you want to do?"

Jason got up and headed to his room and looked back over his shoulder. "I want to go to America. Rachel and I are going to start our own company, and she can't do it without me."

Gabi was very quiet during the evening meal and after she had put Sophie to bed, she sat down with the Borrellis. "I have something I need to tell you."

Vanna took a seat next to Gabi and said, "I thought you were quiet tonight, and you had something you wanted to tell us. What is wrong?"

Gabi gave a weak smile. "What makes you think something is wrong?"

Alonso looked at the two women sitting on the couch. "Is there something wrong?"

"I had a visitor today. Jason is back in town. He came to see me at the hospital. After I finished my shift, we went to have a drink and we talked. He wants us to get back together."

Alonso scoffed, "Surely you told him no."

"No, I didn't tell him no. I did love him before he left me, and I still love him."

Vanna stood up and walked over to look at the painting. "I would say that when you two were married, he must have loved you very much. You can see the love in this painting. Have you told him about Sophie?"

Gabi got up off the couch and came over and stood by Vanna. "I didn't tell him about Sophie. You did."

"How could I have told him? We have never even met."

"He came here, and you let him into the house. He saw Sophie and asked her what her name was? There is a lot you don't know about Jason. I have told you that he has a villa just outside of Caseno. I am going to take a leave and take Sophie there and let him get to know his daughter. I want you to get to know him too."

Alonso Borrelli had been sitting quietly in a chair and had said nothing. "Gabi, you have got some big decisions to make. Vanna and I will support you the best we can. Regardless of what happens, things are never going to be the same."

The next day, Jason pulled out his art supplies and surveyed what he needed. He had to go to Rome to get the fresh tubes of paint he needed. The following day he started his painting of Sophie. In his mind he could see her face clearly. Her eyes were big, and round, and her mouth was small. Her face was round, and she had a cute smile. Her cheeks were rosy in color, and he painted her with her mouth closed. He painted her in a blue gown with some lace near her neckline. Her hair was dark, but not as dark as Gabi's. She was turned slightly toward him with her hand reaching up ever so slightly grasping the top of a chair. He blurred the background with a mingling of colors which gave the painting depth. When he finished, he was proud and considered not giving it to the Borrellis. After all, this is his first vision of his daughter.

Gabi and Sophie didn't get to the villa until the weekend. Sophie had become a bashful little two-year-old and would bury her face into her mother's shoulder when anybody spoke to her. After a half day at the villa, she was walking around following Ana and seemed right at home.

Ana watched after Sophie while Jason and Gabi went to see Father

Borrelli to put their plan in motion. They were greeted in the sanctuary. Father Borrelli took them to his office. "It is so good to see you together, but I must admit when I saw you come in together, I was somewhat concerned. Jason, I assume Gabi has told you of our plan to protect her and your child from the cruel gossip of this world. Now that you are back, how are we going to keep this lie a secret?"

Jason leaned forward in his chair. "We are not, and before you panic you need to hear me out. I know the truth would destroy you. We don't want to tell the truth. We want to correct it."

"How is that even possible? What is done is done. For some strange reason, I didn't think you would ever come back to Caseno. Now that you are here, and you two seem to be together, you are just going to have to live with it."

"Father Borrelli, I said you need to hear me out. Just listen to our plan. We want you to marry us for real. Ana and Michael will be our witnesses. Here comes the real kicker. We want it back dated to three years ago."

Father Borrelli did not say anything for several minutes, and Jason let him think. Finally, he spoke. "There are several reasons this will not work. Neither of you is Catholic. Gabi was raised in and out of the church, but she does not profess the faith. I don't know what you are, but are you willing to join the church? I would have to back date that as well. It would be easier to back date you joining the church than back dating a wedding. I want to help, but this will not work. Your wedding would have to be recorded in Rome."

Gabi spoke up for the first time, "Father, I know you are a kind gracious man. You put your reputation on the line for me. You did not owe me anything. Think about Jason and what he has meant to this town. What would the town of Caseno be like if you had not been here as a priest to heal the wounds of war. Think about this town without me and the medical contributions that I have made. Think about the town without the dam that Jason and his company built. We were told the dam was not going to be built until Jason took over the project. Neither of us would have been here if Jason had not saved us. Jason did not fall in love with the girl in the cave. He fell in love with me. There has to be a way to make this work."

Father Borrelli turned and faced Jason, "I can back date joining the church. Are you willing to allow that?"

"I am."

"The only way we can get a marriage document back dated is to bribe an official in Rome. It will take several thousand dollars. Do you have that kind of money?"

"I am going to donate to your church twenty-five thousand dollars. I think that is more than enough. Use the money to bribe the official, and anything left goes to the church. Do you think it will take more?"

"No, that is far more than will be needed. The church can use this money. Are you sure you can afford this?"

A week later a private ceremony was conducted in the church. Only six people were in attendance. Father Borrelli, Ana, Michael, Jason, Gabi, and Sophie. That night, except for Father Borrelli, they gathered at the villa and were joined by Bonita and Luke and celebrated. Bonita and Luke had no idea what was going on.

Two weeks later, Father Borrelli came knocking on their door. Sitting in the great room, he told them that it was done. They were married, and they could celebrate their third wedding anniversary.

Jason poured Father Borrelli a glass of wine and asked, "How much did you have to pay the Rome official to backdate the wedding document."

Father Borrelli smiled. "Ten thousand dollars. Do you want the rest of your money back?"

"Of course not," he paused for a moment. "Our wine business is in full production. It is doing very well. Bonita and Luke have hired four people to help with the business. One helps with the vegetables and three with the wine. Don't worry about the money. I am doing just fine. Before you leave, I want to give you a case of wine to take with you."

"That is very kind of you. I was told you were rich. You must be." Father Borrelli then asked Gabi a question. "Now the real hard questions are going to have to be answered. What are you going to do?

You and I both know the hospital will hire you back in a heartbeat. Are you going to stay here, or are you going to America?"

Jason started toward the kitchen. "I am going to go fetch Father Borrelli that case of wine. You two can talk. I have to go all the way to the barn."

Once Jason had left the house, Gabi began to cry. "I love him so much. I could not want a better man. I know he will stay in Italy if I ask him, but I also know he does not want to stay here. He loves the people he left behind, and his friend Rachel is waiting for him to start their business. I really don't know a lot about him. I think you could figure out that he is rich, but he has not always been so, and I don't know how he acquired such wealth. I have never been out of Italy. I am scared to get on a plane. I can be a doctor here, but I am not sure if I can be a doctor in America. He has so much money he doesn't even have to work."

"Let's take your last concern first. If he has so much money he does not have to work, then neither do you. You might be a little selfish on that point. If you move to America, you must give up your friends, and if you stay here, he has to give up his."

"He has friends here, and I don't have friends in America."

"When he came here, he had no friends here either. If you are concerned about his wealth, ask him where he got it."

About that time Jason came through the kitchen. "Bonita is putting your wine in your car."

Father Borrelli got up to go. "You don't have to leave. You can stay all afternoon and dine with us tonight."

"No, I have to go. It has been a delight. Will I see you in Mass Sunday?"

Jason looked at Gabi. "Maybe."

Jason, Gabi, and Sophie did come to Mass that Sunday. On the way back to the villa, Sophie fell asleep. Gabi rolled her window up about half way to block the wind from blowing on Sophie. "We have to talk about what we are going to do. I am sure you know that I would prefer to stay here. I can be a doctor and you can oversee the business."

"Luke and Bonita oversee the business. I want to start my own construction firm. You are making a decision on what you want, and you don't even have all the facts."

"What do you mean, I don't have all the facts?"

"I have seen my life from both sides of the Atlantic. I know what it is like here in Italy and what it is like in the United States. You have only seen your life here. What I am saying is, I want to take you to my home in Richmond. It will be like a vacation. I want to stay at least three weeks, maybe four. Once you have done that, then you can tell me what you want to do."

"So, you are going to put the decision on me."

He laughed. "No, I said you can tell me what you want to do. I didn't say I was going to do it."

It took longer than expected to get the necessary papers to allow Sophie and Gabi to travel to the United States.

Sophie took the flight in stride and enjoyed the attention she got from other passengers on the plane. Gabi was terrified. Before the flight took off, Jason ordered a bourbon and coke to help her relax. When the plane landed in New York, the terror turned to amazement. Jason no longer had his apartment, so he took a room at a nice hotel near Times Square. The next day, he took his family to see the sights of the city. Gabi was in total awe.

"So, you lived and worked here. There are so many people, and the buildings are so tall. I don't think I could ever get used to this. What are we going to do tonight?"

"We are going to see Mary. We are going to an Uptown Steak House. It is kid-friendly and has a great atmosphere. You will like it."

When Gabi met Mary, it was like they had been friends their entire lives. Most of the time Jason was left out of the conversation. Finally, Jason spoke to Mary, "Where is JoAnn?"

"She went home to see her parents. She will not be back until next week. When are you going to Richmond?"

"We are flying out mid-morning. We will be back in good ole Richmond by late afternoon."

Turning to Gabi, Mary said, "Are you excited to see where Jason lives? He lives in an American castle. You will have to keep an eye on Sophie. She could get lost in that house."

She then turned to Jason. "Jake was a great guy. He really treated me well, and that Christmas dinner our freshman year is one of my favorite memories. Gabi, has Jason told you about Jake?"

Gabi looked at Jason as she said, "No, he has not told me about Jake."

Before she could say anything more, Jason interrupted her. "One of the purposes of this trip is for Gabi to get to know about me. In the next three to four weeks, she will see what she has gotten herself into."

Gabi didn't say anything for a few minutes while Jason and Mary continued their conversation. She drifted off in her thoughts. *Jason is right, I really don't know him. He knows far more about me than I really know about him. He likes New York, and all I see is a sea of people who never look you in the face, and they always in a hurry and often are pushing to get by you. I like seeing the sights, but I would never want to live here. Sophie does not need this. I hope Richmond is better. This is a great place to visit, but who would want to live here?*

The next day they were on their way to Richmond. Sophie was tired and was soon asleep in her seat. Gabi lay back in her seat and closed her eyes. It was too early to order bourbon and coke, so she tried to drift off in her thoughts. She thought about Jason. *I fell in love with a man in Italy. Is the Jason who lives in America the same as the one I fell in love with in Italy?* She opened her eyes. "Jason, how did you get so rich? Were your parents rich?" She already knew that he grew up poor.

Jason knew she was trying to find out more about him, and he did not want to keep anything from her. "I grew up poor. My father was a carpenter. When he died, I joined the army. When I came back to Richmond from the army, I used the G.I. Bill to go to school. I lived and worked part-time for a man named Jake Winston. He became my second father and good friend. He had no family, and when he died, he left me his house and all his money and investments. It was in the millions. When I went to work in New York, I learned how to invest and met people who gave me sound investment advice. I made even more money."

"You joined the Catholic church. Did you go to church in Richmond and in New York?"

"My father never took me to church. My mother was a Baptist. I have never been to church in Richmond, or at least not to go to a worship service. There is a Catholic church about a half block from our home. If you want to go, I will go with you."

"You said the house was big. How big is it really? I can't believe it is as big as you said."

"You will see it for yourself soon. I wish we could move the villa over here. It is a whole lot more livable."

When the taxi pulled up in front of the house, Gabi couldn't believe her eyes. The house had four levels. The first level was a walk out basement which was ground level in the back and part of the front. It had an entrance on the right side of the house. A set of steps led up to the second floor to a large porch. The front door was on the right of the porch. Two people were standing on the porch, smiling and waving. "Who is that?"

"That is Billy and his wife. I told you about them. Billy takes care of the place, and his wife is our cook."

"You did tell me about them, but you never mentioned that they were black."

Jason motioned to Billy to help with the bags and with a big grin on his face said, "You mean they are black? I had never noticed."

Gabi reached in the back seat of the cab and pulled Sophie into her arms. She smiled at Billy coming down the steps. *This is why I fell in love with Jason. I might not know the Jason who lives in America, but I do know he is a good man.*

Epilogue

After Mass, Father Beasley stood in front of the Catholic church greeting members as they left the church. The congregation could exit one of two ways. Those who drove their cars to church would exit through the side door which opened into the parking lot, and the members who lived close who walked to church would go out the front doors.

As Gabi approached, Father Beasley said, "Dr. Terry, it is so good to see you and Sophie in church. Sophie, you are really getting to be a big girl. How old are you now?"

Sophie gave the old priest a smile. "I am nine, but I will soon be ten."

Seeing that there was no one behind them, he continued the conversation. "I understand that you are taking a leave of absence from the hospital and going to Italy. I don't know how the hospital is going to get along without you."

"They will do just fine. Jason has a business there, and I want to see my family, so we are going to spend a month in Italy. It will give Sophie a chance to use her Italian, and she just loves the villa."

"Speaking of Jason, where is your husband?"

"He went to the nursery to get Jake. He will be here in just a few moments."

Just about that time, Jason and Jake came out the front door of the church. "Father Beasley, I really enjoyed your service today. I guess Gabi has told you we will not be here for the next four weeks."

"She has. I hope you have a nice trip. Bring me a bottle of that wine you produce. It is the best."

Holding Jake in his arms and taking Gabi by the hand, they started walking home. The first half of the walk they didn't talk, and then Gabi broke the silence. "I am really looking forward to seeing Mom and Dad. I know they are not my real parents, but in a sense, I feel like they are. I never thought that I would say this, but I like living here. I am glad they come to visit us as often as they do."

Jason let go of Gabi's hand and gave her a slight bump with his shoulder. "I wish you could have known Jake Winston. I would describe him as more like my grandfather. Dad worked hard for me. He had to be both a mother and father. I would like to sit down with him and say, 'I know you and I didn't get to go into business, but I have done okay. I have a great business with my partner Rachel. I have a winery in Italy that produces over three hundred thousand bottles of wine each year. I have two beautiful children and the most beautiful wife you could ever imagine. By the way, Dad, we met in a cave.'"

Printed in the United States
By Bookmasters